THE DEVIL'S DUE

Stephen Banister

(C) 2000

ISBN

Hardcover: 978-1-969733-27-7

Paperback: 978-1-969733-26-0

THIS BOOK IS DEDICATED TO MY SON, RYAN,
WHOM I LOVE VERY MUCH. IT WAS HIS
QUALITY TIME I BORROWED FROM TO WRITE
IT. I JUST HOPE IT ISN'T TOO LATE TO
REPLENISH THE SUPPLY.

I'D RATHER BE SORRY FOR SOMETHING I'VE
DONE, THAN FOR SOMETHING I DIDN'T DO.

KRIS KRISTOFFERSON "I'D RATHER BE SORRY"

1

Bear Dalton was only twelve when a bullet went through his head and ended his life. Reid Dalton died the same night, only his life went on.

SAN ANTONIO, TEXAS

"Come on, Mom. I'm only going over to Jason's. It's not like I'm going clear across town," Bear Dalton told his mother as he carried his supper dishes to the kitchen. Jason was his best friend and only lived six blocks away in Deer Run, an upper-middle-class section on the northwest side of town.

"I don't care. It's already dark out, plus you've got homework to finish," Kathy Dalton told him. "And you were just over there after school."

"That's the point. We have got a science project due and we have to work on it together. We're a team."

"You should have thought of that this afternoon."

"We had other things to do then."

"Then you can do it tomorrow, after school."

"But it's due tomorrow."

"Bear!"

"Ok, so it's not due tomorrow, but we need to work on it. Please, Mom?" Bear begged.

"No, sir. I'll not have you riding your bike around in the dark."

"Unh! Why do you treat me like a baby? I'm almost in high school."

"Not for three more years."

"Pop?"

"Don't drag me into this," Reid said.

"Why not? You let me ride over there the other night."

Reid Dalton hated it when he was called upon to take sides, mainly because he usually agreed with one but had to support the other. He remembered being Bear's age and riding his bike all over the countryside at all hours of the night, but times and mothers were different now.

"You wouldn't have gotten to if I would have been here," Kathy told them both.

"Who runs this family anyway?" Bear said in the direction of his father.

Reid Dalton thought it was a fair question and one that he had asked himself on more than one occasion, but never out loud.

"That'll be enough, young man," his mother said. "You are not going out at this time of night and that's final!"

Bear stormed out of the dining room and down the hall to his room, where he slammed the door to close off his territory from the rest of the world.

"It's only a couple of blocks," Reid told his wife. "And we don't exactly live on the Southside."

"If I left it up to you, we'd be lucky to see him at all.

You'd let him run around all over creation."

"I think you're exaggerating somewhat. He's a growing boy and needs a little freedom."

"I don't care. I don't want him roaming the streets at night."

"He's not roaming, he just wants to go to Jason's, for Christ's sake."

"The answer is no, so drop it."

Reid Dalton thought of storming out himself and slamming the door to the den behind him, but adulthood had its drawbacks, so he stayed at the table and finished his coffee.

Kathy Dalton did a quick rinse of the dishes and placed them in the dishwasher. Neither one made any attempt at conversation during the process. When finished, she walked back through the dining room and stopped long enough to tell her husband she was going to an Orchid Club meeting and to make sure Bear got his homework done before he went to bed. "You think you can handle that?"

"Probably not, but thanks for asking," Reid told her.

The electric garage door opener was still in the process of closing the door, when Bear exited his room.

"Mom leave?"

"Yeah, she had one of her meetings to go to," he told him, but wanted to say, "Yeah, like you didn't know."

"When's she gonna be back?"

"Couple of hours. Probably about nine or so," he said and waited for his son to drop the next shoe.

"Can I go, Pop?"

"You know what your mother said."

"I know, but what do you say?"

"I say if you can get there and back by eight-thirty, you can go. II

"Thanks, Pop."

"Wait a minute," Reid said. "You got your homework done?"

"I did it in Homeroom."

"OK, but do us both a favor and make sure you are back here and in bed before your mother gets home."

"No, problemo." Bear went through the kitchen and out the door to the garage. He pressed the button to open the garage door and grabbed his bike. He hit the button again and rode under the door as it was closing.

Reid stood by the dining room window and watched his son head off down the street. It wasn't as if he had betrayed his wife but rather strengthened the bond between he and his son. After all, she had left, and in doing so, had relinquished her control. It was an abdication of sorts, just of a lesser degree.

He made his way into the den, opened his briefcase and took out a stack of claim files he had brought home to review. As Senior Claims Examiner at Union Mutual Insurance Company, it was his job to make sure the larger cases in his district never made it to the courthouse.

Bear Dalton rounded two corners and was half a block from his destination when a slow-moving car approached him from behind. He moved to the right and hugged the curb so the car could pass, as he needed to cross the street to reach Jason's house.

Bear Dalton never heard the shot that killed him.

* * *

BOERNE, TEXAS

Doobie sat in one of the few items of furniture he had taken with him in the divorce, a dark green, metal patio chair. The chair dated back to his oldest memory, when as a child he had sat in the broad seat, his legs dangling off the front, and tried to rock by forcing his weight against the back. It wasn't until he had grown tall enough to plant his feet firmly on the ground with his back against the smooth shell-shaped chair back, that he was able to make the tube-like metal legs give under his weight. It was more of a slow, smooth bounce rather than a rocking motion, but it offered him the comfort and relaxation he yearned for.

The chair was old, to say the least, but he had taken care to protect the metal against the killer rust. Just like the rings of a tree told its age, the layers of paint on the chair held stories of their own.

Five years ago, just after the divorce, he had carried the chair to the edge of the cliff that overlooked a lush valley of the

Cibolo Creek. He had sat in the chair for weeks on end and stared into the valley for answers that never came. Progress came instead. Progress under the name of the Tapatio Springs Resort and Country Club. The valley became a golf course and houses sprung up where deer once fed. The deer were still allowed to roam freely about the course, or to Doobie's way of thinking, the deer allowed the golfers to play on their feeding ground. Neither disturbed the other, however, if a golfer found himself coming down eighteen as the sun set to his right, his chances of finishing the round were as remote as the resort itself.

The deer seemed to know when the course was, or should be, theirs. At one sunset, Doobie had counted as many as two hundred deer grazing across the four fairways that led away and back to the clubhouse.

It was such a sunset that Doobie was enjoying across the valley. The fifteen acres of hilltop land where Doobie's one-room, log cabin stood were just outside the northeast perimeter of the resort and high enough that not even his chair, on the leading edge, could be seen from down below.

It was the sunset that Doobie enjoyed every night, along with Sweet, his chocolate Lab, two dog biscuits and two home-grown cigarettes, rolled and filtered by a Laredo cigarette machine he had found still in working order at one of the weekend flea markets in town.

Doobie took one of the cigarettes from his shirt pocket, along with a silver-plated Zippo lighter. He lit the end, inhaled deeply and held it in until he felt the familiar burning sensation in his lungs. He rubbed his thumb lovingly over one side of the lighter before returning it to his pocket.

"Not a bad batch, Sweet," he said as he reached down and scratched behind the dog's ears. He then reached into the same pocket and took out one of the biscuits and gave it to the dog.

"Sorry," he said. "Almost forgot."

Sweet knew and loved the drill and accepted his part with as much anticipation as his master did his.

"They just don't learn, do they, Sweet?" Doobie said and pointed toward the eighteenth fairway with his cigarette before bringing it to his mouth for a long drag. A few seconds later, he exhaled and continued. "There's a group back there on the box and a whole shitpot full of deer around the corner. They might as well just head them carts on in right now."

Sweet lifted his head like he understood and then went about his own business with the biscuit.

Down below, the sound of a car leaving rubber on Cliffdweller Drive drew both their attention.

"Looks like the Jenkins have had another one of their fights and I'll bet you this other biscuit here that Dave is headin' straight for Leon Springs to drink up enough nerve to come back home."

He took another lengthy drag and held it in before letting it out slowly. "Some people just don't understand what they got or what to do with it if they do," he said through the smoke.

Doobie turned his attention back to the course. The first group had rounded the dogleg and come face to face with the end of their round. They didn't even bother looking for their balls and headed on into the clubhouse instead. "What'd I tell you, Sweet? They just never learn."

The sun had gone down in front of him when Doobie took out their last two treats. He handed the dog his and reached in for the lighter. Although it was dark, he knew what was engraved on each side. He gave one side a gentle rub again before firing up the homegrown roll.

He put the old chair into a slow-motion rock and finished his smoke in a dark silence. His life was full of dark silences, but he knew what he had and knew what to do with it.

"Come on, Sweet," Doobie said when he rose from the chair. "Let's go say good night."

The one-room cabin was built in the center of a grove of pine trees. Doobie found comfort in the sound the trees made when even the slightest breeze blew through them. In the spring, when the wind was high, it was almost like the roar of the ocean.

A lone sycamore tree stood guard at the outer edge of the small pine grove. Doobie stopped long enough to run his hand over a carved-out section of bark. Even in the dark, he knew exactly where to touch.

"Made it through another one," he whispered.

2

Reid Dalton half-expected to be sold something as he walked to the front door in response to the chime that had taken him away from his necessary reading. He was a pushover for that sort of thing. He had read in the paper recently that the Girl Scouts were gearing up for their annual cookie drive, which meant it was time for him to open his wallet for each of the half a dozen or so who lived in the neighborhood. The mints were his favorite.

Bear liked the peanut butter and chocolate ones. Kathy favored her diet over the cookies but always managed to sneak some of each when she thought no one was looking.

The last thing Reid Dalton expected to find on his porch was the first thing he saw when he opened the door.

"Is this the Dalton residence?" the uniformed officer asked politely and with a reserved tone in his voice. It was almost as if he wanted the answer to be no.

"Yes, sir," Reid answered.

"Do you have a son named Bear?"

"Yes, sir. Has he done something? Is something wrong?" Reid Dalton looked over the officer's shoulder to where the police car was parked. It was too dark to make out whether Bear was sitting inside.

"I'm afraid I have some bad news, Mister Dalton. There's been..."

"Not Bear. No, he's just at a friend's house around the corner."

"That would be Jason Watson. Yes, sir. That's how we found you. You see..."

"He's all right, though. He's with Jason?"

"Sir, I'm afraid I have to tell you this and it isn't going to be easy, but your son was shot," the officer said.

"Shot? What do you mean? Were he and Jason playing with guns? What's going on? Where is he?" All kinds of things were rushing through Reid Dalton's brain and none of them good.

"Sir, I'm afraid your son is dead," he said in not much more than a whisper.

Reid grabbed for the door to steady himself. "Where?"

"If you'll come with me, sir. I'll take you to him." The officer took him gently by the arm.

Reid allowed the officer to close the door behind him as he walked toward the car parked by the curb. His knees felt like they were about to buckle under him with each step, but they somehow held up. The officer opened the front passenger door to let him in, then crossed in front of the car and got in himself. Neither one spoke during the short drive.

They rounded the two corners, the same route Bear had taken, and from half a block away, it was obvious that something was dead wrong in the neighborhood.

Reid Dalton didn't wait for the officer to stop the car. He pushed the door open and jumped out. He stumbled over the curb and fell onto the grass. He should have felt the pain as his ankle twisted but the numbness in his body deadened the sense before it reached his brain.

The small crowd of police and medical attendants parted just long enough to let him through, then closed ranks again. A blanket covered a small form on the grass, but Reid recognized the Nikes he had helped his son pick out for basketball.

"No!" Reid Dalton shouted as he knelt by the blanket that covered his son.

A female officer took him by the arm. "Sir, we need for you to identify him. We have to make sure." Before he could respond, she peeled the blanket back and uncovered Bear's face.

Even with half the side of his head gone, he knew it was his son. Tears welled up in his eyes and flowed down his face.

The officer knew from his response that the identity had been made but was required to ask. "Is this your son?"

"Yes," he whispered between gulps of air.

The officer covered Bear's face again. "What are you doing?" he asked.

"We have to take him now, sir," the female officer said.

"You can't. He's, my son."

"I know that, sir, but we have to."

Reid leaned back on his knees. "Why? Who did this?"

As if on cue, a plainclothes detective knelt down beside him. "Mr. Dalton, my name is Sergeant Montalvo."

"Where are they taking Bear?" he asked as a group of ambulance attendants lifted the body onto a stretcher.

"He'll be all right, Mr. Dalton. They'll take good care of him. They're very good at this sort of thing."

"This sort of thing? What is this sort of thing? What happened to my son?"

"From what we've been able to determine, someone in a passing automobile shot your son. It looks to be a random drive-by shooting."

"Not here. Not in this neighborhood. That doesn't happen here. You don't understand. We moved here to get away from that sort of thing."

"Did your son have trouble before?" the detective asked.

"What? Of course not. He was just a boy."

"Well, you said you moved here to get away from that."

"I meant we moved to be sure nothing like this would happen. My wife..." Suddenly, Reid Dalton remembered his wife. Kathy had told him that Bear was not to leave the house. That it would be dangerous riding his bike around in the dark. "Oh, my wife."

"Where is your wife, Mr. Dalton?"

"Some meeting. I don't know. She left. She told Bear he couldn't go. She told me..."

"Do you know how to reach her?"

"No."

"Would you rather we went back to your house and waited for her. We can do that. We can talk there."

"No, I need to go with Bear."

"I'm sorry, sir. We can't let you do that."

"Why? He's, my son? Where are you taking him?"

"Sir, they have to do an autopsy. We can't let you go."

"An autopsy?" Reid Dalton thought about his son's body being torn open and taken apart. "Why? You know what happened. You can see."

"I'm sorry, sir. It's the law."

"What kind of a law allows you to do that to a little boy?"

"It's necessary for when we catch who did this. It's something that must be done." It was times like these that Detective Sergeant Eric Montalvo hated his job. He knew how the boy had died, but he knew just as well that without the proper evidence, any good lawyer would be able to get his client off if the authorities didn't follow procedures to the letter. He had seen it happen too many times and it wasn't going to happen in this case.

"Do you know who did it?"

"No, sir. So far, all we know is it was a dark colored car. Probably a Chevrolet or Oldsmobile. We got that from your son's friend. He had been waiting for him on his front lawn."

Reid Dalton remembered Bear coming to him and asking if his mother had gone. He knew then that Bear already knew she had and must have called Jason to tell him he was on his way. Bear knew his father wouldn't say no. He never said no.

"I shouldn't have let him go," Reid said to himself.

"It wasn't your fault. There was no way you could have known this would happen. You said yourself, this doesn't happen around here," the detective told him.

"But it did, didn't it?"

"Yes, sir. I'm afraid it did."

* * *

Ashley Jenkins was sixteen going on seventeen. Her parents were of mixed religion. Belinda Jenkins was a Baptist and believed God was God. Dave Jenkins was a golfer and believed golf was God. Theirs was the first house built on Cliffdweller Drive, a year before the course opened for play. Dave Jenkins wanted to be able to walk out onto his back porch and touch his god in the truest of religious experiences.

Ashley Jenkins followed in her mother's footsteps, not that she was given the option to choose. Her father believed that women had no place on a golf course. They played too slow, talked too much and if they had anybody at all, they were too much of a distraction.

Belinda Jenkins saw to it that her daughter was raised in the proper Baptist venue. Church on Sunday morning, church on Sunday evening, church on Wednesday evening and church whenever the doors were open. She prayed when she got up in the morning, before every meal and when she went to bed at night.

Dave Jenkins prayed too, but usually for a putt to drop or the sun to come out. He even prayed once for lightning to strike his playing partner, who was standing over a two-foot putt on the eighteenth hole to win a fifty-dollar match play bet. It was a blind faith prayer since they were playing under a cloudless sky. It also went unanswered. Still, he believed.

When Dave Jenkins sped away from their house on his way to Leon Springs to drown his daughter's recent news in a glass of ninety proof, Belinda Jenkins marched her daughter to her room and knelt with her by the bed. Her years of religious manipulation of her daughter had just backfired with the announcement that she was loading up her belongings in her Mazda Miata convertible, a sweet sixteen birthday present from her father, and heading off to Comfort to become the newest member of the Kingdom of Lambs.

Dave Jenkins, who had never heard of the Kingdom of Lambs, first thought his daughter was quitting school to go to work for some sheep farmer over in the next county and strictly forbid her to go. When she had enlightened him to the fact that the Kingdom of Lambs was a religious commune dedicated to God's work in the healing of the spiritually underprivileged, the only words he heard were religious commune.

"Ain't no daughter of mine is going off to some hippie commune to be banged by every horny, Bible-thumping, white trash who lays down a blanket in front of her," he had said. He could see visions of his petite, red-haired daughter lying on a pallet with her legs spread open, while a horde of long-haired freaks dressed in tie-dyed robes lined up beside her, waiting their turn.

When she had informed him that all the members of the congregation were not white, he had flown into a rage, grabbed his favorite putter and broke three lamps, a mirror, the glass coffee table and the putter itself. His last words as he left the house had been, "I catch you anywhere near that sheep kingdom, I'll take you to the hospital personally and have that little snatch of yours sewn shut permanently!"

Belinda Jenkins had heard of the Kingdom of Lambs, not from the local paper or even her own Pastor Phipps of the Right Avenue Baptist Church, but from the very mouth of Sally Kuntz, the owner and sole operator of the Hill Country Styling Salon.

Sally had told her, and anyone else who sat in her chair, about a friend of hers in Kerrville whose daughter had spent the past summer in the Kingdom of Lambs and come home pregnant with what her daughter claimed to be the new baby Jesus.

And Sally Kuntz, who was a member of the Right Avenue Baptist Church choir, wouldn't lie about something so reverential. For that reason, Belinda Jenkins knelt with her daughter by the bed.

"I know it's going to be hard after all you have been taught, but I want you to pray to the Lord to give you a sign. A sign that will show you your path to eternity does not lead you through the Kingdom of Lambs, even though they profess to be of the spirit," she said as she gently laid her hand on her daughter's head.

"I have been praying," Ashley Jenkins told her mother. "I've been praying for a week now. Ever since I met Reverend Daniel."

"Who is this Reverend Daniel?" her mother said, with her hand still on her daughter's head.

"He's the Lambs' spiritual leader. He's everything I could ever want."

"Where did you meet him?"

"You remember last Sunday afternoon when I told you I was going to a prayer group meeting. Well, what it really was, was a revival meeting for others, not members of the Kingdom of Lambs, who wanted to know more about their work."

"They didn't...didn't do anything to you, did they?" "Oh, mother, it was nothing like that. They are truly

wonderful, spiritual people. I want to help them spread the word."

"That is not at all what I have heard and you are much too young to be involved with such a group."

"They're no different than your church." "It's your church too."

"I want to choose my own church." "Did you receive a sign?"

"No, not really," Ashley Jenkins said.

"Then pray for one now. If you really pray for one, it will come," Belinda Jenkins told her daughter. "I know it will, and it will be a true sign."

"It's too late for that. I'm already packed and I'm going."

Belinda Jenkins looked around her daughter's room and saw the suitcase standing by the closet door. She got up and grabbed the case. "I won't let you. Not until we have prayed together for a sign."

Ashley Jenkins jumped up and reached for the suitcase. They lunged back and forth until the latch gave way and the suitcase sprang open. Clothes flew about the room. A sweater landed on Ashley Jenkins' shoulder.

"Now see what you've done," her mother said. "Mother?"

"What?"

"This sweater...it's lamb's wool."

3

Kathy Dalton knew there had to be a reason for a police cruiser to be parked in front of their house. Twice before, neighbors had reported high school kids speeding through their quiet streets and each time a cruiser had been posted in an attempt to catch them in the act. But this time the marked police car was accompanied by an unmarked sedan, obviously belonging to a detective or some other such official from the police department. Maybe a prowler had been reported. It had happened in their old neighborhood, but never in this one. If nothing else, it would be more ammunition for her to use when Bear wanted to venture out into the streets at night.

When she clicked open the garage door from her car, the first thing she noticed was the absence of Bear's bike, which he always left leaning against the workbench on the back wall. She remembered vividly it being there when she left. Her immediate thought was that Bear was missing. Reid had gone against her and let him leave. It was a thought that shouldn't have surprised her. He usually always went against her wishes where their son was concerned.

She got out of the car and slammed the door. Even though she was motherly concerned about her son, she wanted her husband to know she was home and to be very afraid.

Reid met his wife at the kitchen door. It was guilt he felt, not fear.

"Where's Bear?" Kathy Dalton said with a clenched jaw. Reid Dalton tried to reach for her. He wanted to hold her, brace her for the news.

"Get away from me, goddammit! Where is Bear?"

Her husband tried again to embrace her, but she hit him with a roundhouse slap to the face. "You tell me where my son is right now or, so help me, I'll tear your face off!"

Kathy Dalton was startled by a voice from the dining room. She hadn't noticed anyone else being there. "Mrs. Dalton, please sit down."

"Who are you and what the hell are you doing here? Do you have my son? Did this bastard let him get into some kind of trouble?"

"My name is Sergeant Eric Montalvo, ma'am, and again, please sit down."

"I'm not sitting down until someone tells me what's going on."

"There's been an accident, Kathy," Reid Dalton said.

"If Bear's hurt, you're going to pay," she told him.

He reached for her again but backed away when he saw her hand go into motion. The slap missed his face by inches.

"Get away from me!" she screamed.

Reid Dalton took a deep breath. When he exhaled, these words came with it. "Bear's been killed."

Kathy's arms went limp at her side and all the air left her lungs. Her face took on a pitiful look, one that her husband would never forget.

No one moved. Kathy Dalton couldn't and her husband dared not to. Sergeant Montalvo had been a party to this scene before and knew the hesitation would pass and pass it did.

Kathy Dalton moved first and with deadly accuracy. She swung her purse by the long strap and hit her husband square in the face. She let the purse go when contact had been made, jumped into him and dug the fingernails of both hands into his cheeks. Reid Dalton made no attempt to defend himself. He knew it wouldn't be right.

Sergeant Montalvo didn't see it that way. He threw his arms around her from behind and pulled her away.

"It's OK," Reid Dalton told him. "Let her finish."

"I'll never be finished with you," she said and spit in his direction.

"What about your son, Mrs. Dalton?"

The same deplorable look returned to Kathy Dalton's face and she became dead weight in the sergeant's arms. He pulled a chair out with his foot and placed her in it. Her arms went immediately to her lap.

Reid Dalton looked down at his wife. He knew he had done this to her. Not the person who shot and killed their son, but him. He had let him go. If he had listened to her. If he had been more of a father instead of a big brother, Bear would still be alive.

They would still be a family. Maybe not the happiest of families, but still a family. Still together.

Although his face was bleeding and swollen, Reid Dalton felt no pain, only guilt.

* * *

Not a morning dawned that Doobie didn't get up and think how easy it would be to just put a gun to his head and end it all. He didn't consider himself a coward, but he had still died a thousand deaths in his own mind. One thousand eight hundred and sixty-two to be exact. Counting today. A shrink would say if he had thought about it that many times and hadn't done it, it was obviously just a bluff. To Doobie, it was an option.

He stuck that thought in one of the dark closets in his brain, along with the other one thousand eight hundred and sixty-one, scratched Sweet behind the ears and got out of bed. Sweet rose to his feet, bowed his back in a long U-shaped stretch, and then followed.

He switched on one of the few electrical appliances he owned, a coffee percolator he had bought for a buck at a local garage sale. The owner had assured him it was still in good working order, and after two years of daily use, it had proven the man true to his word. Unusual for this day in time.

He dumped the last of the fifty-pound bag of dry dog food into Sweet's bowl, which meant a dreaded trip into town was going to be necessary.

He ran his hand across his chin. The stubble told him another week had passed. Doobie had long since stopped paying attention to what day it was. Monday could have been Thursday for all he cared. He owned neither a TV nor a radio. His only contact with the outside world came when he was forced to venture into the small town of Boerne for supplies. It wasn't that he didn't like people in general, he just didn't care for them, nor did he care for what they had to say.

His world, the inside, was his little hill and the small valley it dropped off into. While it used to be his alone, he had grown accustomed, forced actually, to the fact that others shared the part down below. It was from those people that he earned what he needed to survive. A job mowing an adjacent fairway yard, trimming a hedge or even minor handiwork here and there. He accepted what payment they offered, which was usually more than he would have asked for. The offerings also usually included a meal, although he never ate inside. It wasn't that they didn't offer him the comfort of a patio table or even a dining room seat, but rather his own wish to be left to himself.

No one was ever offended by his refusal and some were probably just as happy that he didn't accept. His excuse was that he liked sharing his food with his dog and it wouldn't be safe for Sweet, who was the size of a small hill country deer, to be bounding around in their house.

Doobie's log cabin, which he had built himself solely from the trees that had to be uprooted to construct the golf course, was a one-room structure. Two, if you considered the small, door-less bathroom set off in one corner. The floor was made from scrap lumber left over from the construction of · the resort clubhouse.

The fireplace was made from hill country stone gathered from his own fifteen acres. In the outside world, the fireplace alone would be worth more than the entire cabin itself. It was a far cry from the tent he had lived in when the valley was all his.

All the furnishings, a double bed with a bookcase headboard, a brown, vinyl couch and a rocking chair, had once belonged to someone else. Several, someone else's to be exact. Even the toilet and tub, one white and the other a dirty beige, had seen use before retiring to the cabin. The kitchen was nothing more than a large, warped, yet new, stain-less sink dropped between two hand-built rows of cabinets. He had found the sink in with the discarded clubhouse lumber. The contractor had obviously meant for it to be installed in the resort kitchen but had damaged it somehow in the preparation. The oversize sink, though not manufactured for the purpose, also doubled as Doobie's one-cycle washing machine.

While the dog was eating and the coffee percolating, Doobie drew a bath and climbed in, straight razor in hand. He applied a weak lather of hand soap to his face and shaved without the use of a mirror. With no mustache or other such vanity growth to work around, the job was a simple one. Routine, even though not practiced much more than fifty times a year.

After soaking long enough for the coffee to be done, Doobie removed himself from the tub and toweled off. It was a procedure that was less than time-consuming, due to his six-foot frame being wiry, yet muscular, from eating little and working hard. He ran a comb straight back through his dark brown hair. Once dry, it would fall, from years of training, into a later years Elvis look. Unruly straight, with a mind of its own.

Doobie dressed in faded black jeans and a grey T-shirt that had once had the name of the San Antonio Spurs on the front, but too many hand washings had erased that memory.

He took two cups of black coffee out to the chair by the cliff. The first one would go quickly. The second, he would savor. Taking two at a time saved him an early trip back. On the way, he ran his hand over the carving on the sycamore tree. There was a light haze just above the tree line, which meant the first golfers out had to fight an early morning fog, which crept into the valley during the night this time of year. By mid-morning, the sun would have erased any evidence, as well as the hiding places of golf balls produced by errant shots in the earlier rounds. They would, of course, be the possession of the finder. The first was a law of nature, the second a law of golf.

From his vantage point, Doobie saw that Dave Jenkins had made it home in one piece, or at least his car had. He was probably out on the course somewhere, sweating alcohol through his golf shirt.

Doobie finished off the first cup of coffee and set the mug down by Sweet. He scratched the dog behind the ears, grabbed the second cup, and put the green chair into a slow rock. While things were at least comfortable in Doobie's world, they were far from being right. They hadn't been right for quite some time.

4

The slaying of Bear Dalton made the front page of most every newspaper in south central Texas, including a color photograph of his bicycle with his covered body in the background. The citizens of San Antonio were so outraged that such a hideous event had escaped the inner city and Southside crime areas, that the mayor had called a press conference and sworn to bring the criminal element to justice, regardless of the manpower it would take.

The manpower promised turned out to be no more than a few extra hours of overtime for Sergeant Montalvo, once it all trickled down to his division. It was an election year, so the speech was all that mattered. After all, within the week, another murder or two would take place, demand center stage, and Bear Dalton would be all but forgotten. Life in the big city would go on. No one knew that any better than Sergeant Montalvo.

"We just don't have a whole hell of a lot to go on here," he said to his partner, Jess Ramsey, from across his desk. Ramsey had been on loan to another department the night before and was being brought up to speed on the case.

"We got a dark colored car. That's a start," he said and ran his hand over the top of his brush-cut head.

"More like an end. Hell, we don't even know what he was shot with. We got no shell casing, and the slug is probably buried two feet deep in the yard somewhere."

"We know it wasn't a shotgun," Ramsey said.

"Always the optimist," Montalvo muttered and twisted at the end of his thick, black mustache, a nervous habit he had acquired the day the city banned smoking in all public buildings.

"And we got the kid. The one he was going to see. He could remember something. You know, once things return to normal."

"He saw his friend get killed. When do you expect him to return to normal?"

"You know what I mean."

"Yeah, I know. I also know we got over thirty other unsolved murders turning yellow in the files. What hope has this one got?"

"It's got us," Ramsey said.

"Tell that to the kid's parents. I thought I was going to witness another one last night. I don't see that marriage lasting a month after the funeral."

"That bad, huh?"

"Worse. If the mother had her way, she would have us arrest her husband and charge him with the murder."

"Any other kids?" Ramsey asked.

"Just the one and I don't see any more in their future."

"So, where do we go from here?"

"Canvass the neighborhood, I guess. Those people should be pissed off enough not to be scared to tell us almost anything," Montalvo said. I know I would be."

"You're different. You see this shit on a daily basis. Those folks are probably just happy that it wasn't their own kid who ended up on page one."

"What happened to Mister Optimistic?"

"I guess you're beginning to rub off on me," Ramsey said.

"Don't let that happen. We have enough trouble getting things solved around here as it is."

"Speaking of which," Ramsey said. "We've still got that convenience store murder witness to talk to."

"Yeah, you're right. What time were we supposed to meet her?"

"Ten minutes ago."

"Shit. That's all we need. It took us a week to get this meeting set up so her priest could be there with her, and now we're gonna blow it. The lieutenant's gonna have our ass. Why didn't you remind me sooner?" he said as he grabbed his jacket from the back of his chair.

"Well, you know. Time flies."

Sergeant Montalvo threw the thin file that held what little evidence they had on Bear Dalton's murder on the stack at the corner of his desk.

"Yeah, but we don't."

* * *

When Doobie opened the door of the 1978 Ford Bronco, Sweet jumped clear across the driver's seat and into shotgun position. He didn't need to be told twice that they were going for a ride, whether it was just down the hill to work or the five-mile winding road into town.

They had to stay on the back roads since the Bronco hadn't seen the inside of a vehicle inspection station in a decade. It had been retired to a hunting lease until Doobie called it back into action. The rear license plate had also been dead for several years. It had come off a fire-damaged Plymouth van Doobie had run across at the Exxon station off I-10 going into town.

Nothing about the vehicle was street legal, including the driver. Doobie's driver's license renewal had been returned to the Texas Department of Public Safety in Austin, marked "Addressee Unknown" by his former wife. It hadn't been a lie either.

The Bronco started without hesitation and Doobie kept it in second gear--first gear needed too much dental work to be bothered with--until he reached the cattle guard that marked the entrance to his property. He took the key from the ashtray, exited and unlocked the gate. He reversed the process after driving through.

"You know, Sweet, it sure would make life a lot easier if you would learn how to operate that gate," he said when he pitched the key back into the tray and drove onto the cracked asphalt roadway that meandered into town.

When he got to the I-10 crossing, he pulled off the road long enough to make sure there were no troopers in the area that might hinder his progress as he crossed the overpass. While the Bronco was in good running order for a vehicle of its age, it would be no match against a souped-up DPS Camaro, if push came to shove. He would have to surrender, plead insanity and throw himself on the mercy of the court. Sweet, on the other hand, could head for the hills and evade arrest, but probably wouldn't.

He crossed the interstate and through the old residential section of town until he came to Bradley's Grocery and Bait Shop. He parked behind the store, where Jake Bradley kept his own car and exited the Bronco with Sweet at his heels. Unlike the chain stores in town, Jake Bradley didn't mind the occasional animal wandering about the store, so long as its master was wandering along with it.

Doobie had made a mental note of the provisions they needed, most of which he still remembered. He nodded at the proprietor when he entered and then went about the business of locating what he needed. Again, unlike the chain stores, Jake Bradley was not prone to changing aisles or rearranging the stock on a regular basis, so Doobie wasted no time filling his list.

The store was small by most standards. Jake Bradley knew what his customers needed and saw no reason to stock in excess. They were not impulse shoppers, more into the staples. Therefore, any conversation being had was anything but private.

Such a conversation was presently underway at the checkout counter, and being that the main converser was Sally Kuntz, it could hardly fall into the private category anyway. While Doobie was not interested, he had no alternative but to hear.

"And I suppose you've heard about Reverend Daniel and his Kingdom of Lambs? That man should be horsewhipped for what he is doing over there. It is blasphemy, I tell you. There ought to be a law."

"Yes, ma'am," Jake Bradley said with an unconcerned nod as he tried to ring up her purchases.

"He's telling those young women that he was sent by the Lord to spread the word. Why, all he's doing is spreading his seed and impregnating the lot of them."

"Yes, ma'am."

"Why, just the other day, a customer of mine told me he had some kind of revival meeting and after it was over, three girls, or was it four? I don't know. It doesn't matter. One is too many for the likes of him. Anyway, they went to live with him in some kind of commune. Well, you know what he has in store for them, don't you?"

"Yes, ma'am."

"Why, sure you do. And I tell you; it is just not right. Why, if I had my way, I'd see him tarred and feathered. No, that would be too good for his kind."

"Yes, ma'am."

"Telling those girls, they should give themselves to the Lord when all they end up doing is giving themselves to him. And some of them virgins, too. Now, you tell me, is that right?"

"Yes, ma'am."

"I beg your pardon?"

"What? I mean, no, ma'am."

Doobie choked on a laugh. He coughed several times to hide the evidence and reached on the shelf in front of him for something not on his mental list in case his ploy hadn't worked.

"That'll be twenty-seven thirty," Jake Bradley said.

Sally Kuntz paid in cash and left the store. Doobie returned the unwanted item to the shelf, located a large can of coffee to almost complete his list and walked to the checkout counter.

"Jake."

"Doobie."

"Ring up one of those fifty-pound bags of dog food also. I'll get it on my way out."

"Sure thing. I don't think old Sweet there would let you forget, anyway."

"Dog's gonna eat me out of house and home."

"I tell you what. I think that woman can talk faster than the speed of sound," Jake Bradley said.

"Appears so," Doobie said, though not really interested. "Still, though, she has a point."

"Most folks do."

"Not to take her side, of course."

"Of course."

"But I've had more than one person tell me about what's going on over there and if half of what they're saying is true, someone needs to go over there and straighten that fellow out."

"If you say so," Doobie said.

"What's the damage?"

"Oh, uh, thirty-six oh three. Just make it thirty-six. Three cents won't break the government."

Doobie handed him two twenties and received his change in ones. "Till next time, then," Doobie told him when Jake Bradley pushed the two sacks of groceries across the counter.

"And don't forget the dog food," he said as Doobie walked toward the door.

Doobie held up an index finger as both a thank you and good-bye. When he got to the door, he set the two sacks down, hoisted a fifty-pound bag of dog food up over one shoulder with ease, picked up the sacks and went sideways out the screen door. Sweet had just enough time to make it out before the door slammed behind him.

Doobie never gave the Reverend Daniel or the Kingdom of Lambs a second thought. A person's religion was a private matter, and as far as Doobie was concerned, no religion mattered.

5

Kathy Dalton had spent the night in a sedated coma thanks to Dr. Harlan Pope, their family physician. It was a house call he hadn't given a moment's thought of refusing when Reid had called. It was also a charge that would never show up on the books.

Reid Dalton had spent the same night sitting in a chair by their bed. He had allowed Dr. Pope to treat his facial wounds but had refused any form of medication to relieve the pain. It was a secondary pain at best.

He had just taken a phone call from Sergeant Montalvo, who had informed him that the autopsy had been completed, and he had signed the paperwork to release Bear's body to them. As an afterthought, he had recommended that Reid contact a mortuary to handle the removal in order to spare his wife a visit to the morgue. Neither man mentioned nor questioned the obvious outcome of the autopsy.

Reid was in a quandary. A mortuary was not like a doctor or baby-sitter or favorite restaurant. People didn't keep their numbers under a refrigerator magnet or listed in a book by the phone. By the time their number was necessary, it was already too late. A funeral for a twelve-year-old boy is not something a family plans for; it's something they plan against.

He had never been in charge of burying anyone and didn't want the sad duty now either, but he knew he had no choice. It wouldn't be done *for* him. His wife certainly couldn't handle it, nor would he ask her to. It was, after all, a father's duty to bury his son. It wasn't supposed to be that way. A son should bury his father, but life sometimes plays cruel tricks.

Reid Dalton took out the phone directory and went to the Yellow Pages to find Mortuaries. He found nothing. Not even the word. The thought scared him. He looked again, but there was nothing between Mortgages and Motels, other than a thin yellow space.

He thought of Morticians, but his finger again found its way to that same thin, yellow space. His hands began to tremble. Maybe someone *would* have to do it for him. Someone would have to take him by the hand and show him how to bury his son. Someone else would have to arrange his son's funeral.

Reid Dalton flipped back through the book until he found several pages of listings for Funeral Directors.

The list seemed never-ending. He thought of the joke about it being a dying business or that everyone was dying to get it. The joke was no longer funny and never would be again.

He laid the phone book on the kitchen table and sat down in a chair in front of it. He would have no choice but to start at the beginning. He breathed a sigh of relief, though only slightly, as relief in his situation was relative. At the beginning of the long list was a caption that read QUICK.TIPS. In the caption were more lists, only shorter and more to the point. He got up, took the phone and dialed the number listed for Types of Services. If nothing else, he would at least be able to talk to someone, someone who would understand what he was going through and could help. Someone who could take him by the hand and show him how to bury his son.

* * *

The Reverend Daniel was soap opera-star handsome. Maybe even pretty in some eyes, his own in particular. His hair was long, blonde and with a natural wave that had

44

never been so much as touched by artificial sprays or other such products used by men in his profession. His eyes were a pale blue, like the sky with just the hint of clouds. He stood well over six feet tall in his leather sandals, and his white flowing robe hid the fact that he worked out daily in a hidden room off his bed chamber, which only a few of his chosen had ever seen. Those few, dressed in brown, monk-type robes, were his bodyguards. They, too, held secrets beneath their robes, only their secrets were holstered.

The Reverend Daniel was on one of his spiritual walks about the grounds, content in the fact that his recent revival meeting had five new lambs into the fold. All female, under the age of twenty-two and of Anglo-Saxon heritage. Whether they were yet untouched, in the Biblical sense, would be a fact he would take pleasure in finding. But of more importance, they had each arrived in vehicles of some black-market worth.

Like the other lambs of his flock, each of the new ones would pleasure him in a multitude of ways. To the Reverend Daniel, even business was a pleasure.

One of the monks caught up with him on his walk. "They're ready, Reverend," he said.

"Thank you, James," he said. "Walk with me."

"My pleasure."

Reverend Daniel walked ahead of the monk. It was his rule that no one would be seen walking at his side, only behind. When they reached the end of a metal, dormitory-like building, the monk stepped ahead and unlocked the door. Once inside, the monk locked the door behind them. They made their way along a dim hallway and into another room, even darker than the hall, and stood in front of a window. On the other side of the window were the five new lambs. Behind them was a dark-haired woman wearing sackcloth. The lambs were wearing nothing.

Reverend Daniel touched a switch on his side of the one-way mirror and activated a ceiling sprinkler system in the other room. In the intercom he could hear Arrianna explaining how the water would cleanse them of their external impurities brought with them from the outside world of sinners.

"Not a bad batch, huh?" the monk said as he looked over the reverend's shoulder.

"That will be quite enough, James, unless of course, you would rather take leave of the ritual." His eyes never left the other room as he spoke.

"Yes, sir. I mean, no, sir."

Ashley Jenkins tilted her head back and let the shower hit her full on the face.

The water was warm and she accepted it with outstretched arms. She felt a rush of spiritual freedom as she stood naked and totally without shame. She brought her hands to her face and brushed aside the water and looked into the mirror at her body. Her breasts were firm and high. She brought her hands down over the erect nipples and across her flat belly. Her auburn pubic hair glistened as the water passed over it and dropped in gentle beads onto the floor.

On the other side of the glass, the monk was fondling himself beneath his robe. "The redhead looks to be the pick of the litter, Boss."

"You have such a way with words, James, but I must agree," Reverend Daniel said. "She will, no doubt, become a most satisfying witness to the cause."

"You gonna do her first?"

"I don't *do* anyone, James. I simply teach them the Word. If they desire my comfort, what kind of a father would I be to refuse them? I am nothing, if not freely given."

James Melchor never paid much attention to the ramblings of the reverend. Most of what he said was in far too advanced a language for him to comprehend, but he understood the bottom line. Money and power. He had seen it in Roger Criner's eyes the day he had been arrested in

Joplin, Missouri, for taking pornographic pictures of an eleven-year-old girl in the back of his van. James had been the Assistant Head Jailer and it had been his job to load Criner in his cell.

The arraignment had been swift and the bail so high that Criner had been forced to spend the weeks leading up to his trial behind bars. In those weeks, the silver-tongued Criner filled the jailer's head with visions of power and dreams of wealth. A tenth-grade education and a low-paying, dead-end job had been all Criner had needed to build on.

A week before the scheduled trial date, the Assistant Head Jailer unlocked Criner's cell door for the last time, and the two headed southwest in a Dodge truck that Criner had talked Melchor into buying with his meager life savings. He had paid cash for it at a used car lot in Carthage, under the name of Leonard Mitchell, the day before the escape.

They had worked small cons into larger ones until they had accumulated enough money to go for the big score. On the way, they had picked up two more stragglers, con men in their own right.

They were two semi-professional wrestlers, who went by Mo Morley and Gonzo Drake. The two worked the Oklahoma circuit, doing one-night stands in small, dusty towns. Criner had been amazed by their acting ability, not to mention their size. Each tipped the scales at just over three hundred pounds, but they could move across a makeshift ring with the grace and ease of a Baryshnikov. He knew his future would call for two such men, bodyguards at the very least, and a wad of cash and a promise of more to come had been all the enticement necessary to bring them into the fold.

"So, then you're gonna freely give to the redhead first?"

"In due time, James. In due time."

6

Reid Dalton had been directed to a Funeral Home in nearby Alamo Hills, after giving the QUICK TIPS operator everything from their religion to their annual income. While the operator had been cordial and extremely helpful, Reid had not come away from the experience with the peace of mind he had hoped for. But it was only the beginning.

Lack of sleep began to wear on him. He felt a heavy sensation inching its way up his body. He knew the burden of the day rested on his shoulders. Sleep was out of the question. He decided that before he called the funeral home, he needed something to keep him going. He wasn't hungry and didn't know if he ever would be again. He didn't know if we would ever have the urge to do anything again. Out of habit, he went to the kitchen counter, filled the coffee maker with grounds and water and flipped on the switch. He set a cup under the dripper and allowed it to fill before replacing it with the glass container. He returned to the table and hoped the black coffee would work its magic.

After downing three cups and remembering none of them, he got up and went to the phone. Voices filled his ear before he began to dial. One was Kathy's. He cradled the phone before identifying the other. A feeling of dread mixed with anticipation filled his body. He knew he had to face her and hoped the fact that she was talking to someone meant her state of mind would at least be rational. As rational as any mother who had just lost her only son could be. He felt his hope fading.

He touched the bandage on his cheek and wondered if she would remember any of last night. He would soon know, as the door to their bedroom opened slowly and Kathy Dalton emerged, running a brush through her hair as she walked toward him.

"I'm sorry about your face," she said calmly.

He figured the sedative must still be in control. "It's okay." He caught himself before he could say, "I'll live."

"No, it's not okay. I shouldn't have gone at you like that. I realize that now."

Reid had to choose his words carefully. "You were caught up in the moment." He wanted to tell her that he didn't blame her, but blame was an old wound he didn't want to open back up.

"I heard you pick up the phone," she said as she continued to groom her hair.

"I'm sorry. I was about to call..." He stopped himself short of telling her about the funeral arrangements he was about to make. He wasn't sure the time was right.

"Did you hear any of the conversation?"

"No, I hung right back up. I guess I was startled more than anything. I thought you were still asleep."

"No, I've been awake for quite a while now. I heard the phone ring earlier. I guess it woke me up."

"That was..." Reid Dalton had to think a minute. The sergeant's name had escaped him. "The uh, the policeman from last night."

"Can we get Bear?"

"Yes." Again, he had to catch himself. He started to tell her they were through with him, but the words hurt him enough just thinking them. There was no telling what they would do to her. "Yes, we can."

"Good. That's good," Kathy Dalton said. She was standing stone still. The only movement was the brush as it made its way down her hair.

"I was going to call a mortuary. I've been checking..." This time, Kathy Dalton stopped his sentence.

"There's no need," she informed him. "I called my parents. They'll handle everything."

"How will they do that? They're in Denton. That's hours from here."

"They'll get in touch with the funeral home there and they'll handle everything."

"But how?"

"I suppose they'll arrange to have him picked up and transported back?"

"Back? Back where?"

"Back up there. I want him to be buried in our family plot. They said it's okay. He'll have a place and I'll have the place next to him."

"But we haven't talked about…"

"There's nothing to talk about. I'm going to take Bear back home to be buried. Of course, you'll be there too."

"I thought this was his home?"

"Not anymore. This isn't anyone's home anymore."

"What are you saying, Kathy?"

"I'm going to take Bear back home and you can come, but when we come back, I want you to leave. We'll be together for the funeral. Bear would want that."

"For how long?"

"For how long what?"

"How long do you want me to leave?"

"Forever."

"I don't think you know what you're saying."

"I think I do."

"You're upset, Kathy."

"Of course I'm upset. My son is dead and it's made me realize I don't love you anymore. I haven't for quite some time."

"How can you say that?"

"Surely, you've known that. I used to love you, I did. I guess when Bear was born, I transferred all the love I had for you into him. Now that he's gone, there's no love left."

"But I still love you. I loved Bear too, just as much as you," he told her.

"You might now, but every time you see me, you'll think of Bear. It will eat away at you until you won't be able to look at me anymore. It's better that we do this now."

"Better for who?"

"Both of us. You *will* realize it someday. I know you will. Please don't fight me on this. I just don't have anything left to give you."

"What? What are you going to do?"

"I don't know. I haven't thought it all through yet. I just know what we need to do now."

"We can work through all this."

"We shouldn't have to *work* at anything. Don't you understand?"

"I guess I don't."

"You will. I promise," she said. Before he could say anything else, his wife turned and walked back toward their bedroom, brushing her hair as she went.

Reid Dalton never felt more alone. The house that had once been their home was now nothing more than an empty shell. One fleeting moment in time had gutted it of all life and love and left it to rot.

Reid Dalton, like the house, had also been gutted. Only time would tell if he, too, would be left to rot.

* * *

Dave Jenkins drove his custom-made Melex golf cart across the Number 8 fairway and up into the small shed he had built just for that purpose. He raised the seat and connected the electric battery charger to the post at the end of the tray of three marine batteries. His mood was well below par as he had shot just the opposite on the round.

He left the barn and walked across the porch that overlooked the course and into the house. Belinda Jenkins was in her favorite rocking chair, reading her favorite book, *The Holy Bible*. She didn't acknowledge his entry. She never did. She had learned not to speak until spoken to when he returned from playing. His first sentence would always dictate how he had played and what kind of mood he would be in until the round wore off, which sometimes lasted until his next tee time.

"Worthless, fucking game," Dave Jenkins said as he stormed into the kitchen and grabbed a beer from the refrigerator.

"Bad round?" Belinda Jenkins spoke without looking up from her reading.

"What was your first clue?"

"If you hate it that much, why don't you quit?"

"The same reason you don't quit reading that book," he said. "It relaxes me."

"It sure doesn't look like it."

"What do you know?"

"I know that half the time you come in complaining about how bad you played and threaten to quit. When you play good, you come in with that stupid putter of yours and practice all over the house," she explained.

"Don't talk to me about that putter," he said. "That's why I played bad today. I had to buy another one at the pro shop and it didn't work worth a shit."

"Maybe it's not the putter."

"Damn sure was. I put my life's blood into that other one. It was like family."

"If you cared half as much about your real family, Ashley never would have left."

"What do you mean left?"

"She went to that Kingdom of Lambs place," Belinda Jenkins told her husband.

"You mean she's not in school?"

"No, she packed up and left early this morning."

"She can't do that."

"I'm afraid she did."

"Well, you just get your ass over there and bring her home. No daughter of mine is going to get involved with something like that," he yelled at her. "How would it look?"

"What do you mean, how would it look? Is that all you care about?"

"Hey, I've worked hard all my life to give her the best. I just bought her that new car, gave her money and nice clothes. How could she do this to me?"

"I doubt that thought ever entered her mind."

"Well, it should have."

"Then you go get her."

"The hell I will. She wants to ruin her life like that, then let her. I'll wash my hands of her, that's what I'll do. She wants to come back here, then let her crawl back," he said. "And I'll tell you another thing. If she thinks she can come back here carrying something around in that little belly of hers, she's got another think coming. I'll not have her walking around the club in that condition. I'd never be able to live it down."

Belinda Jenkins went back to reading her *Bible*. After a few minutes she spoke again. "You know, the Lord *does* work in mysterious ways."

"No shit. I missed a two-foot birdie putt on fourteen and then sank a two-footer on fifteen for a double bogey," he explained. "Tell me that ain't mysterious."

7

Denton is north of Dallas and south of Oklahoma, but as far as Reid Dalton was concerned, it might just as well be Bumfuck, Egypt. It was a good three hundred miles ·from San Antonio, whether by car or crow. Kathy Dalton had chosen to ride in the transport hearse with Bear's body. Before leaving, she had purchased a return airline ticket. She had also chosen for her husband to drive himself. He had respected her wishes.

The McLeod Funeral Home had seen to all the arrangements and had taken special care and measures to make sure Bear's body was situated in the casket in such a way that there was no evidence of how his life had been taken.

Reid had been skeptical of having an open casket for viewing, but as he looked down on the lifeless body of his son, his head surrounded by what looked to be a thick cloud of soft pillows, he was thankful for the opportunity.

The funeral was scheduled for two o'clock the following day, but already more than thirty people had come by to pay their respects. They were all people he didn't know and would never see again, and the respects they were paying were to his wife and not him. Sure, they had words to say to him as they passed Bear's casket. Some even shed tears at the sight of one so young in such a final rest. Reid Dalton took no comfort in either.

His Methodist upbringing told him his son was in a better place, but the way he was taken to that better place led him to believe otherwise. The better place would be with him, where he could watch him grow up. Watch him drive a car for the first time, go on his first date, graduate from high school, then college. There was no better place. No one would ever be able to convince him of that again. His son was gone, period. No reason.

"Oh, he looks so at peace," an elderly woman said to her companion as she laid her hand on the edge of the open casket. "Don't you think so, Mildred?"

"Oh, yes. They did a wonderful job. He looks like he's just sleeping."

"He's not sleeping, he's dead. Half his head is blown off," Reid Dalton wanted to say. He wanted to rip the pillows out of the casket and show them what his son really looked like. Tear away the disguise and get down to the actual reason why he was there. Show them he wasn't at peace. He wasn't asleep. He was dead. Lifeless.

Gone. He wasn't in a better place and he wasn't going to a better place. He was going to a hole in the ground. A hole in the ground, half the state from home.

It was then that Reid Dalton came to the realization that not only was his son dead, but as far as he was concerned, so was God. God would never let something like this happen to his son, to anyone's son. He had seen it too many times in his line of work. Children were killed needlessly in car wrecks. Fathers were taken away from their children. Whole families were wiped out in mere seconds. Teenagers were burned alive in fiery crashes on prom nights. Mothers were beheaded while their children watched in horror from the back seat. None of it made any sense. One minute they were here, enjoying life, and the next minute they were mingled in twisted metal.

It had all been eating away at him for too long. He had run from the truth his entire life. The only truth was life. When life was gone, so was truth. Death kills truth. In the end, death becomes truth. Nothing starts over.

Bear was dead. That was the truth. That was Bear's truth and truth wouldn't set him free. It would be up to him to set Bear free. Bear was his son and he would always be his son. Death couldn't destroy that. He wouldn't let death take him away, any more than he would let Kathy take him away. He would see to it that Bear was with him. The funeral, his burial, would all be temporary. Bear was his life and Bear was his death. They would be close again. That would be his truth.

* * *

Doobie was hard at rest in the green chair at the edge of the cliff, with the second cup of coffee in his hand. Sweet was next to him, gnawing on a bone. He had spent the last two days in the employ of Bob Lansing, laying a split-rail fence across the front of his property on the thirteenth fairway. The work had been hard for the first few hours, until Doobie convinced Bob that his time would be better spent on the golf course. Without Bob's help, Doobie completed what would have been a weeklong project in two days. For his efforts, Doobie received two lunches, four T-bone steaks, three one-hundred-dollar bills and Bob Lansing's undying gratitude.

Doobie had fired up the stove, a gas grill he had received as payment for a previous job, and laid waste to one of the steaks when he got back to the cabin. He shared the bone with Sweet, who had earned his keep by keeping Doobie's work area free of the ever-present and always-nosey squirrels that shared the course with the golfers and the deer.

Unlike the deer, who ignored the golfers, the squirrels were much more brazen. Any food left open and unattended in a golf cart was considered fair game to the vermin. Peanuts, of course, were their favorite meal and they had been known to carry them away, bags and all.

The three hundred payment would have been enough to keep Doobie on his hill and gainfully unemployed for at least two weeks, but further duty had called in the form of Belinda Jenkins. She had caught him on his short drive back the night before and asked if he could please mow their yard at his next available opportunity. She hadn't demanded it be the next day, but from the looks of the yard, the sooner he did it, the easier it would be. And, she had said please.

Sweet also liked it when Doobie worked around the Jenkins' house. Their porch was covered with a thick, straw mat he could roll around on and scratch places he couldn't get to otherwise. Belinda Jenkins would also spend time with him throughout the day and always managed to bring a treat with her. Doobie knew the Jenkins' had no dog of their own, which meant she would undoubtedly buy the biscuits for the sole purpose of pleasing Sweet.

Doobie never shared many words with the people he worked for. He preferred to find out what they wanted done, do it and be gone. He wouldn't ignore their attempt at conversation, but would rather find a tactful way to end it in the early stages. In Dave Jenkins' case, it was unnecessary. The two hadn't exchanged a dozen words in the entire time Doobie had done work for them.

Belinda Jenkins had always been the one to seek out his services. If left to her husband, nothing around the house would ever get done. Doobie didn't care one way or the other. He did what was asked of him, received payment and was gone. What happened in their house was none of his concern.

"We're going down to see your friend this morning," Doobie told his dog when he rose from the green chair with two empty cups in his hand. "And you better leave that bone up here, otherwise she may not think you need anything else to chew on."

The chocolate lab looked at him with not so much as an inclination that he understood and got up with the bone in his mouth.

"Drop it, Sweet," he ordered.

The dog opened his mouth and let the bone fall to the ground in front of him.

"That's better. You won't regret it." On the way back to the cabin, he ran his hand across the trunk of the sycamore tree, just like he had done on his way out. Just like he had done every time he passed the tree thousands of times before, to let him know he was still there.

Belinda Jenkins was busy watering an assortment of potted plants on the porch when the two of them arrived. Sweet headed for the porch, waited long enough for Belinda Jenkins to acknowledge his presence with a pat on the head, then went to his side on the thick straw mat and began doing half-circle slides.

"Morning, ma'am," Doobie said.

"Why, good morning, Doobie," she answered. "I hope I haven't put anyone out, but I'm afraid this yard will go to seed if I wait too much longer. I should have gotten hold of you last week. It's all my fault."

"No problem, ma'am. I'll get right on it and it'll be good as new in no time."

"You're so kind. I was just about to get everything out for you. Let me set this down and I'll..."

"No, no. You just go about what you're doing. I know where the mower is," Doobie said. "And if old Sweet gets in your way, just give him a little nudge."

"Oh, he's just fine. I have a little something for him in the house," she said. "It's okay, isn't it?"

"I don't know that I've ever seen him complain, ma'am."

Doobie left the side of the porch and went through the back door of the garage and located the mower. Like everyone else he worked for, the Jenkins had their own lawn equipment and much more elaborate than he could have afforded. While he made use of their equipment, he always treated them like they were his own. He checked the gas, oil and spark plug, even though he knew full well he had left them full, clean and ready the last time.

Doobie pushed the mower out the back door and started it with ease. He let it idle while he made a thorough sweep of the yard in search of hidden golf balls that would damage the blade. As usual, the hunt was productive. He took three balls into the empty cart shed and laid them by the battery charger where Dave Jenkins could find them. He had no doubt he would probably find them again in someone else's yard, but he had no use for them himself.

At one time, he had thought about marking them somehow, just to see if golf balls had any migrating pattern, but figured the game was confusing enough for those who played it, and he surely didn't need to get caught up in it.

The only yard to speak of was in the back of the house. The front was a circular drive that surrounded a rock garden; the cart shed and a flower garden ate up the sides. It took Doobie just under two hours to mow, trim and return the equipment, cleaned and ready for his next visit, to the garage.

Belinda Jenkins was sitting in a wrought iron, patio chair on the porch. Sweet was at the other end, asleep in a patch of bright sunlight. As always, a plate of sandwiches was on the two-by-twelve railing that surrounded the porch.

"I hope you like the ham," she said. "It's honey-glazed. And I added just a touch of Dijon mustard. I think it brings out more of the flavor. I hope that's okay. "

"I'm sure it will be, ma'am, but you didn't need to go to all that trouble."

"It was no trouble at all. I enjoyed doing it. I had one myself just a few minutes ago. I would have waited, but I know you like to eat alone."

"Just something I'm used to."

While Doobie would have rather taken the sandwich to go, he knew it wouldn't have been proper under the circumstances, plus he hadn't yet been paid, at least not in coin.

"Do you mind if I ask you something?" Belinda Jenkins said. "If you do, I'll understand."

While he did, on both counts, he said he didn't. It would be like biting the hand that fed him.

"Are you a religious man?"

Doobie was quick to answer and hoped his response would bring an end to the topic. "No, ma'am."

It didn't. "Do you mind if I ask why?" He did. "Yes, ma'am."

"Oh."

Not knowing what day it was, Doobie figured it must be Sunday, from her pointed question. Then he remembered watching the golfers during his morning coffee in the green chair by the cliff. There weren't nearly enough of them crowding the course for it to be Sunday. He began chewing faster, but not fast enough.

"I don't know that you've ever met my daughter, Ashley," she started again.

While Doobie had never been formally introduced to Ashley Jenkins, he had met her on one occasion and seen her on others. That one occasion, right at four years ago, had led to one of the few bright spots left in his life.

As Doobie recalled, he had been patching ball dents in the stucco retaining wall belonging to Rich Casterwine. The wall bordered the left side of the number 6 fairway about a hundred and fifty yards from the tee box and was hit more times than it was missed. The golfers played up the left side on purpose, as the fairway sloped right, all the way down to the creek. The job turned into an annual toil.

It was only natural to hear screams, both of disgust and jubilation, on a golf course, but the scream that had stopped Doobie in his work that day had been made by a young girl. Three fairways over, he could see the girl chasing after a golf cart. At first, he figured she must have just fallen out of the cart until the cart started meandering from one side of the fairway to the other.

When her screams continued, Doobie jumped up onto the retaining wall for a better look. Out in front of the cart was a small dark animal, too small to be a deer and too large to be a squirrel. What's more, the cart seemed to be chasing the animal. Even back then, Doobie had made it a point not to get involved in the business of others, but the odds in this situation didn't seem to be fair.

Doobie jumped from the wall and ran across two fairways. Luckily, it had been a dry summer and the creek was shallow enough to retrieve golf balls by hand. He was in and out of the water before he even knew it was there. When he reached the top of the bank, the cart was headed in his direction, not more than a yard behind a small, brown puppy.

The driver of the cart must have sensed his fun was over. He made an immediate right turn and headed toward the number 4 green. Doobie knelt down and the puppy ran into his arms. By the time Ashley Jenkins reached them, the bond had been set.

"Oh, thank you," she said, out of breath. "I think they would have run over him."

"Looked like it," Doobie said. "You might want to keep him on a leash."

"Oh, he's not mine. I was just out here trying to see if I could see my daddy when I saw what they were doing."

"Who does he belong to?"

"I don't know. I've never seen him before."

"Do you live around here?"

"Yes, sir. Over on Cliffdweller Drive."

"I tell you what. Why don't you carry him home? I'll watch to make sure nothing else happens. Your folks'll be able to find out who he belongs to."

"Oh, no. I couldn't do that. Then my daddy would know I had been out here. He told me

I wasn't supposed to come out onto the course."

"Just tell him you found him by your house."

"I couldn't do that either. That would be lying and he spanks me when I lie."

"Well, what are we going to do? We can't just leave him here."

"Why don't you take him?"

"I'm afraid that's out of the question," Doobie told the young girl. "There wouldn't be anyone to take care of him."

"You can take care of him," she said. "See how he trusts you?"

Doobie had been too deep in conversation to notice that the puppy had snuggled its way deeper into his arms and was resting with its eyes closed.

"He's too young to know any better."

"You have to take him, please? I don't want him to get hurt."

Doobie knew his choices were limited. He could at least take the dog to the cabin, where it would be safe for the rest of the day. Surely after the owner realized it was gone, he would come looking for it and probably even post signs. From what he could tell, the puppy was a Labrador and probably had cost the owner a few dollars.

"Okay, but when you hear of someone looking for him, you tell your daddy. He'll know how to find me."

"Can I tell my mama instead?"

"Deal."

Ashley Jenkins skipped her way back across the fairway and up the hill. Doobie watched until he lost her in the trees. He stood up with the small dog in his arms. When he tried to put him down, the puppy jumped up against his leg and yapped.

"What, you can't walk?"

The puppy yapped again. "I think someone's already got you spoiled," he said and picked him up again. "I bet they'll come looking for you before the sun goes down."

After giving the puppy its first of many rides to come in the Bronco, Doobie gave him a bowl of water and left him yapping in the cabin. Before he returned to his job, Doobie took a detour down Tapatio Drive West. He parked and walked into the trees on the side of the hill where Bob Lansing's house would later be built and waited.

The thirteenth hole was a five hundred and fifty-nine yard par five that dog-legged left around the hill. The safe shot off the tee was down the middle to the dogleg, however, that would leave over three hundred and fifty yards to the green. Most golfers, thinking they were more powerful than they actually were, tried to drive over the hill and cut off a good hundred and fifty yards. They usually never made it to the top of the hill, much less over it and onto the fairway. Nevertheless, they tried time after time.

Doobie watched two groups flail off the tee box and fail on the hill before the group he had been waiting for arrived. The first one off the box was the one he wanted. He watched him rear back and swing out of his shoes. The ball sailed over the side of the hill, hit a tree and came to rest on the down-slope at least thirty yards from the fairway. Doobie walked over, picked up the ball and put it in his pocket. Two of the others hit to the safe spot. The fourth drove the cut and ended up in the dry creek bed on the far side.

The first man drove the cart to the center of the fairway, let his playing partner out, then headed toward the hill. The other cart was parked by the shallow ravine that led to the creek. Doobie's man drove his cart as far up the hill as the boulders would allow him to go, then got out in search of his shot. Doobie made his way to the cart, using the trees for cover, extracted a metal driver from the man's bag and walked slowly up the hill. When he was no more than two steps from the man, he looked back onto the fairway to make sure he hadn't been seen.

"Looking for this?" Doobie said quietly.

The man turned, but before his eyes could tell his brain their foursome had added a fifth, Doobie laid the metal driver against the side of his head with an evil ring. The man fell hard against a tree before he hit the ground.

Doobie returned the club to the bag and was about to leave when he remembered the ball. He reached into his pocket, took out the ball and put it in a zippered pocket with the others.

Doobie didn't consider himself a thief.

He also didn't consider himself a master, but when a week passed and no one came looking, he named the chocolate lab Sweet and took him to raise.

"No, ma'am, but I do recall having seen her on occasion," Doobie said.

"I've tried to raise her with the right Christian values. Lord knows Mister Jenkins hasn't been much help, but he does his best to provide, so I can't complain. I just worry about her, that she'll grow up to make the right decisions."

"I'm sure she will."

"Well, right now I'm not so sure. *I'm* even torn between what's right."

Doobie knew he was already just short of too late to back out of the conversation, so he swallowed the last bite of sandwich and made the best of it. "How's that?"

"I don't suppose you've heard about the Kingdom of Lambs, have you?"

While he had, he figured any knowledge he might admit to might prolong the conversation. So, he lied. "No, ma'am."

"I guess you wouldn't have. It's some sort of a religious organization. I'm not really sure what denomination or even if they are one, but to make a long story short..."

"Please do," Doobie thought to himself.

"...she left the other day to become part of their congregation."

"I take it you don't agree with her decision."

"I'm not sure. I've heard some things, just gossip, mind you, but upsetting, still."

"I've never put much stock in gossip," Doobie told her.

"Oh, I don't either. It's the devil's work and I want no part of it. But she's so young and naive. I don't want her to make the wrong decision."

"That's part of life," Doobie said, knowing but not wanting to admit to himself where his words were coming from.

"I know it's hard for you to understand, being that you don't have any children..."

Her words hit Doobie hard.

"...but I wish there was some way I could make sure she was all right."

"Just go see her."

"My husband would never allow it," she said. "He's all but disowned her."

"Ah, he'll come around," Doobie said.

"Oh, you don't know my husband. He's as hard-headed as the day is long."

"Still, she *is* his daughter. You'll see."

"You think so?"

Doobie didn't know one way or the other, but the conversation had drawn him into a reassuring mood. It had also given Sweet enough time to wake from his nap. He got up and walked over to him with his tail wagging. "Sweet does, don't you, boy?"

"I guess I'm just being a worrywart," Belinda Jenkins said. "No, sounds to me like you're just being a mother."

8

When Reid Dalton returned to the house in Deer Run, he did so alone. He had seen no point in staying in Denton after the funeral. Kathy had taken to her old room in her parents' house and had shown no sign of wanting him around. One night sleeping in the hide-a-bed in her parents' den had been more than enough to convince him that he would be better off anywhere but there.

On his way out of town, he had paid a visit to Bear's grave, not to say good-bye but to get his bearings. He would be back to do what he needed to do.

An assortment of plants and flowers met him at the front door. Cards, both stamped and unstamped, were crammed into the mailbox. While he was grateful for his friends' acts and thoughts of sympathy, Reid Dalton wanted no part of it. He made three trips through the house and into the garage before his porch no longer bore testimony to the fact that Bear was gone.

He went to the desk in his den next and pulled open the bottom left drawer. It had been almost a year since he had kicked the habit, but he had kept the remains of the last pack of Camels he had opened as a reminder. On top of the pack was the silver-plated Zippo lighter Bear had given to him for Father's Day the month before he had quit. Bear had told him he would rather that he not smoke and that every time he used the lighter, he would be reminded of that wish. Engraved on one side was "Bear" and on the other "Pop". He picked up the lighter and rubbed his thumb over the engraving of his son's name.

Bear's ploy had worked. He had quit smoking to ensure he'd be around to watch his son grow up but that particular policy got cancelled before either had a chance to mature.

Reid reached back into the drawer and took out the stale pack of smokes. Flakes of tobacco fell onto the desktop when he pulled out a lone nail from the coffin. He walked out of the den and down the hall to Bear's room. Nothing had changed. It was just as Bear had left it before going to Jason's. His backpack with his finished homework inside was on the desk next to his computer.

The covers on the bed were ruffled where he had obviously waited for his mother to leave. It was there that he had planned his strategy, the words he'd used to get his father to let him go. He had known the answer would be yes. It always was.

Reid sat on that very same spot, the cigarette in one hand and the lighter in the other. On the wall facing him was a team soccer picture from four years back. He had known nothing at all about the game, but had agreed to coach when Bear had told him how much fun it would be for the two of them to learn together. Their record had been two and eight but Bear hadn't cared. In the picture, there was evidence of that fact. Bear stood next to his father, wearing a proud smile.

Reid Dalton looked around the room at other team pictures.

There were basketball and baseball, even one from the year he had spent learning karate. He had made it to the green belt stage before giving it up to make room for other things. Reid Dalton kept going back to the soccer picture, the only one where they were both together. Bear's smile was different in that picture.

Brighter, even happier, than in the others.

He leaned over the end of the bed and threw the cigarette into the trash can by the desk. With the lighter still in his hand, he lay down where Bear would have and let the long drive and the days passed ease his weary body into a deep but confused kind of sleep.

                    ⋆ ⋆ ⋆

The House of Lambs compound was far enough
in the hill country off Highway 27 to go
unnoticed by the everyday traveler. No
signs pointed the way and even the
entrance to the twenty-four-hundred-acre
grounds, surrounded by barbed wire fence,
fit into the countryside. It was nothing
more than the usual cattle guard below a
metal push-gate. While there was no lock
on the gate, the entrance was guarded by
one of the monks, positioned in a
camouflaged deer stand in the scrub brush
no more than fifty yards away. A caliche
path led around two hills to an old cattle
ranch that had been made up of the main
house, a barn and a grain silo when it was
purchased under the name of the House of
Lambs Evangelical Church from the estate
of Ben Ryder.

The estate was made up of Ben Ryder's two
daughters, who hadn't cared who the
purchaser was. They had long since left
the ranch and were only concerned with the
financial arrangement, which would allow
them to continue living the way they had
grown accustomed to in a small community
outside of Phoenix, Arizona.

It had been a cash transaction handled by
the realtor. All the required signatures
had been handled by mail and the money had

been deposited into the estate's account by wire.

Had the daughters ever cared to visit the ranch again, they would have given up trying to find it and returned home. With the exception of the silo, nothing of the old homestead remained. In its place were two large, metal, warehouse-type buildings, one being the church and the other a storage facility for the many automobiles that passed through the compound. Another four-story metal building with wrought iron, screened windows was the dormitory. A fourth, where the Reverend Daniel and his monks resided, was made of Austin stone. The buildings formed a four- sided compound with the silo in the middle of the quadrangle. The church building was at the front and the reverend's quarters were at the rear.

A ten-foot chain link fence with three rows of barbed wire at the top surrounded the immediate twenty acres. With the exception of a large neon cross from the roofline down to just above the front door of the church, the facility resembled any other

modern-day minimum-security prison.

Unlike a prison, the security measures were there to keep people out, not to keep the congregation in. While the gate was kept locked, it only took Reverend Daniel's blessing for someone to leave.

Very few had sought his permission to make a permanent exit, and when they did, they left with only what clothing they could carry. Everything else they had donated to the church when they arrived.

A chosen group made excursions into the surrounding communities, and only then for the purpose of revival meetings to add to the flock. The chosen had reached such a pinnacle of trust that nothing said by the outside world could sway them from their dedication and beliefs.

Regardless of their gender, they were all married to the church; some more than others. The chosen females, once they had given themselves wholly and freely to the Reverend Daniel, were considered to be his wives. To them, to be married to the church was to be married to him. He *was* the church. None denied the existence of the others. If jealousy became evident in one, she was deemed to be impure and was given in marriage, so to speak, to the monks, until her penance was complete. No one had yet done penance more than once.

To the monks, a penance was a perk. One they accepted with open arms.

<h1 style="text-align:center">9</h1>

Detective Sergeant Eric Montalvo knew the only way to negotiate a brick wall was to hit it head-on. If he could make even the smallest crack in the surface, he could eventually penetrate the entire structure. He had been up one side of the block where Bear Dalton had been killed and had banged on every door, but so far, the only crack he had been able to make was in his own head-on, and he had a splitting headache to prove it. The wall was winning.

Detective Sergeant Jess Ramsey had covered the other side.

They stopped at the corner to compare notes. "Any luck?" Montalvo asked.

"Not yet."

"What about the kid? The one he was going to see?"

"He's having a rough time of it. His folks have him seeing a shrink. Poor guy's been having nightmares like you wouldn't believe."

"I guess I would too if I were his age and had seen my best friend blown away right in front of me."

"Who are you kidding? You would've chased the car down and pistol-whipped the lot of 'em," Ramsey said.

"Not back then. I would have hidden in the bushes till hell froze over. Just like most people."

"I can't see you being afraid."

"Well, right now I'm afraid we're not getting anywhere with this investigation, and that scares the hell out of me."

"You think the shooter will do it again?" "Why not? He's gotten away with it so far." "Maybe next time he'll get careless."

"Now that's a comforting thought," Montalvo said. "We just gonna let him keep killing kids till he screws up?"

"Maybe the shrink will help the friend remember something."

"I don't think that's what his parents have in mind. If I were them, I'd want to help him forget."

"So, we've still got nothing," Ramsey said. "What's next on the agenda?"

"As long as we're here, we might as well wake everybody up. You take the next block and I'll go back and start on the other end. Who knows, maybe someone's just sitting there waiting for us."

"That's what I like about you, amigo," Ramsey said.

"What's that?"

"You don't like the taste of defeat."

"Shit, defeat only tastes bitter if you swallow it," Montalvo said. "And I ain't chewed on this long enough yet."

* * *

Ashley Jenkins had never worn sackcloth. The closest she had come was a cotton nightshirt and that wasn't even in the same ballpark. Her nipples were raw from direct contact with the coarse material and she itched so bad that even scratching no longer brought relief. A dark-haired woman with green eyes, who introduced herself as Sister Arrianna, saw the trouble she was in and told her she could help.

"Come with me," the woman said.

"But I have to finish sweeping the floor and then I have the scriptures to read."

"They will both still be here when you return."

"Where are we going?"

"Just to the infirmary. It's on the first floor."

"Are you sure it'll be okay?"

"Don't worry. It's what I'm here for."

Ashley Jenkins set the broom against the wall and followed the woman down three flights of stairs and into a room next to where she had been cleansed the first day. The room looked just like any other medical examining room. The walls were white, the tile floor spotless. In the middle of the room sat a padded table with a broad strip of paper covering the black vinyl.

"Take off your dress and let me have a look at you," the woman ordered.

"Can we close the door first?"

"I'm sorry, but Reverend Daniel doesn't allow it."

"But what if someone comes by?"

"Are you ashamed of your body?"

"No, but..."

"Then do as I ask or I won't be able to help you."

"Are you a nurse?"

"Among other things," she said. "Now hurry and slip out of your dress."

Ashley Jenkins lifted the shift-like frock over her head and dropped it on the table.

Her milky-white body was covered with red splotches from her shoulders to her knees. "Ew, what is it?"

"Just chafing. You'll get used to it. We all do."

The nurse touched her left nipple. Ashley Jenkins pulled her shoulders inward and winced at the cold touch of the woman's hand.

"And you've got a pretty bad case there."

"I'm not used to not wearing underwear," she said. "It makes things easier," the nurse told her. "What things?"

"Oh, just things. You'll understand by and by." Arrianna walked over to a cabinet and took out a can of baby powder. "Here. Let's try some of this." She shook the contents of the can onto Ashley Jenkins' shoulder and then over her breasts. "You rub that around lightly while I get your back."

She rubbed the powder in like she had done many times at home.

Arrianna nudged her into a half-circle move and began to powder her back. The effects of the powder masked the coolness of her touch. She laid a blanket of powder at the base of her back and rubbed it smoothly across her buttocks and into the crevice.

Ashley Jenkins jerked away. She had never been touched there before, at least not in her young adult life. Before that, it had only been by her mother's hand.

"You needn't be afraid," Arrianna said. "I do this for all the girls."

"I'm sorry. It's just...I'm just...It's the door being open, that's all," Ashley said nervously.

"That's quite all right. I'm done," she said. "Hold out your hand."

She did as instructed and Arrianna shook a small mound of powder into it.

"You'll want to put some down there, too."

Ashley Jenkins forced an embarrassed smile, then turned to the side and rubbed the powder between her legs and down her thighs.

"You'll need to do this every day until you get used to the material. It won't take long."

"Can I take some upstairs?"

"Reverend Daniel wouldn't approve, I'm afraid. He's very strict about what you keep in your living quarters. Just come by here after you shower and I'll see to it that you're made comfortable."

"Am I the only one?"

"Of course not. They all come to me from time to time. That's what I'm here for. To keep you ready."

"Ready for what?"

"The special things," Arrianna said. "You'll know when it's your time. Now, go on back upstairs."

Ashley Jenkins was confused. It was all too new to her. She imagined it was what college would be like. Living in a dormitory. Showering with a group. The clothes were not what she had expected and certainly not being allowed to wear underwear.

But Reverend Daniel was something else. So far, he had been everything she had imagined. A loving father. A father who would recite scriptures with her. Not just with her alone, but with everyone. Yet, even when the congregation was together, his words were directed to her. She had felt it the first time at the revival meeting. It was what had brought her to the Kingdom of Lambs. It was what would keep her there.

She *was* ready.

10

Reid Dalton woke refreshed and with a new attitude, not necessarily better, just new. He hopped off the bed and made his way through the house into the garage. He grabbed the cord that hung from the ceiling and pulled down the ladder that led to the attic. He climbed up and switched on the light. He stepped carefully from one joist to another until he found the neatly folded pile of moving boxes they had saved when they moved into the house. He grabbed as many as he could muster and balanced his way back to the opening and down again, careful not to harm himself or his cargo.

He took the boxes into Bear's room, where he unfolded and then folded each one. He hit the walls first, taking down all evidence of Bear's existence and loading them into the boxes. The dresser was his next target. He pulled out the drawers one by one and dumped the contents into more boxes. By the time he had cleaned out the closet, he was in need of more cartons. He made his way back to the attic for reinforcements, then returned to complete his mission. After emptying the desk, he made a final sweep under the bed, where he found Bear's ball glove and bat.

Reid carried the loaded boxes back to the garage and up into the attic, where he stacked them neatly and in plain sight near the opening. He switched off the light, climbed down the ladder and lifted it back up into the ceiling.

His job was only half done. He hurried to the den, pulled out all the drawers **in** his own desk, took them to Bear's room and loaded the contents into the smaller desk. When he ran out of room, he dumped the rest into one of the remaining boxes. He disconnected his computer and phone and reconnected them in the other room. He tested both, found them in working order, then went to the bedroom he had shared with Kathy and removed all his belongings. It was her room now, not theirs. It was what she had wanted. She had made it perfectly clear. And it was what she would find when she returned.

The clothes that wouldn't fit into the closet and dresser in Bear's old room found a new home in the boxes. The room was his now, but Bear still shared a space on the wall. The soccer picture was all that remained of his son. It was what he wanted now. Everything was perfectly clear.

* * *

Doobie couldn't remember the last time he had climbed into the Bronco without Sweet riding shotgun. He had explained to him that a tent revival meeting was no place for himself, much less a dog, but Sweet wasn't buying his act. All he knew was that when Doobie was behind the wheel, he was supposed to be in the seat beside him. That's the way it had always been from the first day Sweet had latched onto him. Doobie hadn't taken him to raise. Sweet had taken him to protect. It was his job, just like it was his job to sleep close to him when the nights got cold and the fire in the fireplace went out. To sit close by the green chair near the cliff and make sure Doobie didn't get too close to the edge. He considered the cookies his reward for a job well done. He had never asked for a reward. He would have done it for just a scratch on the head or even for nothing. Now he was being told his services were no longer needed.

"Look. I'm not going to be gone that long and you wouldn't enjoy it anyway," Doobie told him. "It's just gonna be some guy trying to feed a load of shit to a bunch of people who are already so full of it they're fartin' angels."

Sweet tilted his head to the side.

"Besides, someone has to stay here and guard the homestead, such as it is, and since you haven't learned to drive yet..."

Sweet wagged his tail in the dirt.

"Is that a yes?" Sweet wagged harder.

"Well, it's gonna have to do. If I wait around here much longer, I'm gonna miss the opening hymn, and you know how much I love to sing."

Sweet barked loudly when Doobie started the engine of the old Bronco.

"Sorry, boy," Doobie said reluctantly, "but this is just something I've gotta do alone." It was a thirty-thee-mile drive to Bandera, and one that would take him a good hour and a half on the back roads with no one to talk to. While he hated to do it, Doobie barked an order of his own. "Sweet! Stay!"

Doobie took the Bronco into a U-turn and headed out toward the gate. He knew the dog wouldn't follow. He had given him the only command he had ever taught him, but in the back of his mind, he wished he would refuse. The dog was a part of him now, the best part, for that matter. Without him, he would be back to the way he was before. No one to care for and no one to care for him. He had lived, no existed, that way for a short while. Going from one day to the next with no direction. No reason. He

still lacked a good part of direction, but
Sweet had given him reason.

When he got out to unlock the gate, Doobie
looked back up the path. Sweet had obeyed.
He drove over the cattle guard, got back
out and re-chained the gate to the fence.
Not to keep Sweet in, but to keep everyone
else out.

11

Reid Dalton had demanded they buy Bear a double bed once he had outgrown his baby bed, bars and all. He had told Kathy his son needed a bed he could grow into. When Bear reached the age of sleepovers, he had complained that he needed two beds. It just wasn't right for two boys to be sleeping in the same bed.

"The guys are going to think I'm a fag, Pop," he had said. "Can't we sell this one and get me a bunk bed?"

Reid had rectified the situation with a hunting cot, which the boys usually fought over to see who got to sleep on it rather than the larger bed. He'd moved the cot into the garage, where it was about to start gathering dust. Bear was gone and the bed was now his. He put the bed to overnight use and managed to pass through the dark hours in an unexpected, restful sleep.

He'd just gotten off the phone with his office. Buster Horton, the District Claims Manager and his immediate superior, had told him in no uncertain terms that he was not to be seen in the office until he was ready to come back, regardless of how long it took.

Buster had asked about Kathy. Reid had said she was doing as well as could be expected. He hadn't offered any more information than that. He hadn't lied; he just hadn't given himself a chance to. He was sure the company had sent some sort of floral arrangement to the funeral home in Denton. It was their usual procedure. He hadn't paid any attention at the time, but thanked Buster for what he knew had been there.

He was on his third cup of black coffee at the kitchen table when he thought he heard a light knock on the front door. It wasn't loud enough for him to be sure, so he waited to make sure it wasn't just his imagination. When he heard it again, he walked through the living room to the door.

Jason Watson looked up at him as he eased the door open. When words failed them both, he moved to the side and Jason walked in. He took small steps, apprehensive, almost afraid, yet there he was.

"You want a Coke or something?" Reid asked, for the lack of anything else to say and because he and Bear, once inside, usually went straight to the refrigerator.

"No, thanks," Jason said.

Reid Dalton had always been more of a big brother than a father to Bear. He had tried to make Bear's friends his friends, especially Jason, but without Bear around, it just wasn't the same. There was a void no one alive could fill.

"You sure? I'm going to have another cup of coffee and I really hate to drink alone."

"Well, okay," Jason said. "But I'll get it. I know where they're at."

"Have at it, son," he said and topped off his own cup.

They both sat down at the table and fiddled with their respective containers. Neither one spoke for several minutes while Jason looked around the room like he expected Bear to jump out and tell him it had all been a joke. A cruel joke.

Reid Dalton broke the ice first. "No school today?"

"Yeah, but I have an appointment."

"Oh, yeah? Dental checkup or something?" To Reid Dalton, small talk was better than no talk.

"Or something," Jason said. He paused for a few seconds, then continued. "I have to see this doctor again."

"You sick?"

"No, sir. He's a kinda psychiatrist or something. I'm supposed to talk to him."

"Oh, uh, yeah. That's good. I, uh."

"He wants me to talk about Bear."

"Well, that's okay. You need to be able to talk about him."

"No, it's not. He's a stranger. He didn't know Bear. He doesn't know anything," he said with a sad look on his face. "Well, I'm sure he means well."

"No, he doesn't," Jason said. "He wants me to tell him about that night and I don't want to. I don't even like to think about it.

"I know, son. I don't either, but it'll be good for you in the long run."

"How?"

"They say talking helps."

"Can't I just talk to you?"

"Well, sure. We're talking right now. Are you gonna talk to someone else, too?"

"What do you mean?"

"Are they gonna make you talk to a psychiatrist too? Talk about Bear, I mean?"

"Well, I guess if I felt like I needed to, I probably would."

"Do you?"

"I don't know. I haven't really thought about it."

"Why can't we just talk to each other?" Jason said. "I don't want to talk to someone else. They might tell. You won't tell."

"Tell what, Jason?"

"About what happened. About what I saw. They want to know what I saw."

"The doctor does?"

"And the cops," he said quickly.

"They're just trying to find out who did it."

"But I don't want them to. Then they'll find me."

"Wait a minute. Are you afraid whoever did this will come looking for you? That's not going to happen," Reid told him.

"It could. It happened to Bear. Those Mexican boys could come after me, too." Jason moved the still-unopened can of Coke from hand to hand.

"I won't let that happen. I..." Reid Dalton started talking before what Jason had just said reached his brain.

"What'd you just say?"

"Huh?"

"Did you say Mexican boys? How do you know?"

"They were yelling something in Spanish, I guess. I don't know."

"Are you sure?"

"Well, it sounded Spanish and the accent and all."

"Could you be mistaken? I mean it all happened so quick."

"No, I recognized some of the words. I hear it on the school ground all the time...*pinche puto*. I think it's slang or something. I know you get in trouble if the teacher hears you say it, so it must not be nice."

Reid Dalton had heard similar words when he grew up in south Texas, even used them himself. They wouldn't be found in a dictionary, at least not defined as they were used in common Tex-Mex fashion. They were meant to be derogatory and nothing more.

"What did the police say when you told them?"

"I haven't."

"Why not?"

"I dream it and then I wake up and remember."

"What about the psychiatrist? Have you told him?"

"I don't like talking to him," Jason said. "I told you that."

"I know, but..."

"I'll only tell you."

"But it could be important, son."

"Then you tell them." Jason looked at his watch. "Uh, oh. I gotta go. My mom doesn't know where I'm at."

"Oh, man. Don't do that. She'll be worried sick, especially now. From now on, you tell her when you're coming over, okay?"

"So, it's okay if I come back?"

"Any time you want to. I'll keep the Cokes on hand," Reid Dalton said.

"Oh, sorry. I forgot," Jason said, looking at the unopened can in front of him. "I'll put it back in the fridge."

"It'll be there for you when you come back," Reid Dalton said. "And we can talk?"

"Yeah. We can talk, but don't forget about your mom."

Jason ran to the front door to let himself out, then turned back toward the kitchen. "I miss him, you know?"

"Yeah, son. I know. We both do."

* * *

By the time Doobie located the revival tent on Highway 173, just north of Bandera, the show was in full swing. He pulled off the road and into the field by the tent, where no less than forty other cars had been left. He parked between a van and a stake truck on the back row, hidden from view.

Doobie got out and ran his fingers through his windblown hair.

He had never been to a revival before, much less one in a tent. He wasn't sure how he should dress, so he had worn his newest, old blue jeans, a faded, blue denim shirt and his brown, soft leather, Durango boots. The boots had pointed toes; the kind no self-respecting cockroach would ever try to escape from by hiding in a corner. If nothing else, Doobie looked like a local.

The tent was a big-top type made of a dirty white canvas. The side flaps had been left rolled up due to the afternoon heat and little or no wind to speak of. Doobie could hear the gas-powered generator that ran the lights inside and the cross at the top of the tent.

The congregation was in the midst of some hymn he didn't recognize when he walked up to the entrance. An extremely large man, who resembled Friar Tuck in an old movie he had once seen, held a wooden plate filled with money out in front of him.

"For me?" Doobie said.

"For the Lord," the monk known as James said back.

Doobie reached into his pants pocket and pulled out a dollar bill. "Got change?" he said.

The monk gave him an evil stare and shook the plate. Doobie wadded up the bill and tossed it in.

"Praise the Lord," the monk said as he let Doobie pass. "Yeah, and pass the tambourine," Doobie said under his breath as he made his way to a wooden folding chair two rows from the back. An elderly woman, dressed pretty much like himself and standing in front of the chair next to him, offered to share her hymnal.

"No, thanks," Doobie said. "I'm into classical myself."

After two more long and drawn-out verses, the woman behind the upright piano ended the song with an off note. She got up and motioned downward with her hands. The small crowd took their seats on cue.

A restless and impatient feeling hung in the air around Doobie like a bad aftershave. He had no idea what to expect next. He had heard about such off-the-wall religious meetings where the preacher would come on stage wearing a live rattlesnake for a necktie and test the faith of the congregation by having them kiss the snake on the mouth. If this turned out to be such an occasion, he had every intention of exiting before he was called upon to swap spit with any form of reptile. He hadn't driven by himself for an hour and a half just to lock lips with tomorrow's road kill.

Before Doobie had a chance to dream up some other useless act of offertory worship, a spontaneous hush fell over the gathering. It was like someone had turned on a giant vacuum and sucked all the air out of the sides of the tent. He expected to see the roof collapse at any moment, bringing the cross down with it, and making shish kebab out of the people three rows up. That would be a true test of faith for those who survived. The snake would have to take a back seat in that bus.

"The Lord be with you, my children," an extremely handsome man in a pure, white robe said from behind a glass pulpit.

The hair on Doobie's arms bristled. A chill slid down his spine like a falling icicle. The man's voice was calm, yet strong. He stood like a rock with a white *Bible* clutched against his chest. He made a visual sweep of the tent and looked deep into each and every eye before moving to the next.

"After all, you are my children," he said as he surveyed the gathering. "Just as you are His children."

A host of "Amens" spewed forth into the late afternoon. Doobie held his in abeyance. Not that it wouldn't have been easy for him to speak. His mouth was locked so steadfast in the open position that his jaws ached. He hadn't yet heard a word the Reverend Daniel had spoken. His eyes were riveted to the man's face. It was a face so natural, so beautiful. No lines. No blemishes. Only strength.

Doobie knew it was a face he wouldn't trust his back to.

12

Reid Dalton grabbed the phone on the first ring. He figured it would be Jason's mother calling to either apologize for her son's intrusion or to thank him for telling Jason of her concern for his whereabouts. Maybe even both. He was prepared to tell her Jason was welcome anytime and that he would have him call her when he arrived and again when he was about to leave. He was prepared to tell her almost anything if she would agree to allow him to return. Reid didn't know who needed the visits more, Jason or himself. His preparation had been for naught.

"Hi," the caller said. "It's me."

He had recognized his wife's voice after the "Hi". He always did, but she had always gone on to identify herself anyway. That much hadn't changed. "How are you?"

"Better," she said. "But not much."

"I'm sorry for not sticking around."

"You don't have to be. I understand."

"I went by to see Bear before I left,"
Reid Dalton said. "That's good. I figured
you probably would."

"And I had a visitor this morning."

"Oh, who?"

"Jason."

"Really? Is he okay?"

"He's a good kid. We had a long talk. I
can see why Bear liked him so much."

"That's good," she said, then paused. Reid
Dalton could hear his wife take a deep
breath on the other end of the line.
"Reid, I've spoken to an attorney."

"You didn't waste any time." He wanted to
say that Bear wasn't even cold yet, but he
didn't.

"I want to get it over and done with, so
we can get on with our lives."

"You don't even want to think about it a
while?"

"No, and he agreed with me that a quick,
clean break would be the best in our
situation."

Their marriage was no longer a marriage.
It had been downgraded to a situation
faster than a hurricane becomes just a
tropical storm. One by an attorney and the
other by a weather forecaster, and neither
was right more than half the time.

Kathy Dalton continued. "I'm going to stay up here for a few weeks, so you can go ahead and stay in the house."

"Your attorney's not afraid I'll load everything up and haul it away?" Reid said.

"He did mention that, but I assured him you wouldn't stoop to something that low."

"Well, thanks for that."

"I just wanted to tell you first. I didn't want them to just serve you with the papers out of the blue," she said. "You might think about who you want to represent you. I know you deal with a lot of attorneys at work. You should be able to find a good one."

He wanted to tell her that there was no such thing as a good attorney, but she wouldn't understand. Instead, he said, "I don't need one. You just tell yours to draw up whatever it is you want and I'll agree to it."

"I don't want everything," she said.

"Just do it," he said. "You're the one who wants it over and done with. I'm not going to do anything to stand in your way."

"I guess I expected more of a fight."

"I'd give you one if there was something worth fighting for, but you've made it perfectly clear that there's not."

"I'm sorry, Reid. I really am."

Reid Dalton remembered the line from *Love Story,* but somehow the words didn't fit their situation. "You'll get over it," he said. The anger in his voice echoed in his head.

"I guess I better go now," Kathy Dalton said. "Mom's driving me out to the cemetery."

"Yeah, I guess you better," he said. "I'll be expecting the papers."

"Okay."

"And Kathy."

"Yes?"

"Give Bear my love," Reid Dalton said. "*He* still needs it."

* * *

Doobie was underwhelmed by the message the Reverend Daniel had fed to the cluster of people gathered under the tent. He had to give the man credit though, he knew all the buzzwords and exactly which buttons to push to excite the crowd into a giving frenzy when the plates were passed around. So as not to call any undue attention to himself, Doobie had placed another dollar bill in the plate and shuffled the other bills around to make it look like he was giving at least as much as he was supposed to be receiving.

The elderly woman sitting beside him had smiled at his alleged generosity before placing a rather thick wad of twenty-dollar bills on top of the stack herself. Doobie had rebounded with a sheepish grin of his own.

Doobie stayed seated when the performance ended and watched the others as they filed out. When the tent was empty, he got up and walked toward the stage. Monk James grabbed him by the collar about halfway down the aisle.

"Going somewhere?"

"I thought I'd pay my respects to the reverend," Doobie said without turning around.

Monk James let loose of his shirt and walked around to face him. "Reverend Daniel has left the tent."

Elvis has left the building would have been a more appropriate response. Even Elvis would have managed at least one encore. "Surely he's around back somewhere."

"He's tired. These meetings take a lot out of him. He needs time to meditate, if you know what I mean."

"I just want to tell him how much I enjoyed his sermon. It won't take a minute."

"I'm sorry. Maybe some other time," Monk James said.

"I've still got some money left. I couldn't find it when the plate was passed. I checked all my pockets, then remembered I had stuck it here in my boot. By the time I got it out, the plate was gone." Doobie used a buzzword of his own.

"How much?"

Doobie reached into his pocket and came out with one of the hundred-dollar bills he had received from Bob Lansing for laying the split-rail fence. He showed it to the monk.

"I'll take it to him. I'm sure he will be pleased with your benevolence."

"I think I'd like to give it to him myself, if you don't mind."

"He may not be back there. He sometimes chooses to meditate while he is being driven back to the church instead."

"Then maybe I *will* wait for another time," Doobie said. He folded the bill up and slid it back into his pocket.

"Wait... Wait a minute. I'll go see if he is still available. I can't promise anything, you understand."

"Oh, I understand completely," Doobie told him. "I'll just wait here. If you aren't back in a minute or so, I'll presume he's gone and I'll be on my merry way. I can always put the money in my church plate on Sunday. After all, it all goes to the same place, doesn't it?"

Monk James turned and marched hurriedly down the aisle, across the stage and through the back curtain. Doobie didn't bother checking his watch. He knew the hundred was a goner the minute he pulled it out.

Doobie saw the opening in the curtain move ever so slightly and knew a second pair of eyes were on him. A wave in that direction would have been a bit much, so he looked around the empty tent and shuffled his feet, acting very much the lost soul.

Monk James opened the curtain and allowed Reverend Daniel to pass through without touching the flap. He stayed behind him until they reached Doobie.

"My follower tells me you enjoyed my sermon," he said.

For the first time, Doobie noticed the blue of his eyes. He hadn't been able to see them from his seat near the rear of the tent. It was easy to see how a girl Ashley Jenkins' age could get lost in their clouds.

"I don't know that I've ever experienced such an exhortation."

"Bless you, my son, but I owe it all to the Lord."

"I can see that," Doobie said.

"I'm also to understand that you missed your donation. That is truly a sin on our part. I will have to speak to my helpers about that. They, too, sometimes get caught up in the moment and get lost in the words of the Lord."

"Oh, yeah." Doobie reached in and pulled out the bill. He held it out for the reverend to take, but his bands remained at his side. Monk James reached for it instead.

"I never like to handle the money," Reverend Daniel said. "My work is sharing the word. The offering is but a means. I would gladly go about preaching for mere food and clothing, but what kind of example would I set if I refused to accept what is freely given for the Lord's work?"

Doobie wanted to add an "Amen" to what he had just heard but was afraid he would laugh between syllables.

"While your generosity is well received, my son, I would be remiss if I didn't inquire as to whether you can afford to part with such a gift."

"What? Oh, you mean these clothes. I didn't want to miss your sermon, so I didn't take time to change. Working at my ranch like I do, I lose track of time. As it is, I missed the first couple of hymns. I'm sure you understand, with your own busy schedule and all. I barely have time to get over to the club on any regular basis," Doobie explained. "And I'm sorry about the hundred. I thought I grabbed more than one when I was leaving. The things are so thin, I hardly ever know how many I'm carrying around in my boot. Here, why don't I sit down and take the thing off? There might be some more hiding down there. I've gone for days sometimes with three or four of them folded flat under my foot. Course, with me living alone like I do on my ranch and all, it's hard to keep track."

"That won't be necessary, my son, but I would encourage you to attend some of our other meetings. I'm sure it would be a blessing," the reverend said.

"If I can find the time, I surely will," Doobie said. "But you understand, I love what I do. I just get caught up in building things and working with my hands. Sometimes the sun goes down and I don't even know it. I'm sorta like you. I'd work for nothing and just give all the money away. It's the root of all evil, like they say, but in the right hands it can do a lot of good." Doobie couldn't help but notice the sparkle in the reverend's eyes at the line he was handing him.

"And you have no family to share it with?"

"None at all. Like I say, I've never found the time. I'd dearly love a family, but I guess it's probably too late for me now."

"Nonsense. It's never too late to be surrounded by loved ones. As a matter of fact, I'd like to invite you to visit our home. You'll find it's much like your own. We have several thousand acres of land and we're always in need of someone with your joy for working," he said. "However, I should warn you our family is quite large and could be overwhelming, but love abounds from each and every one of them."

"You know, I might just take you up on that offer. I'll surely pray about it," Doobie told him.

"You do that, my son. I'm sure the Lord will guide you in the right direction." When Reverend Daniel held out his hand, Doobie took it and noticed he had an unusually strong grip for someone wearing a white robe and sandals.

The reverend turned and headed back down the aisle with Monk James following in his footsteps. Doobie shook his head at the sight and was about to turn and leave himself, until he remembered something.

"Oh, uh, reverend?"

Reverend Daniel stopped and turned.

"Is it okay if I bring my dog along? He's all the family I got and I'd sure hate to leave him."

"By all means. We welcome all of the Lord's creatures."

Doobie was relieved by his answer. He would have had to think long and hard about leaving Sweet again, especially if his stay turned out to be a long one.

13

Detective Sergeant Eric Montalvo was in the bullpen when the desk sergeant called to inform him that a Reid Dalton was there to see him. He told him to send him on up. He dreaded the fact that he had very little to tell him about his son's murder.

Actually, he had nothing to tell him, which was even worse. He hoped it wouldn't turn out to be one of those what-the-hell-are-we-taxpayers-paying-you-for meetings, but he wouldn't blame him if it was.

He got up from his desk and walked over to the door to meet him and was surprised by the smile on the man's face and an obvious spring in his step. He had expected a more somber greeting. The two shook hands and exchanged the usual pleasantries while they made their way through the maze of detectives. Reid Dalton took a seat in the metal chair by the sergeant's desk.

"What can I do for you, Mister Dalton?" he asked as a courtesy.

"I think it's more of what I can do for you," he answered. "How's that?"

"I understand Jason Watson's been seeing a psychiatrist."

"That's what we've been told."

"You didn't set it up?"

"No, sir. It's not our place to do something like that. While we surely don't disagree, especially in circumstances where a witness might be helped to remember things, we still have the doctor-patient thing to contend with. In this situation, I'm sure the boy's parents would be willing to share anything that might be beneficial. But no, this wasn't our call. As a matter of fact, we don't even know the name of the shrink. It's a private matter."

"It may not turn out to be," Reid Dalton told him. "I thought if ya'll were behind it, I was going to see about getting you to call it off. You see, Jason's not too keen on the idea."

"How do you know?"

"He came by to see me, and to be honest with you, the kid is scared."

"Of the shrink?"

"No. He's scared that he's gonna be next," Reid Dalton said. "I don't follow you," Montalvo said.

"He's, uh... he's remembered some things about that night, but he doesn't want to tell anyone."

"Has he confided in you?"

"Yep, and I'm here to make sure that he's not going to get into any trouble by telling me and not you."

"Why wouldn't he want to tell us?"

"Let me finish and you'll understand," Reid Dalton explained. "He's just a kid and sometimes their imagination can cause them to think all kinds of things. Right now it's telling him that if he helps to identify the boys, they'll come after him, and remember, he saw my son get shot. He can see the same thing happening to him."

"*Can* he identify the ones who did it?"

"Not yet. Things are coming back to him, like he told me he remembered one of the boys yelling something in Spanish. Now, I know that doesn't help narrow things down that much, but he could remember more if we let him do it his way."

"That's a damn sight more than we had before you came in here, but what do you mean by letting him do it his way?"

"He only wants to talk to me. He'll tell me when he remembers something, that way I'm the one giving you the information, not him," Reid said. "He'll be out of the loop, so to speak."

"I've got no problem with that," Montalvo informed him.

"But what if he has to testify?"

"We've got ways to handle that, especially where minors are concerned."

"Good. I was hoping you would see it his way."

"But I still can't do anything about the shrink."

"I know, but he's a smart kid who's been thrown into an adult world. I got an idea he can handle it."

"I hope you're right," Montalvo said. "In the meantime, we'll get to work on this other matter and you let us know if he recalls anything else."

"Don't worry. You'll be the second to know."

* * *

Reverend Daniel always finished his revival sermons on an emotional high, not so much from the spiritual conquest, but from the smell of legal tender and the power it possessed. His favorite dive from such a high was the kind that emerged him deep into the vaginal recesses of a chosen lamb. Tonight would be no exception.

Arrianna was in charge of the concubine department, as she and the monks referred to it, though never in the presence of the reverend. She was in charge of their first sin-cleansing shower, and from then on, it was up to her to make sure they stayed clean, though not necessarily in the biblical sense. It was a duty she enjoyed, being somewhat of a confused sexual deviate herself.

Monk James liked to refer to her as their token greedy, little, double-gated, sexist, bisexual, but only in quiet conversation with the other bodyguards, and certainly never in the confines of her own quarters, which he had frequented on occasion for something other than a religious experience.

Melissa Nicole Reynolds hadn't always been held in such regard. She had been born an only child into a rather well-to-do family in New Braunfels, Texas. Her father was a prominent physician who put his small-town practice above his family, never understanding that money couldn't always buy everything. Her mother was the typical physician's wife. A socialite who favored the bright lights of the big city over the existence she had been forced to endure in a town of lesser standing. With San Antonio less than an hour's drive away, she accepted her fate and a new Jaguar every three years gracefully.

Melissa had been well-behaved as a child, but at the age of fourteen and with no structured parental guidance to speak of, her hormones took over and sent her through puberty on a jet plane. She had been blessed with her father's raven black hair and her mother's eyes that were as green as the stem of a fresh cut flower.

While watching her mother, she learned how to apply just the right makeup to bring out what nature and good genes had provided.

She began hanging around with an older crowd and although her mother and the Catholic church had preached the virtue of virginity until the marriage vows, she saw nothing wrong with allowing boys to touch her in forbidden places. At fifteen, she lost her virginity in the back seat of a 1972 Ford Torino. Three months later, just before her sixteenth birthday, she discovered she was pregnant. Rather than face her parents and the wrath of small-town gossip, she took matters into the hands of a doctor in Seguin who specialized in helping girls out of their family way.

Melissa traded virginity for promiscuity and never looked back. Each time she allowed a man inside her, it was for her own benefit, not theirs. They were just the means to an end that was nowhere in sight.

Arrianna's first choice for the reverend's pleasure that night would have been the young redhead, who had arrived with the most recent herd of lambs, but there were others whose turns came first. There was also her sackcloth rash, which would have to be taken care of before she was given the honor of being bed and bred by the reverend.

She chose instead a dark-haired lamb with big brown eyes. She could not be considered a black sheep, as she had taken her medicated vitamins as instructed, without question. The glassy look Arrianna saw in her eyes as she bathed her before the reverend's return told her so.

She helped the young girl from the tub and toweled her off, until every inch of her body was dry. She took pride in her work and very seldom complained. The young girl stood perfectly still and in a cloudy daze while Arrianna rubbed a light coat of powder over her. No spot was left untouched. She then applied a fine spray of Fire and Ice perfume, the reverend's favorite scent, in special areas. When this was done, she took the girl by the hand and led her down the hall and into the bedchamber, where she helped her onto the bed and covered her to the neck with a white satin sheet.

Before she left, she checked the girl's eyes again to make sure the drug was in complete control. Like all the others, this lamb would never know she had been slaughtered. After a few missed periods and the proper chosen verses of scripture, she too would embrace the theory of the Immaculate Conception.

14

Jason Watson was twelve and should have been going on thirteen, instead, he was beating a path to twenty-one, thanks to the recent events in his young life. While most kids his age were busy figuring out how to jack with their teachers and stay out of D-Hall, he had been forced to step it up a notch in order to jack with a child psychiatrist and stay out of an early grave.

Jason hated Dr. Wilfred Honniker's office. He imagined it was what a rich kid's room probably looked like right after Christmas, only not quite as messy. There were entirely too many toys in too many rows on too many tables. There was a place for all of them and they were all in their place. He had outgrown most of them, had never played with some of them and had never seen the rest of them. Having grown up in the age of computers and the games they screen-generated, he had lost interest in manually operated toys at an early age. The doctor, Jason figured, still lived in the Dark Ages of his own childhood.

The chair he had been made to sit in was shaped like a large, over-padded baseball glove. The signature below the thumb said Yogi Berra. Not Cal Ripken, Jr. or even Deion Sanders, but rather someone his grandfather had probably watched on a black and white TV.

Dr. Honniker sat down in a rocking chair next to a large, stuffed, purple dinosaur. "And how are we today, Jason?"

"He was a catcher, you know?" Jason answered.

"I beg your pardon?"

"A catcher. The guy behind the plate."

"Yes, go on."

Jason hated that phrase. "Yes, go on" had come to mean "You still haven't answered the question, stupid, and I'm going to keep saying it until you do." So, he went on. "Yogi Berra was a catcher. This is a fielder's glove, not a catcher's mitt."

"Ah, I see. And what does that mean to you?"

"It means you don't know anything about baseball."

"And does that bother you?"

"Not if it doesn't bother you. I just thought you might like to know, that's all."

"Would you rather sit elsewhere?"

Jason looked around the room. His options were a rocking horse, a small swing that looked to have a weight capacity of a normal size six-year-old or a black, wicker chair with a back in the shape of Mickey Mouse's ears. Behind Dr. Honniker he saw a fourth. "How about over there?" he said and pointed to a leather chair behind a mahogany desk.

"I'm afraid that's out of the question. That's the doctor's chair."

"Aren't you the doctor?"

"Why, yes."

"Then let me sit in your chair."

"That wouldn't be proper."

"Why?" Jason said, turning the tables and taking an offensive posture.

"Because I'm the doctor."

"Then you sit over there and I'll take the rocker."

"That's where I make my notes after our session."

"I know. I can see the computer. What's the byte capacity?"

"Is this meant to be a stall tactic?" Dr. Honniker asked.

"You asked if I wanted to sit somewhere else."

"I was being polite. Now, shall we proceed?"

"If I said no, would that make any difference?"

"It would only prolong the inevitable."

"But don't you get paid by the hour?"

"That's not the point."

"What is the point?" Jason said. "I'm not sick. You can't make me any more well than I already am."

"The point is, your parents are worried about you. You don't want them to worry, do you?"

"Again with the questions," Jason thought. "They don't need to worry. I can take care of myself," he said.

"I'm sure that's what your friend thought," the doctor said, pointedly. "Why don't we take up where we left off the last time you were here?"

"Where was that, exactly? I forgot." Jason hadn't forgotten; he was still jacking. They had spent the first full session discussing what the doctor referred to as his relationship with Bear. It wasn't until the second visit that they had ventured into the night it had all happened. It was then that Jason chose to clam up.

"You were waiting for Bear on your front lawn," the doctor told him.

Jason clenched his jaw. He had been over it all before. In conversation with the police. In his dreams. In real life. Now, he was going to have to go over it again. Here in a room full of toys, sitting in a baseball glove that bore the name of someone who wouldn't be caught dead wearing it. It was all the same.

Nothing had changed. He had seen Bear riding down the street. A dark, two-door car with the left headlight out had driven up beside him. +Why had he suddenly remembered that?" he caught himself mouthing the words and stopped.

"Just think back," the doctor said. "Were you standing or sitting?"

"I was standing in my yard. I saw Bear coming. Then this car comes down the street real slow, and when he gets next to Bear, I heard a loud noise, like a backfire, and then the car drives away real fast. Then Bear wasn't there anymore," Jason said in rapid succession.

"What about the car? Think about the car."

"Dark. Black or blue. I don't know."

"What else?"

"Nothing else."

"What about the driver? Think about the driver."

"I couldn't see the driver. It just happened. I wasn't looking. I just saw."

"That's okay."

"How can you say it's okay? They killed Bear. It's not okay."

"I meant it's okay that you weren't looking. No one expects you to have been looking."

"Then why is everyone questioning me about it?"

"You need to talk about it. You need to get it all out in the open. What did you think after it happened? Were you aware of what had happened?"

"I couldn't see Bear. I saw his bike on the curb, but he wasn't on it."

"Where was he?"

"Two-door car. Left headlight out. I've got to tell Bear's dad," he told himself. To the doctor he said, "On the Casper's yard. He was lying down. I thought the car backfiring had scared him."

"What did you do?"

"I ran across the street to see if he was okay, but he wasn't and there was a lot of blood."

"What did you do then?"

"I ran back to my house and got my mom." Jason paused.

"Yes, go on," Dr. Honniker said.

"No. I've told you everything, now I want to go home."

"We still have some time left."

"I don't care. I want to go home and I don't want to come back."

"I'll talk with your parents," Dr. Honniker said. "We'll see what they say."

"Fine. Can I go now? I really need to get to school. I've got a math test."

"Sure, and ask your folks to come in."

Jason pushed himself up to the front edge of the glove and stood up. The only thing on his mind now was to get to Bear's dad and tell him what he had remembered.

* * *

It was well after dark-thirty when Doobie pulled the Bronco up next to the cabin. He was mildly demoralized not to find Sweet waiting for him. Even a half blind and deaf dog would have known he had arrived and at least let out a bark of some sort in acknowledgement. He thought about calling him, but if he was somewhere pouting over being left behind, he wasn't about to respond to the gesture.

Doobie had a fairly good idea where he would find his four- legged companion, so he went into the cabin and opened the lids of the twin coffee cans and extracted their usual sundown treats. He gave the Zippo lighter a gentle rub and did the same to the sycamore tree on his way out to the edge of the cliff.

Doobie was relieved when he saw a dark mound next to the green chair. He sat down in the chair, rubbed the dog behind his ears, and then balanced the cookie lengthwise on the dog's snout. He waited until he could hear a crunching sound before firing up the Zippo at the business end of a filtered homegrown.

Before he had stumbled on the Laredo cigarette machine, Doobie had rolled his usual nightly dose in Zigzag paper. The machine had allowed him to manufacture a monthly supply in one sitting.

The filter just made him look legit and Sweet was never the wiser.

Doobie had been careful not to plant his meager crop on his own land. Instead, he had chosen an overgrown patch of ground below a cliff on the far side of the valley. While it was actually on the golf course, it was on the opposite side of the widest and deepest bend in the creek and behind a row of pampas grass. Just to be safe, Doobie had hand-painted a "Beware of

Rattlesnakes" sign and stuck it in front of the pampas grass.

Both the sign and the crop of stalk-like plants, he kept trimmed to just below the top of the pampas grass, were still standing. His annual harvest was done by the light of a full moon.

Doobie toked for medicinal purposes only and limited himself to two a day. Even when he had added the filter, he didn't add to the number to make up the difference. For some people, it was an apple a day, for others, a six-pack or a dry martini. For Doobie, it was a pair of doobies. All is fair in love and war and the eternal search for peace of mind.

"You can forgive me anytime now," he told Sweet. "That is, if you want this other cookie."

The dog's tail cut a swath in the grass behind him at the sight of the second treat.

"I knew you couldn't stay mad long. You're too damn spoiled."

Doobie looked out over the valley. The golf course was hidden in total darkness. It was like a dark hole in the center of a small galaxy of house lights. The night was still and clear. He could hear the faint sound of laughter emanating from a television set somewhere down below. Doobie tried to imagine the valley as it had been when he first pitched his tent among the pine trees. It was all dark then. No roads. No houses. No people. Just he and the valley. It was easy to imagine. All he had to do was close his eyes and cover his ears, but eventually he would have to open them all again.

Life was like that. He could only close himself off for so long. Eventually, he would have to open himself back up, and that eventually was near. He knew he couldn't just sit there on the edge of the cliff and hope for the better. Hope that someone else would come along before it was too late. Too late for Ashley Jenkins. Too late for someone else who might have fallen for the Reverend Daniel's words earlier. Someone was under the tent with him.

He knew the reverend's game and it was time for him to play. He had sat on the bench and watched for too long. The splinters had taken root and before long, the rings would choke him out forever.

"You know what, dog?" Doobie said. "I think it's about time you repaid a debt."

15

Jason Watson had lied to Dr. Honniker about not knowing more about the car. He had lied about the math test. Upon leaving the child psychiatrist's office, he had also lied to his mother about feeling sick. He was on a roll, but for good reason.

Jason knew his mother's remedy for almost any illness was chicken noodle soup, so when they got home, he requested a bowl immediately, downed it almost as fast and declared himself cured. He knew it would be too late for her to take him to school now.

"Mom? Can I go to see Mister Dalton?"

"You were just over there this morning."

"I know, but he told me I could come back any time I wanted to."

"I don't know, Jason."

"Oh, please, Mom. I went to the doctor like you wanted me to and I'll call you as soon as I get there. I promise."

"I don't want you bothering him. I'm sure he has a lot on his mind and would probably rather be alone."

"No, he wouldn't. He told me so."

"Are you sure?"

"I'm sure. Bye." Jason ran from the kitchen and into the garage. He was on his bike and out the open door before his mother had a change of heart.

Reid Dalton had only been home long enough to throw together a ham and cheese sandwich when he heard the knock. He opened the door where Jason dashed in, out of breath, and headed for the phone in the kitchen. He dialed home, told his mother where he was and hung up before she could get a word in edgewise.

"I remembered something else," he excitedly told Bear's father.

"Settle down, son," Reid Dalton told him. "I was just fixing to eat lunch, you interested?"

"No, thanks. I've already eaten."

"Then sit down while I do."

They both took a seat at the kitchen table.

"Now, tell me what you're talking about," Reid said.

"I was at the psychiatrist's office. Boy, did I fake him out. Anyway, he wanted me to talk about the car and I remembered. It was a two-door and the left headlight was out."

"You sure?"

"Positive. I remember cause I thought it was a motorcycle at first. A guy up the street has a motorcycle and I thought it was him, except he usually goes a lot faster. My dad complained to him about it once, but it didn't do any good. He still rides by fast, only it wasn't him."

"Slow down."

"But that's good I remembered, right? It's gonna help?"

"You did good, Jason. I told you talking with someone about it would help."

"I didn't tell him. I did just like we agreed. No one knows but me and you," Jason said.

"That was the deal," Reid said. He was surprised by Jason's enthusiasm. He had come a long way in just a few hours. He was no longer a scared little kid.

"We're gonna get 'em. You and me. Just wait, you'll see. We'll make 'em pay."

* * *

On occasion, Doobie had been asked to do various forms of light carpentry work around the resort. The kind of work a contractor would have charged an arm and a leg for just to make the trip. The resort always furnished what material he told them was necessary and he only asked to be paid what they thought was fair. Neither side had ever been guilty of gouging or slighting the other. It was therefore not out of the ordinary for him to be seen on the grounds.

Doobie had raided another coffee can for a pocketful of change and with Sweet running interference, they made their way on foot down the backside of the hill and across the creek to the clubhouse. It was a warm and cloudless day and Sweet needed the half mile walk to keep him in shape.

Sweet had been there before and knew on instinct that his place was beside the side door. He sought shelter from the sun under a bush. Saliva dripped from his tongue as he panted.

"You been riding in the truck too much, dog," Doobie told him as he entered the building. He walked through two vacant meeting rooms, around the dining room and into the men's locker room, where a pay phone hung on the wall. He emptied the change from his pocket into an ashtray by the phone, stuck a quarter in the slot and dialed the operator.

"Information. What city, please?" a male voice asked. "Hondo."

"And your party?"

"The Cross Timber Ranch."

"Thank you. Have a nice day."

When a recording came on with the number, Doobie realized he had come unprepared. He reached for a scorecard pencil on a nearby table and when the recording gave him the number a second time, he wrote it on the front of the phone book in the shelf below.

Doobie slid another quarter in the slot and dialed the number. When a female voice came on the line, she asked if it would be a credit card call?

"No, ma'am. Cash money."

"That will be one sixty-five for the first three minutes," the operator said.

"How much for ten?"

"We don't usually get that kind of request. I'll come back on after three minutes, if you aren't done, and tell you to remain on the line afterwords for the total charges."

"Just tell me how much for ten minutes." Doobie didn't want his conversation to be interrupted.

"But what if you don't use the full ten minutes, sir?"

"Then it's my loss," Doobie said.

"If you say so, sir. That'll be four-eighty."

Doobie began dropping coins into the slot and listening to the bells as each one fell.

"Thank you, sir," the operator said. "And have a good day."

"You, too," Doobie countered, but by that time the phone had already begun ringing.

"Cross Timber Ranch," a female voice answered on the third ring.

"Is Donnie there?" Doobie asked. "Can I tell him who's calling?"

"I'd rather it be a surprise."

"Just a minute."

The line was silent for almost that long. "This is Donnie Hubbell."

"You still smoking pasture vine, Hub?"

There was a slight pause on the other end of the line. "You son of a bitch. Is it really you?"

"Only my hairdresser knows for sure."

"Where the hell have you been?" Donnie Hubbell was Doobie's oldest friend, going all the way back to the fifth grade when they had found the remains of a still unidentified, dried-up vine in a field. They had thought it would be cool to smoke it, since they were too young for the real stuff. They paid for their act of defiance with heat blisters on their tongues that took two weeks to heal. They had gone on to puke up their first beer together and had even been Best Man at each other's wedding. Both of which had ended in divorce, but that's what friends were for.

"Here and there mostly," Doobie said.

"I ain't heard from you since...", Hub started.

"Yeah, I know. I been meaning to write."

"Bullshit."

"You always did have a way with words, Hub."

"I hope you're calling from around the corner."

"I'm a few hills away from there," Doobie said, "but not far."

"You coming by? Damn, I'd love to see you again."

"I'll get there one of these days, but right now I need a favor."

"Shit, name it."

"I need to be you for a while."

"Say what?"

Doobie went on to explain to his friend about the charade he had instigated and the need to step into his boots, at least in name only.

"Sounds to me like you're about to step into some shit you might not be able to clean off," Donnie Hubbell told him.

"Smells like it, doesn't it?" Doobie said.

"So, how about it?"

"On one condition."

"I'm afraid to ask."

"You bring my name back here when it's all over. No phone call. Nothing that easy. I want to see your ass right here when the smoke clears. Deal?"

"Do I have a choice?"

"Nope. Use of my name don't come cheap."

"I'll try not to use it too long," Doobie told him.

"Take all the time you need," Donnie said. "I'll be keeping an eye out for you."

"Just look for me when you see me coming."

16

Detective Sergeant Eric Montalvo always hated it when a crime, especially one as serious as murder, involved someone from the Latino community. He considered it a dishonor to himself. Since San Antonio was predominately Mexican-American, he had been dishonored more times than not, but he never got used to it. In Bear Dalton's case, the fact that their only witness had heard his second language was nothing more than a needle, and the entire city of San Antonio was its haystack.

Bear's file was still on his desk when Reid Dalton reached out and touched him. He grabbed the phone on the first ring.

"Montalvo," he said.

"Sergeant, this is Reid Dalton again."

Montalvo couldn't figure out why he would be calling so soon after his visit. "You leave something?" He looked around the top of his cluttered desk.

"No. As a matter of fact, I've got something else for you," Reid Dalton said.

"Speak to me."

"According to Jason, the car was a two-door."

"Well, that narrows it down by about half." "With the left headlight out."

"Hello!"

"He thought that might be worth something," Reid said.

"Is he sure?" Montalvo asked.

"Says he is."

"He just up and remember it?"

"No, the psychiatrist pulled it out of him or at least that's where he remembered it. Course, he didn't let on."

"Of course," Montalvo said. "I gotta hand it to him. The kid's got gumption."

"More than you know," Reid said.

"I'll get right on this," Montalvo said. "We can get an APB out in just enough time for the night patrol and notify all the shops in town to report any headlight replacements or purchases. This may turn out to be the break we've been hoping for."

"I hope you're right."

"Hey, that's the way these things usually turn. We cops would like to think it's our doing, but luck plays a major role when it comes right down to it."

"Luck and a smart, little kid out for revenge," Reid Dalton thought. To Detective Sergeant Montalvo he said, "I'll tell Jason you owe him one."

"If this turns out to be the nail in the coffin," Montalvo winced at his poor choice in hyperboles, "the kid'll get my own personal GET OUT OF JAIL FREE card."

"I hope he never has to use it."

"You and me both, my friend."

* * *

Monk James' primary duty the day after one of Reverend Daniel's revivals was to count the take and have it stacked and ready for the man to examine. It was also his favorite duty. He had built up quite a nest egg of his own by skimming ever so carefully off the top. At last count, he had over a hundred thousand dollars in hundred-dollar bills stuffed in the mattress in his private quarters. While cleanliness had never been a watchword in his previous life, he had made a point of seeing to it that his sheets were changed twice a week and by his own hands. The girls assigned to laundry duty never complained.

It was one less bed they had to make.

Monk James lifted his robe and slipped four bills under his gun belt just before the reverend entered the room.

"Good morning, James," the reverend said. "How did we make out last night?"

"I was about to ask you the same question," he said. "Let us just say she rendered unto the Lord what is the Lord's."

"Yeah, Hail Caesar." While Monk James was not altogether comfortable with what the reverend did in his own quarters, he found a measure of solace in the rejects he was sometimes, though not often, allowed to taste. And the job paid well, even without the occasional perk.

"A measure of tact would be beneficial at times, James. After all, it is the Lord's work we are doing here."

Monk James was also beginning to doubt his partner's attitude toward his present vocation. Reverend Daniel had taken to being the reverend even when they were alone together. The act used to be played only to an audience, but now it seemed to him that he actually thought he was who he claimed to be. He was now totally the Reverend Daniel. Somewhere along the line, Roger Criner had ceased to be. He preferred Roger to the reverend, but so long as the bottom line remained green and his mattress lumpy, he would play along.

He could always hatch his nest egg and fly away, but just like Roger Criner, James Melchor had trouble knowing how much was too much.

"Eleven thousand, three hundred fourteen dollars and seventy-five cents, to the penny," Monk James told him. "Praise the Lord," the reverend said.

"Uh, huh."

"Anything else?"

Monk James froze. He could feel the bills pinching his belly beneath his gun belt. "Had he seen?" he thought.

"I was sure I saw some jewelry in one of the plates."

"Oh, that." Monk James' barrel chest heaved with a quick and thankful breath.

"It's over there." He pointed toward a small, blue bag on the table.

"Two rings, a gold chain and a watch."

"Rolex?"

"Timex."

"The Lord does accept small favors," the reverend said with a sigh.

"One of the rings has a four-carat+ mount," Monk James informed him.

"And a cheerful giver."

17

Several days had passed since Carlos Cuevas had performed the ritual of human sacrifice. He was now a blood member of the Mayas. He gritted his teeth as the tattoo needle etched the gang's symbol, a multi-bladed, war axe, on his right arm, just below the shoulder. He felt no remorse in the fact that his victim had been a young boy, not much older than his own little brother, Vicente. He was now a Maya and that was all that mattered.

Hector Calderon was working on the front of the midnight blue Monte Carlo. He had just returned from Wal-Mart, where he had purchased a headlight to take the place of the burned-out one on the left.

"You should have been there, *cholo,*" Calderon said to Juan Mata, who was working the tattoo needle into Carlos' arm. "He blew the little fucker's head off."

It was all Calderon had been talking about since they had returned to the abandoned vegetable shed deep in the south side of town. "And the cops don't got a clue. The fuckers don't know who done it. Shit, man, we're the kings."

Mata continued to work on Carlos' arm. When the axe was done, he wiped the needle on a rag and exchanged the black cylinder of ink for a red one to add just the right touch of dripping blood.

"How many is that now, *cholo*? Seven?"

"Six," Mata answered. "One of them lived, remember?"

"Oh, yeah. Bustos didn't get a good shot on the little *negro*. He couldn't see him in the dark. "Fucker should have waited for him to smile, no?"

Mata was the leader of the Mayas and the oldest at nineteen.

He was also the wisest and was none too happy at Calderon's choice of neighborhood for their newest member's rite. Up until that point, they had remained on the south side of San Antonio, where they could get lost quickly, if need be. But the Monte Carlo belonged to Calderon as would any implication in all the murders. Mata could be held accountable for only two, his and Calderon's. He had only driven the one time and only because he didn't think Calderon could drive and shoot without getting the both of them killed in the process.

"There," he said to Cuevas as he pulled the needle away. "Now you are one of us. You're a Maya."

"Fucking-A, brother," Carlos said, glad that the ordeal was over.

Calderon finished replacing the headlight at the same time. He threw the burned-out beam in a pile of bushel baskets. "You done, man? Let me see?"

Carlos got up and held his right arm out proudly.

"*Bueno*. You done good, *cholo*. It looks better than mine. Now I got to go out and kill me another one so you can do me more better."

"Why don't we just celebrate instead?" Mata told him.

"Yeah, let's get some beer," Carlos said.

"You gotta buy, *vato*," Calderon said. "You're the man."

"But I'm not old enough," Carlos, who was barely seventeen, told him.

"Then give Mata some money, but enough for all of us."

"Where are the rest of the guys?" Mata asked.

"Chuey's."

"You got any money?" Mata asked Cuevas. "I've got a ten."

"That's good enough. Me and Hector will take care of it. You go show the others your mark and tell 'em to get over here if they're thirsty."

Carlos handed him the ten-dollar bill and Mata asked, "You got a preference since it's your party?"

"Any kind. Beer's a beer, isn't it?" The tattoo on Carlos' arm made him talk beyond his years.

"You're the man," Mata said.

* * *

Doobie understood the saying about "Money talking and bullshit walking" as well as anyone. He had lived by it back when times were different. He had given Reverend Daniel a taste of both in their first meeting, but knew he would have to talk louder the next time.

His premature retirement money had been enough to buy the fifteen acres and build the cabin with right at three thousand dollars left. He had earned enough doing odd jobs to keep him from having to open that particular non-interest-bearing coffee can. As a matter of fact, Doobie hadn't even seen the money in almost four years, but he knew exactly which can it was in.

He went to the cabinet and reached to the far back of the top shelf until he felt cold metal. He dragged the can out and set it on the counter. A layer of dust covered the plastic top. He pulled the cover off and turned the can upside-down. A heavy fold of hundred-dollar bills held together by a rubber band plopped out in front of him. He counted out thirty to make sure his memory hadn't failed him, then stuck ten of them back in the can and the can back on the shelf.

Sweet had been watching him in anticipation of a possible early sundown. Doobie noticed the disappointed look on the dog's face when he turned around empty-handed.

"It ain't that time yet," he told him. "Besides, we got some work to do around here before tomorrow."

Sweet barked loudly.

"You back-talk me and I'll make you stay here and eat squirrel every day, and I've seen you hunt. You'll starve before the week's out."

Sweet barked again.

"Okay, so Mrs. Jenkins might feed you, but her old man's liable to have a word or two to say about that. Then where would you be?"

Again, Sweet echoed his sentiments.

"Okay. You can have one if you get out of here and let me be," Doobie said, "but you'll only get one later on, not two. Deal?"

Sweet answered in his usual manner and watched as Doobie entered another can and pulled out a biscuit. He handed it to the dog. "Eat it outside. I don't want you to make me hungry."

Sweet exited by the open front door and took the cookie to the cliff. Doobie rummaged through his belongings and found barely enough clothes for a week. He didn't feel in the mood to wash, so he emptied the drawers into a canvas bag and threw it on the bed.

He walked outside and shook his head when he saw Sweet by the green chair. He went around to the Bronco to see what tools were in the back from his last job down the hill. Pickings were sparse and with no knowledge of what he might be called upon to do or what the reverend might have to do them with, Doobie decided to pile everything he had to work with back there and let Mother Fate handle the rest. She couldn't stay a bitch forever.

18

Reid Dalton could feel the walls closing in on him. Two days had passed since he had any contact with the outside world.

Jason's absence meant that maybe he had found a little peace in his world. Nights full of pleasant dreams, instead of nightmares filled with one-eyed cars.

He hadn't heard a word from Detective Sergeant Eric Montalvo since he had filled him in on Jason's recollection about the car. No news was simply no news. He wasn't altogether sure what good news would be. If they did catch Bear's killer, the good news would be that he wouldn't be able to kill someone else's son.

For Reid Dalton, the news would just be the beginning. The headlines. The trial. It would all have to be re-lived again. Then, the waiting. The years of waiting until the killer got his just desserts. Surely a jury wouldn't give him life, even life without parole. Not for killing a twelve-year-old boy in cold blood. It had to be pre-meditated. A person just doesn't ride around and all of a sudden think, "Hey, time to kill somebody."

Reid Dalton would accept nothing but death. If he had to wait, so be it. If he had to watch, so be it. If he had to do it himself, so be it.

It was that last thought that made him decide he had to do something with himself. He had to put a coat and tie on again and get back out amongst them. He had to go back to work. At least there, he could immerse himself in other people's problems. It wasn't much of a commentary, but it was all Reid Dalton had.

He went into *his* room and dressed hurriedly before a different mood swung in his direction. He grabbed the last of the coffee for the road and shut off the machine.

It was already after ten, so traffic was fair to moderate, not the usual bumper-to-bumper caravan. The half-hour trip took only twelve minutes, barely enough time for him to change his mind. He brought the car to a stop in his assigned space and exited after taking a deep breath to prepare himself for the onslaught of pity he knew awaited him inside the Union Mutual Building. He had to take that first step. The one that would lead him to the next step and then the next. It was all a matter of just doing it.

Just jump in and do it.

Reid Dalton stepped out of the elevator and into the familiar surroundings of the Cave, as the Claims Department was lovingly referred to by those who were proud of their profession. To an outsider, it was nothing more than a cluster-fuck of cubicles. An endless maze of desks and computers, manned by people who, for the most part, would rather be anywhere but there. His own cubby, as Bear had called it that Saturday morning he had come in, with his dad, to pick up a file before heading for breakfast at Shoney's, was on the perimeter. It was quieter out there. Out away from the trenches. Out where the supervisors could think about what they needed to say before they actually had to say it. The only problem was that Reid Dalton's cubby was on the window perimeter across the Cave.

He knew the way through by heart. He could make it with his eyes closed and walking backward. But the semi-direct route meant he had to pass by seventeen cubicles, whose tenants knew him up close and personal. Granted, most of them would be on the phone and some of them on break, but those who weren't would leak his presence to the others.

His only other option was to circumnavigate the Cave along the wider perimeter aisle. He could walk much faster and maybe not be noticed as easily. This route would also take him by Buster Horton's office. If Buster was in, he could always seek shelter if the trip proved to be too much. He did need to check in, if nothing else but to let him know he was giving work the college try.

Reid began his journey around the block. To his surprise, he was met with little or no resistance, only sad looks and nodding heads. It was obvious that they had no more of an idea what to say to him than he had to them. He traded nods, but tried not to look sad.

Buster's light was on but his office was empty, so he remained on the course he had chosen until he reached his own window cubicle. He found his desk clean of any files. His IN basket was filled with un-postmarked envelopes. The kind he would usually find there around Christmas, only Christmas was still too many shopping days away.

He laid his briefcase on the desk, opened it and took out the files he had taken home to review. He replaced them with the cards, shut the case and set it on the floor.

"I didn't expect you back so soon," Buster said from the cubicle entry.

"I didn't either, but I have to do something to get me back on track."

"You sure?"

"Now that I'm here, I don't know."

"I think you need to be home with Kathy," Buster said. "Yeah, you would think so."

Reid Dalton knew his comment had no meaning to anyone other than himself, but since he had blurted it out, he owed Buster an explanation. "Kathy's not home and it doesn't look like she'll be coming home anytime soon."

"Is she okay?"

"You'd have to ask her attorney. She's filing for a divorce."

"Jesus, Reid, I'm sorry. I didn't know."

"No problem. I sorta left you in the dark when you called the other day anyway. She stayed with her folks after the funeral."

"Hasn't been easy, has it? I mean, with no one there and all," Buster said.

"That's why I'm here. This seems to be pretty much all I've got left," Reid said.

"Is there anything I can do?"

"Yeah, dump everything you got on me."

"If that's what you really want. I've been giving your stuff to Rudy and Clark, but if you think you're ready, I'm sure they'll oblige."

"Just do me one favor."

"Name it."

"Let everyone know I'm gonna be okay and to treat me like none of this ever happened."

"I can tell 'em, but I can't make 'em."

"Sure, you can. That's why you get paid the big bucks."

"I'll see what I can do," Buster told him, "and I *am* glad you're back."

"Of course you are. I'm the best you've got," Reid said.

* * *

Doobie had never cared too much for sunrises. They came too early in the morning to suit him. He was also afraid that if he turned the green chair around to watch, he might forget he had done so and walk off the cliff instead of back to the cabin when he got up.

Today was different. Today had reason. He had to have today so Ashley Jenkins and others like her would have tomorrow. Doobie wanted to meet today head-on. Face to face. He wanted to look today square in the eye and dare it to try and stop him. Dare it to kick him in the nuts when it thought he wasn't watching.

The cabin was locked and the Bronco was loaded. Sweet, for the most part, was confused, but when Doobie had opened the door to the Bronco and ordered him in, he had obeyed without reservation.

When the first glint of sunlight came up over the hills behind the cabin, Doobie stared straight into it with a glare of his own that said, "You ain't fuckin' with me no more."

He laid a hand gently on the sycamore tree. "I'll be back," he whispered and walked to the waiting Bronco.

Belinda Jenkins was standing in her driveway, shucking the morning paper from its plastic wrapper, when she saw Doobie come down the hill and turn onto Cliffdweller Drive. She stepped into the street and motioned for him to stop.

Doobie hadn't expected to cross paths with anyone at this hour, other than a possible small herd of golfers, who had nothing but time on their hands and metal sticks to beat it to death with. He brought the truck to a halt next to her.

"You're up mighty early, Doobie," she said.

"Yes, ma'am," he answered.

She reached in and patted Sweet on the head. "I'd appreciate it if you could help me put some bushes in around the porch. I swear that ground is rock hard."

"It may be a week or so, ma'am. I've got a job to do out of town that may take me awhile to finish."

"I guess it'll wait till you get back."

"I'll put you first on the list. You have my word on it." He expected her to accept his promise and back away; instead, she brought up a subject that was heavy on his mind.

"Our conversation the other day?"

"You remember Doobie could have asked which one, but he knew."

"Yes, ma'am."

"Well, I still haven't heard from Ashley and I'm really getting worried about her."

"I wouldn't worry too much if I were you, ma'am," Doobie said. "I expect she'll be coming home any day now."

"You think so?"

"You have my word on it," he said again.

Belinda Jenkins gave him a strange look, then smiled. "Well, you just be careful and don't let anything happen to my friend here."

"Yes, ma'am," he said. "I'll be real careful."

19

Reid Dalton had done three weeks' worth of work in three days.

He had developed a vampire-like work ethic, arriving at work before the sun came up and not leaving until it had gone down. The only light of day he had seen was through the shaded window at the back of his cubicle.

While Buster Horton was far from being a slave driver, he knew a good thing when he had it. He also knew it wouldn't last.

Therapy only lasted until the patient was either healed or had reached a maximum plateau of improvement. For his employee and friend's sake, he hoped for the former, but would accept the latter.

When his phone rang, Reid picked it up instantly. It was the receptionist, Lucy Woolard.

"Mister Dalton, there's a Mister Ammonds here to see you."

Reid had been over so many files since his return, all the names had run together. The name Ammonds didn't ring any bells, but at this point in time, he would be lucky to remember his own name. "I'll be right there."

He took the semi-direct route through the Cave and out the glass doors to the receptionist's desk, where a thin, mousy-looking man in a seersucker suit was waiting.

"Mister Dalton?" the man asked and made no attempt to shake his hand.

"Yes?"

"Mister Reid Dalton?"

"Correct again."

The man reached into his inside jacket pocket and pulled out a fold of papers and handed them to him.

"Consider yourself served," he said, then turned and walked away.

Reid Dalton unfolded the papers and, from experience dealing with lawsuits, knew exactly where to look first. He folded them back up after reading all he needed to read.

"Who was that?" Lucy asked.

"Process server."

"One of your cases, huh?"

"You might say that."

"Oh, well. I guess that's what they mean by job security."

Reid Dalton didn't respond. Instead, he rolled his wife's divorce petition into a tube shape and carried it back through the glass doors to his desk. He pulled out his briefcase, snapped it open and threw the papers inside. With nothing else to look forward to, he went back to work.

* * *

Doobie had to take two back roads to reach Comfort. For all he knew, he might have driven past his intended destination before he hit town, but that had been his plan. He had thought better of asking anyone around Boerne, even Jake Bradley, if they knew where the House of Lambs was located. He didn't need the attention in case his visit went south. He was sure any good citizen of Comfort would probably be able to head him in the right direction.

He drove slowly around town until he located a laundromat, where most small-town gossip is known to run rampant. Doobie had decided against a beauty parlor. The last thing he needed was to run into Comfort's answer to Sally Kuntz. He left Sweet in the Bronco and went inside. No fewer than five women came to his aid and all with the same answer. They all followed with the same question.

"Why?"

"Delivery," he said and returned to the Bronco before their conversation had ended.

Doobie backed out, took a left at the next intersection and headed the Bronco west on Highway 27. The gaggle of women had been correct. Exactly two point four miles later, he turned left again and stopped in front of the metal gate that hung above the eleventh cattle guard he had come to. He exited the Bronco out of habit, but found the gate unlocked. He jumped back inside, gave the gate a gentle push with the truck's bumper and drove on through. The gate swung closed behind him.

Doobie drove just fast enough to stay ahead of the trailing caliche dust, but not so fast as to appear anxious. He had the feeling of being watched, but it was a feeling he was sure he would have to get used to in the days ahead.

The first things that came to Doobie's mind when he rounded the second hill was that he had miscounted the cattle guards and he needed to have his odometer checked. While he really hadn't known what to expect, the ten-foot chain link fence topped with three strands of barbed wire wouldn't have been on the list.

The only thing that kept Doobie from turning around and re- tracing his steps was the large neon cross that stuck out like a bad omen on the front of the nearest building.

"Doesn't exactly look like the travel brochure, does it, dog?" he said when he shut the engine off outside the locked gate. He exited the Bronco and held the door open for Sweet to follow. He knew immediately that his feeling of being in someone's eyesight had been correct, when an extremely large man in a Friar Tuck outfit came toward him from inside the yard. The man was carrying what was either a walkie-talkie or a very good imitation. The fact that he was talking into it was a dead giveaway.

"You lost?" Gonzo Drake asked. He had a wide grin of a permanent nature on his face. The kind that won't wash off, even in the meanest of fights. Although not of oriental extraction, the man's grin reminded him of Goldfinger's man-servant, Odd Job. That thought didn't rest too comfortably on Doobie's mind.

"Hope not," Doobie said.

"If you're sellin', we ain't buyin'."

"I'm here by invitation."

"Whose?"

"I believe he introduced himself as the Reverend Daniel, but I could be mistaken. I'm not good with names," Doobie said. He watched the man's expression, in search of a frown. He got none.

"You stay where you are," he said. "I'll check." He turned with his back to Doobie and spoke into the radio. After a few nods, he turned back around.

"You got some I.D.?"

"I'm sorry, but I seem to have left it at the ranch."

The man turned again, but only for one nod this time before he whirled back around. Doobie noticed he moved quickly for someone his size. "Cop a squat. It'll be a few minutes."

"If it's all the same to you, I think I'll just stand here and stretch my legs. It's been a long drive."

"Suit yourself."

"I don't think he likes you," Doobie said to Sweet, but not loud enough for Gonzo to hear.

While he waited, Doobie surveyed the grounds from one end of the fence to the other. At the far left, he could make out what looked to be a garden of sorts. People were milling about as if in labor. Some were hoeing and others just looking. None of them seemed to be hard at it enough to break a sweat. With the sole exception of his immediate host, who took up quite a bit of space in his own right, the front

grounds were empty. To the right, Doobie
noticed tracks that seemed to lead off
around the building, but other than that,
it was just wasted land. He half expected
to see a basketball court for the inmates'
recreational purposes. It would have been
more in tune with the surroundings.

"Here comes the cavalry now," Doobie said
to Sweet, when the front door to the
church opened.

Reverend Daniel exited first, followed
close behind by Monk James. They were both
attired in what was obviously the uniform
of the day everyday; the reverend in his
white flowing robe and James in his usual
brown outfit. He and the grinning mountain
shared the same tailor.

"Ah, yes. Our friend from the other
night," the reverend said.

"And I brought my dog," Doobie said. "You
did say it was okay."

"That I did," he said to Doobie. To Gonzo,
he said, "Open the gate so our friend can
pass through."

"Yes, sir," Gonzo said. He opened a metal
box near the gate, but not near enough to
be accessible from outside, and pressed a
button. The gate, some twelve feet in
length, wheeled itself parallel to the
fence.

"I decided I'd take you up on your invitation to be part of your family," Doobie said.

"Praise the Lord."

"Him, too. I brought all my tools and I'm ready to go to work. I'm yours for the taking."

The reverend looked beyond him to the Bronco. "Looks like your vehicle is on its last legs." He figured scrap metal at best.

"Her? No way. I've had her since she was a pup. Never a lick of trouble, besides, I couldn't haul all my tools over in the Lincoln. Them leather seats are hard to keep clean as it is," Doobie explained.

"Still, you might consider bringing it here for safe-keeping."

"Now, you do have a point there. I never thought about that. I

may just take you up on that offer. I'd hate to see anything happen to that car or the Mercedes, either, for that matter. It's something to think about. It surely is."

"In the meantime, why don't you go ahead and pull that one in. James will show you where to park."

"I'd be much obliged," Doobie said. "And, oh yeah, I almost forgot. I brought a little something for the church." He reached into his jeans pocket and came out with a fold of bills. He made a weak attempt to hand it to the reverend, but Monk James intercepted the move.

"Sorry, I forgot. You don't touch the money."

"That's right, my son. It isn't pure," the reverend said. "And I must apologize deeply, but in praying for your arrival, I realized I never got your name."

"Donnie. Donnie Hubbell. Actually, it's Donald, but I've never been one to stand on ceremony and my mama, God rest her soul, always called me Donnie."

"Then Donnie it is," he said. "And I'm sure your mother is smiling down from Heaven at this very moment. She, no doubt, directed you to us."

"I'd surely like to think that. Yes, sir, I surely would."

"Amen," the reverend said. "Now, if you'd just drive on around, James will show you to your quarters."

"I'll do that right now. Yes, sir, I'm ready to get to work." Doobie turned and headed back to the Bronco.

Reverend Daniel looked at Monk James. "How much?"

"Two grand." The opportunity hadn't been ripe for him to palm a bill or two for his mattress.

"Praise the Lord."

Doobie opened the door to let Sweet jump in and climbed in after him.

"If I ever hear of you telling anyone how you heard me talk, I'll see to it that you live out your golden years in the pound," he told him.

He gunned the Bronco's engine and eased it through the gate. Gonzo saw to it that the gate rolled closed behind him and went back to walking the perimeter. Reverend Daniel returned through the front door of the church. Doobie followed Monk James around the right side and parked in front of a closed bay door that hung on a metal, warehouse-type building.

"What's in there?" Doobie asked when he exited the Bronco.

"The shop."

"Tools, huh?"

"Yeah, tools," he said. "Grab your gear and I'll show you where you'll be staying."

"Have you been here long?" Doobie asked as they walked between the two buildings and into the quadrangle.

"Ever since we started."

"That long, huh?" Doobie suddenly caught sight of the concrete silo.

"Whoa! Where'd that come from?"

"That's all that's left of what used to be here. It would have been too hard to take down, so we just built around it."

"Good place to keep provisions."

"You could say that."

Doobie noticed the heavy iron door with double padlocks at the base of the silo. "Mind if I take a look around inside? Sorta reminds me of the one I got back home."

"Another time."

They entered the four-story dormitory from the front and walked up the stairs on the immediate right. When they reached the second-floor landing, they entered a large room on the left that took up the entire end of the floor. Doobie counted thirty military-type beds, fifteen on a side. The six on the far end were made, while the others held bare mattresses.

"I didn't bring any bedclothes," Doobie said. "Bedclothes?"

"Sheets and stuff."

"They're provided."

"Which one's mine?"

"Take your pick of those," he pointed to the bare mattresses.

Doobie threw his canvas bag on a bed beneath one of the barred windows facing the quadrangle.

"I like fresh air at night," he said.

"The showers are on the other end of the floor. Toilets,too," Monk James told him.

"Cleanliness is next to godliness, I always say."

"What about the dog?"

"Sweet? He won't be no bother, will you, boy?" Doobie said.

"These little beds might take some getting used to, but we'll manage."

"If you say so."

"Where do I put my stuff? I don't see any chests."

"You won't need any. We'll also provide you with clothes to wear. After you unpack, just leave your clothes on one of the beds. You can take your utensils to the showers. There's cabinets in there."

"And here I went to all the trouble of packing."

"Sorry, but the reverend has his rules."

"Rules are rules, I guess. There's a lot to be said for order."

"That's what they say. You go ahead and get settled in. Take your time, just stay here on this floor until you hear the dinner notice, then come to the cafeteria."

"Is it a bell or what?"

"You'll know, and the cafeteria is on the first floor. You'll see the crowd."

"What's upstairs?"

"Women's quarters and don't get any ideas. They're off limits. You aren't allowed above this floor."

"They have two floors?"

"You'll understand why at dinner," he said. "Now, if you'll excuse me, I need to take care of your donation."

"By all means," Doobie said. "And you say I'll know when chow's ready?"

"Unless you're deaf," Monk James said, then left.

Doobie walked over to the window at the head of his twin bed and watched as Monk James exited the dormitory and headed to the Austin stone building at the rear of the quadrangle.

"Well, Sweet. Looks like our sleeping arrangements have gotten a little cozier."

20

Hector Calderon was half drunk and halfway through waxing the Monte Carlo. None of the others were allowed the privilege and none of them wanted it, no matter how shitty a job Hector did.

The more beer he consumed, the worse the car looked when he was done, and he was well on his way to a total waste of wax. The rain that was dripping down from the dilapidated roof of the vegetable shed was hardly Hector's ally in the battle.

Chuey Arrendondo had waited for his mother to fall asleep before he slipped into her purse and stolen the last of the food stamps that were to be used for the next week's groceries. He had exchanged the coupons for cash, at thirty cents on the dollar, and had given the money to Juan Mata. It was enough for two cases of Lone Star. With Eddie Bustos, Chuey and Juan blocking the cashier's view, and Carlos Cuevas running interference, Flaco Dominguez had escaped with a third case. Hector had been behind the wheel of the getaway Monte Carlo the whole time.

That had been three hours and a little
more than a case ago and they were all now
pretty much in a talkative mood as they
headed toward an alcoholic induced coma.

"It ain't my fault the little nigger
moved," Bustos said, referring to his
first botched attempt at human sacrifice
six months before. "But I got the other
one and he didn't move none after that.
Killed him clean, man. Right through the
heart.

Actually, the young, black boy had been
gut-shot and had died alone in an alley
after five hours of excruciating pain.

"Shit. How could you miss with me and
Hector holding him down?" Dominguez said.
"Mine was more better, no? I cut that
little, fat fucker's throat from ear to
ear. He didn't breathe no more after
that."

Dominguez and Calderon had followed a
young, Anglo boy as he left school in the
dark after a late band practice. They had
waited for him to cross the street and ran
him down in the Monte Carlo. Before he
could get up, Dominguez had jumped from
the car and stuck a knife in the side of
his neck. The boy had drowned in his own
blood, as the blade had actually severed
the artery and the windpipe, causing the
blood to flow, at will, into his lungs. He
had lived long enough to crawl, with his
clarinet case in hand, the final two

blocks to his house. Death came on his own front porch.

Chuey Arrendondo, who was every bit of six feet tall and two hundred and fifteen pounds at the ripe age of eighteen, wasn't about to be outdone. He crushed his empty beer can across his forehead and grabbed for another. "You're all pussies. At least I gave mine a fighting chance."

"Fuck you," Bustos said. "Yours was a faggot. He shouldn't even count."

"Up yours. He wasn't no *puto*."

"Then why did he say he would suck your dick if you would let him go?"

"He was just scared, man. You saw him. The guy pissed himself. It was funny. I told him to run. He just wouldn't do it."

"That's because he wanted you. He wanted your *chile*."

"And I gave it to him, man. You saw me give it to him. I stuck the pistol right in his mouth where he wanted it. I made him lick it till it came. I told him not to swallow."

Chuey's story had been closer to the truth than the rest, though not entirely. Hector had driven the two of them to the Pink Stallion, a known gay bar in the *barrio*. Chuey had gone inside and, mostly due to his muscular build and boyish face, had been propositioned almost immediately.

The two had left by way of the back door, where Bustos was waiting. The man, who was a college student at St. Mary's, hadn't just offered to go down on Chuey, but both of them. While on his knees, he had been forced to perform on the gun barrel instead. After Chuey had tired of the foreplay, he had shoved the barrel as far down the man's throat as he could and pulled the trigger. The shot made no more than a coughing sound, as did the man, who died with his eyes and his mouth wide open.

"He was a faggot and you know it," Bustos said.

"Okay, so maybe he was, but he still counted," Chuey told him.

"What about you, Hector?" Bustos said.

"What about me, what?" he said in the midst of fighting with the raindrops on the hood of the Monte Carlo.

"Your kill, man. Ain't you been listening?"

"Shit, no. Can't you see I'm working, *cholo?*"

"You ain't doing no damn good. It looks worse than when you started."

"Fuck you, *pinche hoto.* I don't need to talk about mine to make it real."

"That's okay with us. You couldn't tell it right anyway. Mata can tell it more better than you," Bustos said. "Can't you, Juan?"

"It's not mine to tell," Mata said. "Come on, Hector. Join the fun. Your car's not going anywhere."

"Ah, fucking rain. We need to find a better place. This place ain't worth a shit." He threw his rag onto the hood and joined the others, who surrounded the remaining cases of warm beer like a campfire.

"About time," Bustos said. "Shut up and hand me a beer."

Bustos obliged and Hector began. "Like I said, vato, it was real. Before you guys even knew about the Mayas. It was just me and Juan and the car. It didn't even have our symbol like it does now. We were just driving around. Juan had already done his the night before. It was my turn." He paused. "I can't believe I let you drive," he said to Mata.

"I had to, *cabron*. You were too drunk."

"Only because you drink too slow. You always do."

"At least *I* know what I kill."

Hector ignored the comment and continued. "We were down by the underpass where all the box people live. They were all over the place, man. We would stop and they would crowd around and spit on the glass, man, and try to wipe it off for money. They were spitting on my car, man, and this long-haired one came over and jumped on the hood. It scared the shit out of Juan and he took off with the long-hair still on the hood, man. Wouldn't let go. We went all the way to the water. What's that, six, seven blocks? Juan finally stopped the car. I was pissed. I could see the dents in the hood and the long-hair tried to run away, but I had the rifle. One shot. Right through the back. Fucker shouldn't have jacked with my car."

All but Carlos Cuevas had heard the story before and knew the ending. They watched him as Hector finished.

"I went over there and kicked the body over. I wanted to make sure the job was done, so I put my hand on the heart and felt a lump. It was a girl, man. It wasn't no long-haired guy. It was a girl. I took her pants off and fucked her right there."

Carlos' eyes were wide but his face was blank. "He fucked a dead girl," Bustos said for affect. "Yeah, but she was still warm."

"Until you threw her into the river," Mata said. "It was a good night for a swim, *cholo*."

"If a girl counts, then a faggot counts. Right, Carlos?" Chuey said.

"Fuckin' A," he said. "She never should have done that to his car."

"Now you, Juan," Chuey said. "Yours was the first."

"And the best," Mata said. "It proves the Mayas are brave. We fear no one."

"Fuckin' A," Carlos said again. He was caught up in the moment. He was one of them.

"Even the *negritos* know not to mess with us. Right, Hector?"

"You showed 'em," Hector said.

"Right in their own neighborhood, too. One less black pimp never hurt nothin'. Sucker was standing right there beside his gold pussymobile. Hector pulled up right next to it. Right there in front of... what was that bar?"

"The Black Diamond," Hector said.

"Yeah, The Black Diamond. I got out with the rifle and told him it was time for him to see Jesus and then shot the black piece of shit right between the eyes. The bullet went clean through his head and blew out the window in the bar. Shit. You could hear the music inside, plain as day."

As it turned out, the young black man had been on his way to the store up the block to get his pregnant wife a jar of peanut butter for a sandwich she had been craving. He had only stopped by the gold Cadillac to light up a smoke.

"No guts, no glory," Hector said.

Carlos Cuevas had been waiting for his turn at bat. He was one of them and had the tattoo to prove it. He was a Maya. Still, he waited to be called on. He was the youngest, though only by six months short of Flaco Dominguez. Age made very little difference, but he was also the newest.

Juan Mata invited him in. "What do you have to say for yourself, Carlita?"

"I did mine with honor. Away from our turf. And a *gringo*. I knew the little *pinche* was about to do something. They always do. They give us the finger when they think we aren't looking. They look down on us. They have to be killed while they are young.

Before they can grow up." The beer was doing most of Carlos' talking. "I did what was right and for our ancestors. For the Mayas. I wasn't going to give him a chance to become like the others. We must rule, not them. So, my brothers, I blew him away for you."

What Carlos Cuevas failed to tell them was that later that night, after he had returned home, he had puked his guts up and then dry-heaved until he had seen angels.

"To the Mayas," Carlos said, lifting a half-empty and extremely warm can of beer.

"The Mayas," the others chimed in.

They had each filled in a chapter, but the book was far from being finished.

* * *

Doobie had spent the morning walking from one side of the room to the other and window to window. He knew how to make use of time, when time was all he had. From the windows opposite his bed, he had watched the people, mostly women, working in the garden. He found it was a much more elaborate operation than he had seen from the front gate. He estimated there to be at least four acres of eight, possibly nine, different varieties of produce growing in well-manicured sections. He had studied the movements and noticed that only certain ones worked certain areas. It was definitely no helter-skelter operation.

He had also seen the large monk, Gonzo Drake, make a total of three trips to that side of the compound. Each time he had walked the fence line, never stopping to talk to anyone. He presumed the man's duty was akin to that of a watchman and estimated his total perimeter time to be roughly an hour.

At one point, about mid-morning, Reverend Daniel and Monk James had paid a visit to the workers. They had stopped their toil long enough to gather, on their knees, in a circle around him. It was obvious that he was offering some sort of prayer on their behalf. Doobie had taken the opportunity, while they were huddled together, to try to spot Ashley Jenkins. He remembered her having red hair, but not much else, at least not enough to be able to identify her from fifty yards away. He counted five girls with red hair, which narrowed down the field for later.

From the windows on his bed-side, where Doobie now stood, he had seen very little activity. Reverend Daniel had made two trips from the front building to the Austin stone structure at the rear, and always with Monk James trailing at his heels.

The only other person to enter the quadrangle was a dark- haired woman, probably about his own age. She had left the building he was in and also gone into the one at the rear. She hadn't stayed long, and as she was about to re-enter the dormitory, Doobie was sure she had seen him at the window. She may have even smiled.

Over the last few years, Doobie had taken to depending on the sun to keep him abreast of time, when time had become a factor. Those times had been few and far between. Cloudy days had been no bother, as time, for the most part, had been irrelevant. Today was sunny and the tree trunk shadow the silo had cast earlier was now just a stump of its original self.

Doobie jumped when music screamed at him from a speaker mounted flush in the ceiling. Sweet jumped from the bed and barked even louder.

"Shut up, dog. I don't need you joining in." Doobie recognized the song to be 'Bringing In The Sheaves.' He turned back toward the window and watched as people filed out of the front building and from around the corner of the dormitory; those coming from the garden. While the volume in the room was loud enough to wake the dead, he was sure it couldn't have been heard all the way out there.

Doobie pulled up on the window and was met with even louder music. A quick look across the quadrangle answered his question. Megaphone-like speakers were mounted on both top corners of the building, as well as on the building to his right. He had no doubt they were probably on the dormitory corners also. He shut the window and looked down at Sweet.

"I'd say it was probably time to eat, wouldn't you?"

Doobie took a deep breath. He couldn't remember the last time he had shared a meal with more than two people, not counting Sweet, who he considered to be better than people. People meant conversation and conversation meant throwing away a part of yourself, whether intentionally or not. Doobie considered idle conversation a waste of time. No one really listened or even cared, and usually only talked to hear themselves speak.

Doobie preferred to listen without being drawn in. He relished the role of an outsider, not as a judge, though he *had* taken on that role before and had been made to live with it ever since. He had taken himself away from all that. Removed himself almost from life itself, because of that role. And now, the only one he was made to judge was himself. He had not been, nor was he now, lenient in either case.

Doobie exited the room and onto the landing that divided the sleeping quarters from the showers. Two girls were coming down the stairs above him. He decided to wait and allow them to pass before continuing. Both girls stopped and looked mildly surprised, though not at the sight of a man in the building, as there were obviously at least six who already shared the quarters.

"Look," one of the girls said, "a dog." She walked over and patted Sweet on the head. Sweet, of course, reacted in his normal way by wagging his tail. Then, to Doobie's surprise, the dog jumped up and put his paws on the girl's chest and began licking her on the face.

"Sweet. Get down," Doobie ordered.

The girl backed away, not out of fear for herself, but for fear that the dog might get into more trouble if she let it continue.

"I'm sorry, miss," Doobie said. "He doesn't usually react like that."

"That's okay," she said and followed the other girl down the stairs.

"What's the matter with..." Doobie was about to warn his dog about such action and the possibility that it could get him in a much smaller doghouse, when his brain put two and two together. The girl's hair was red and her voice, even though he had heard it only once, was Ashley Jenkins'.

She had obviously not recognized either of them, and had it not been for Sweet's over-reaction to her affection, Doobie would have probably let her pass without knowing. She was no longer the little girl he remembered. Even in the sackcloth she was wearing, he could tell that she had grown into the young woman her mother had every right to be worried about. With any luck, her memory of their chance meeting on the golf course, when Sweet was just a puppy, would remain locked up in the suitcase of her mind until he was ready to open it.

"I knew there was a reason why I brought you along," he told the dog as they made their way down the stairs.

He waited at the bottom until everyone had entered the cafeteria doors to the left, then went in himself. The room looked like it would seat at least a hundred people. He estimated there to be maybe forty in line against the wall, waiting their turn to fill their trays. Reverend Daniel, Monk James and the dark-haired woman he had seen in the quadrangle were seated at a table away from the rows of others. A young girl had just set a plate in front of each of them.

When Monk James saw Doobie, he pointed a finger toward the end of the line. "I guess two thousand dollars doesn't buy what it used to," Doobie told Sweet, then took his place in line.

He inched his way along the wall with the others and received a generous helping of roast beef, mashed potatoes and green beans.

"Excuse me, but could I bother you for another plate?" he said to the girl who was dishing up the meat.

She seemed surprised that he had even spoken to her. None of the others had. They had just taken what she had given them and gone on their way. "Waste not, want not," she said.

"I assure you it won't go to waste. My friend here knows there are people starving in Africa."

The girl looked behind Doobie, who was still the last one in line and tilted her head.

"Oh, I'm sorry," Doobie said. "He's kinda short." He nodded down toward the floor.

The girl leaned over the counter and saw Sweet for the first time. She broke into a smile and filled a second plate.

"Better not. He needs to watch his weight. Thanks."

"My pleasure," she said.

When Doobie turned, he noticed that all the eyes in the room seemed to be on him. He also noticed that Reverend Daniel was now standing. He nodded toward the back of the room, where a table of boys were sitting with their hands clasped in front of them.

Doobie understood the gesture completely and headed for the table with Sweet in tow.

A pair of green eyes that sparkled like leaves after a spring rain followed him to his seat. Arrianna had seen him arrive, but from a distance. Then, later at the window, she still hadn't been able to make out his features. She knew he was lean and tan with dark hair much like her own, but up close, she could tell there was more to him than his clothes let on. He had a tightened, almost painful, look on his face; more learned than sorrowful. It was a look that told her he had been there and back. And while she didn't know where there had been, she knew he had come away a changed man. She could tell that by the way he held himself and the way he walked. He wasn't stoop-shouldered, but rather tall and proud, yet she saw right off that he was carrying a load.

Something heavy was weighing on him, but that something was what kept him going. It kept him braced against the odds. It kept him coming back. He had crossed a line somewhere and almost dared it to make him cross it again.

Arrianna knew he would be a challenge, unlike the monks who trailed after her like a pack of dogs waiting for her to go into heat. In a strange way, that excited her. A new adventure. One that would take some doing on her part. If she was wrong, if it was some unforgotten pain that drove him on, she would break through it. She would tear the mask away. She, better than anyone, knew pleasure sometimes followed pain; and even if the pain returned, the trip was worth it.

The same familiar stirring rose in her. Just the thought of him inside her sent orgasmic shivers throughout her body. She knew she would have him. She knew she had to.

After Doobie sat down, the reverend began. "Today, we welcome a new member to our flock. Brother Donnie comes to us as a sinner, as you all did. And like you, we welcome him into our midst with open and loving arms. As you partake of this bountiful harvest the Lord has seen fit to bestow upon you, remember that it is the Brother Donnies of this world, who have seen the light and who have chosen to rid themselves of *all* their worldly possessions, that will help us in our quest to bring peace and understanding to those who have chosen to stay behind... Praise the Lord."

The room was filled with a unison of "Amens." It would have been unanimous, but Doobie had come ill-prepared and missed the call. It was something he would have to work on.

Doobie set the second plate on the floor in front of Sweet, who devoured the meat without delay. Not being as hungry, Doobie took a few bites of meat and scraped the rest onto his dog's plate. He then finished off the vegetables and began working the room.

His estimation had not been far off. He counted thirty-one girls, most of whom looked to be college age. A few were younger, but not by much, and three looked to have passed the drinking age twice. Five seemed to be in different stages of pregnancy and with a radiant glow about them. Two others each held a child on their lap, one of whom was nursing while its mother ate. She smiled shamelessly at Doobie when she caught him staring.

Doobie couldn't remember the last time he had seen a woman's breast, much less held one. When the baby was through nursing, the mother laid him crossways in her lap before covering herself. Doobie was pleased to see that they hadn't changed.

The six boys were all somewhere in their third decade and had probably followed their little captains there, looking for a different form of religious experience. After a while, celibacy would lose the hormonal battle and they would be gone, only to be replaced by a new herd of rams. It was reason enough for their poor showing in numbers.

Reverend Daniel declared the meal to be over by action and not words. He stood up with his palms together and his eyes looking heavenward, at which point the first row of tables took their trays to an opening in the wall, laid them down and filed out.

The second row followed and then the third. All the while, the reverend never moved.

When it came time for the last row to follow suit, Doobie grabbed Sweet's plate and headed for the bin. When he was even with the head table, the dark-haired woman smiled at him for what Doobie was now sure was the second time.

<h1 align="center">21</h1>

No matter how deep a trench Reid Dalton dug himself into with his work, the walls still remained shored up with thoughts of Bear. Those thoughts were the only things that kept him going.

Two more days had gone by with no word from Detective Sergeant Eric Montalvo. If the police could spot an expired, three-inch square inspection sticker, stuck deep in the lower left-hand corner of a windshield of a car going in the opposite direction, why couldn't they find a one-eyed car? It wasn't like they didn't know what they were looking for or even where to look, for that matter. It just didn't add up.

If it was a manpower problem, why not deputize the Claims Department for one night? The results couldn't be any worse and the price would be right. Reid knew that thought was crazy, but crazy thoughts sometimes kept you from going insane.

For him, not knowing was making him go insane. He picked up the phone and dialed Montalvo's number.

"Montalvo."

"This is Reid Dalton, Sergeant."

"I was wondering when you would be checking in," he said. "It's been a while."

"You don't have to tell *me* that."

"I'm sure I don't. I just wish I had something positive to report."

Reid Dalton had expected as much. He just didn't want to admit it.

"Nothing, huh?"

"Well, nothing that matters. We *have* stopped seventeen cars with one headlight out and followed up on eleven reported headlight purchases since we last talked. The only one that was even close was a black Olds Cutlass, but it was owned by a little old lady in Oakhaven Heights. And get this, the car was six years old and only had a little over four thousand miles on it. Still, she agreed to let us check around the windows for gunpowder residue. It came out clean, just like we figured," Montalvo explained.

"So, I'm responsible for seventeen people getting tickets?"

"Nah, we let 'em all off with warnings. It wouldn't have been

fair, under these circumstances."

"Well, I hadn't heard anything and I needed to call you anyway and give you my work number. You can catch me here most of the time." Reid Dalton gave the sergeant his direct line in case he called after business hours.

"My guess is they probably bought a light off some discount store shelf and paid cash. I doubt these guys carry plastic, at least not their own."

"But you aren't going to stop looking?"

Montalvo didn't have the heart, or maybe it was the guts, to tell him they already had. The A.P.B. had been wiped off the list after the third night. They were now working with the luck of the draw. "We're still on it," he said instead. "By the way, have you heard anything else from the kid?"

"No, and it's probably better for him that I don't," Reid Dalton said.

"Well, he gave it a shot. That's better than most folks would do."

The second button on Reid Dalton's phone started blinking. Had the conversation been going in a different direction, he would have just let it blink. "Listen, I got another call coming in. I just wanted to check up on things."

"No problem. I'll keep in touch." Detective Sergeant Montalvo cradled the phone and reached for Bear Dalton's file in the stack on his desk. He opened it and looked at the photos taken at the scene. He had developed a gut feeling about this case. The kind that turned his stomach into a breeding ground for premature ulcers. His gut told him it would never be solved, but what was worse, it also told him it wouldn't matter.

* * *

The two hours immediately following lunch were reserved for scripture reading and silent prayer in the church building.

Attendance was mandatory. A medical excuse from Arrianna was the only acceptable means for absence. Doobie had yet to be introduced to the nurse, at least not formally.

Reverend Daniel had stepped in and pulled rank and told Monk James to acquaint him with the various projects that needed his immediate attention. Monk James had been less than pleased by the request. He usually took advantage of that time period to catch up on his beauty sleep or count his money. Both required mattress time of sorts.

Being that the dormitory was empty of any female residents, they started on the fourth floor. Upon entering the living quarters, Doobie noticed they were no different from his. No lace curtains or teddy bears or other such frills one would expect, just two rows of made beds lined up against bare, white walls.

"There's a hole in the wall over there," Monk James said and pointed to a spot about halfway down the right side above one of the beds.

"Nightmare?" Doobie asked and made a mental note that it would take no more than an hour to repair the sheetrock. He would keep that information to himself, in case he needed the time for other things.

"More like a fight, but that's to be expected when you stick this many women in one room together. I'm surprised we haven't had more."

"From what I saw at lunch, it looks to me like they're all fine, upstanding Christian women."

"Uh, huh," was Monk James' only response. "And I believe they have a leaky shower nozzle in the other room." They exited the living quarters and crossed the hall.

Doobie found the area to be spotless. "Looks like they do a good job of keeping the place clean. You could eat off this floor."

Monk James held back a snicker. Doobie's comment had taken on a different meaning when it reached his ears. "I don't know that they've tried that yet," he said.

Doobie missed his point and followed Monk James into the shower. "Yep, that one there," Doobie said. He knew it would require a simple washer replacement, but he didn't let on.

"I think that's all up here," Monk James said. They left the fourth floor and headed down one flight of stairs and again entered the lavatory room.

"All we got here is a broken mirror."

"Another fight?" Doobie asked when he saw the bare wall above one of the sinks.

"Never did find out what happened here. We just came in and found it cracked one day."

Doobie didn't bother to ask why the entire mirror had been removed if it had just been a crack. A small indentation in the wall told him there was more to the story, and there had been.

A month before, one of the girls, upon discovering she was pregnant, had skipped the scripture reading time. She had broken the mirror with a deodorant can and cut her wrists in the shower. Luckily, Arrianna had found her first and had been able to wash the evidence down the drain.

At supper that night, the others had been informed that the girl had chosen to leave and go back to the world of sinners.

And the silo remained locked.

Doobie had already made a thorough inspection of the second floor that morning and didn't recall seeing any repair work that would require his expertise. However, he kept that information to himself and followed Monk James down to the ground floor.

They entered the cafeteria to the left, where Doobie was shown a table with what appeared to be a broken leg. Upon closer inspection, he found the metal folding brace broken and another about to go. He deduced that it would be cheaper to just throw it away and buy another, but decided to hold that decision in abeyance until he was informed who it would be that made the trip into town for the supplies he needed.

When they left the cafeteria, Monk James headed for the front door. Doobie stopped him with a question. "What's in there?" He pointed to the door that led to the other half of the first floor.

"Infirmary and Arrianna's quarters." Monk James failed to mention the one-way, mirrored shower room at the end.

"Arrianna?"

"She's the nurse and I guess you could also call her the house mother to the girls. She tends to their female needs."

"I understand." Doobie started to tell him that he had a sister, but remembered he wasn't supposed to have a family. "I presume that was her sitting at the table with you and Reverend Daniel?"

"You presumed correctly."

"I hope she will forgive my manners," Doobie said. "A gentleman would have introduced himself."

"Oh, I'm sure you'll be meeting her before you know it." Monk James turned and headed out the front door as he spoke; his grin hidden from Doobie's view.

Sweet had been given the liberty of the compound after lunch. He had gone about marking his territory and was now asleep in the shade of the silo. Doobie left him to his dreams and followed Monk James to the Austin stone house, but not inside. They went around the building to the back.

"Reverend Daniel would like a balcony built up there." He pointed to a window on the second floor of the two-story structure.

"How's he gonna get to it?"

"I guess he's leaving that up to you."

"What's up there?"

"His bedroom."

"The whole floor?"

"The rest isn't your concern."

"I see. I'm just trying to get the big picture. I want to make sure I do the job right, being that he's the reverend and all. Can I get a look from the inside?" Doobie had an idea of what the answer would be.

"When the time comes," Monk James informed him.

"What about down here? I could build a mighty fine-looking patio or maybe even a deck where he could meditate while he watched the sun go down. It's my favorite time of the day, watching the sun go down. It's so peaceful, if you know what I mean?"

"I'm sure he'll get enough meditation done up there. Besides, me and two others live down here where we can keep an eye on the bus..." He caught himself before he could say business. "...the operation."

Doobie caught him before he could catch himself, but didn't let on. He stuck a different iron in the fire instead. "Three of you?" Unless the rather large monk, whom he had met first and who he had seen walking the fence line, was a twin, he was one body count short.

"That's right," was the only answer Doobie got, but when Monk James tugged at the rope-like belt around his middle, Doobie forgot about the third man. Something more deadly slapped him in the face. Something he hadn't counted on and wasn't ready to deal with. Not again. Maybe he was mistaken. Maybe the bulge he had seen on the man's hip was just a wallet. Maybe it held the twenty hundred-dollar bills he had given him earlier. He knew he had to find out. He had to be sure.

"Just a second," Doobie said and went around to Monk James' back. "You got a little knot back here." He tugged at the back of the rope-like belt with his right hand to draw attention away from the fact that his left hand had gone to the bulge. It wasn't a wallet. Wallets didn't have grips. He let loose of both together. "There. That ought to do it."

"Thanks. These outfits aren't my idea," he said. "Wait'll you get yours. You'll see what I mean."

His comment concerning his attire bounced off Doobie like grease in a hot skillet. He had another pan on the stove and the fire was white hot.

"Uh, yeah. I'm sure." Doobie paused. "Are we finished here?"

"Yep. All we got left for now is the church building. Everything else is pretty much up to snuff."

They walked back around the same way they had come. When they reached the quadrangle, Doobie noticed that Sweet hadn't moved.

"Looks like your dog's made himself to home," Monk James said. "He's easy to please. Kinda like me. Food and shelter is all we need."

"Well, as you can see, we have plenty of both here."

"What about the silo? It looks like it could use some patchwork."

Doobie had a feeling that he needed to look inside. At the same time, he didn't want to.

"No. Reverend Daniel wants it left alone. It's just a relic. If it falls down, it falls down."

"What if someone's under it when it decides to fall? Could be dangerous," Doobie explained. "I could get in there and shore it up in no time."

"I said no. You've got plenty of other things to keep you busy."

"Just trying to help out. It sure would be a shame if some of these girls got hurt. I don't think I could ever forgive myself if I let something like that happen, especially if I could have done something about it," Doobie said. "You might mention that to the reverend. Tell him how somebody could get hurt. I bet he'll change his mind. He's probably never thought about it that way."

"I'll mention it to him," Monk James said.

They were about to enter the church from the rear when the doors opened in front of them. They backed off to opposite sides and let a stream of mostly women pass between them. Doobie hoped they had learned something from their scriptures, because he was for certain that their prayers had fallen on deaf ears.

When the stream dried up, Doobie followed Monk James inside. He felt nothing when he entered the large room filled with rows of pews. No peace. No comfort. He breathed nothing but dead air.

They walked down the center aisle to the front, where Monk James pointed out a loose board on the wide steps that led up to the pulpit.

"I can see where that could be a problem," Doobie said. "I'd sure hate to see that give way when the reverend was walking down. He could take a nasty fall. I might oughta get on that first thing."

"I'm sure the reverend would appreciate it," Monk James said. "Course he wouldn't get hurt near as much as he would if the

silo fell on him." Doobie had nothing
against dealing from the bottom of the
deck if it helped his hand.

"You just get this fixed first and I'll
see about talking to him about the other."

"Fair enough," he said. "A fella couldn't
ask for more."

22

At the close of the business day on Friday, Buster Horton had ordered Reid Dalton not to come in over the weekend. He had stopped short of demanding that he give him his key to the Cave. It wouldn't have done any good, since all he would have had to do was show his ID and tell the guard he had left his key at home to gain entry. Reid hadn't argued. He understood Buster had done it for his own good.

He had worked until just before midnight, -- any later and he would have been guilty of disobeying a direct order -- gone home and fallen into a temporary coma.

He woke refreshed, eleven hours later, with nothing but idle time on his hands and Bear on his mind. He threw on a gray San Antonio Spurs T-shirt and a pair of jeans. He hadn't eaten in almost a day, and then only a sandwich at his desk. The refrigerator was empty, save for a couple of cans of Coke and a sack of pecans Kathy had purchased to make Bear's favorite dessert, pecan pie. Neither looked appetizing. He made up his mind to just

get in the car and drive until he came to
the first restaurant, stop and eat
whatever the waitress recommended. He had
made so many decisions over the last week
that his brain was in gridlock. He needed
to be told what to do next.

He had taken to leaving his car in the
driveway. It made for a quicker getaway in
the mornings. When he opened the front
door to leave, he came face-to-face with
the friendly face of Jason, who was
startled by the door opening before he had
a chance to knock.

"Sorry. I didn't mean to scare you. I was
on my way out."

"It's okay," Jason said. "Where you
going?"

"Lunch," Reid told him. "You had yours
yet?"

"Hunh, uh."

"You want to come along?"

"To where?"

"It's up to you. I'm not particular."

"How about pizza?"

"Sounds good to me," Reid Dalton said and
realized a pizza actually did sound good
to him.

"Go on inside and..."

"I know, call my mom. Can I leave my bike inside? I left the chain lock at home."

"Have at it." Reid Dalton stepped aside so Jason could walk the bike inside. He waited by the door in case Jason's mother wanted to clear the trip with him. It was something parents were bred to do. It was in their genes not to trust their children when it came to believing they could actually be invited out to eat in a public place.

Jason returned with a smile on his face. "She said to tell you that if I misbehaved, you could just leave me there."

"I'll keep that in mind." They climbed into the car and headed toward a strip center on Bandera Road, where Reid had taken Bear on more than one occasion. "Okay?" Reid asked, pointing at the Pizza Hut sign.

"The best," Jason said.

"You're easy to please," Reid followed.

"You don't understand. My mom was making bologna sandwiches for lunch."

"Ah. Good thing you showed up when you did, then."

"You're telling me."

They drove the next few blocks in silence. Reid was so happy to have his little friend along, he would have agreed to take him to The Tower of Americas Restaurant, if that had been his pleasure. Nevertheless, the Pizza Hut was closer and a lot less expensive. Being a Saturday, the strip center lot was near capacity. They found a spot at the far end and walked along the sidewalk in front of the stores.

They passed the computer store where Reid Dalton had bought Bear's. It had taken him less than a month to fill the memory with games, uneducational, for the most part, but Reid had gladly shelled out the additional funds to upgrade the system. He had thought it would pay off in the long run.

The Pizza Hut was crowded, but Reid Dalton was hungry, so he accepted a table in the smoking section, rather than wait the twenty minutes the hostess told him it would be before they could sit elsewhere. If nothing else, it would test his resistibility. "What flavor?" Reid asked Jason when the waitress stopped at their table.

"Pepperoni, if that's okay with you?"

"Pepperoni it is," he told the waitress. "Large and two Cokes."

"So, how's school?" Reid Dalton asked when the waitress had left.

"Better, now that I don't have to miss any to see that stupid doctor anymore."

"Oh yeah?"

"Yeah. I told my folks I wasn't having any more bad dreams, so they wouldn't make me go back," Jason told him.

"See, it did do you some good."

"No, it didn't."

"But you just said..."

"I said I *told* them that."

"So, you're still having them?"

"Well, kinda. That's why I came by to see you. We're still a team, right?"

Reid Dalton knew he was treading on thin ice. He had to step carefully. The last thing he wanted was to have Jason fall through.

"Sure, we are. That was the deal."

"And you promise you won't tell my mom?" Jason said. "I don't want to have to go back to that doctor."

"I promise, but only if you promise to give it a week. If you are still having them, you'll tell your parents."

"But they'll make me go back."

"We'll leave that up to them," Reid said. "Those are my terms."

"A week, huh?"

"And no lying to me. We're a team, remember?"

"Okay."

The waitress returned with two glasses of Coke. After she left, Jason took a drag on the straw. He swallowed, then continued. "There was something on the car. An emblem or something."

"You mean like a sign or a name?"

"No. Nothing with words. More like a picture."

"Of a person?"

"No, not that either. It was kinda like a drawing or a painting or something like that."

"Can you describe it, Jason?"

"I don't know. It was blurry. It kinda looked like a big stick or a log. Yeah, a big log, only stuff was on it."

"Stuff?"

"You know, shiny stuff like squares or something. They were sticking out of it."

Reid Dalton had no idea what Jason was trying to describe, but he had to keep him going. He grabbed a waitress as she was walking by. "Can I borrow your pen?"

"It's the only one I have?" she said, somewhat politely. "We'll only be a minute."

"Okay," she said and handed him her pen. "But only till I come back. I've got another table to get."

Reid Dalton reached for a napkin and slid it toward Jason, then handed him the pen. "Draw it."

"I'm not very good at drawing."

"That's okay. Just do what you can."

Reid Dalton watched as he tore the pen across the napkin.

"Uhhnn." Jason beat him to the napkin holder and took out another. He applied less pressure with the pen this time and drew a rectangular shaped object, then filled it in with lines running lengthwise. He followed with smaller squares, three on each side of the rectangle. At one end, he drew a smaller rectangle, but no squares.

"That," Jason said.

"That looks like a traffic light," Reid Dalton told him.

"See, I told you I wasn't very good," Jason explained.

Reid had to laugh. And that felt good. "So, it's not a traffic light?"

"No. It was at an angle, like this." He turned the napkin sideways.

"On the door."

When the waitress came back by, she asked
if they were through with her pen. "I'm
afraid so," Reid Dalton said and handed it
to her.

"What are you drawing?" she asked.

"Not a traffic light," Reid Dalton told
her. He and Jason both laughed at the
waitresses' expense.

When their own waitress showed up with
their large pepperoni pizza, Reid folded
up the napkin and stuck it in his jeans
pocket. If it wasn't a traffic light, it
had to be something else.

* * *

The only thing the loose board had
required was a larger nail.

Doobie had seen that right off, but had
kept that under the hat he didn't wear. He
had made a big production out of the
simple job with his toolbox, a circular
saw, an electric drill and a pair of
safety goggles, just in case he was being
watched. He had replaced the nail in
thirty seconds, but had spent the next
half hour running the drill and saw in
order to produce just the right sound
effects. The kind expected in a quality
project.

When he left the church building by the quadrangle door, Sweet met him with his tail wagging. "Woke you up, huh?"

They walked together to the Bronco, where Doobie replaced the unused tools. "It's all in how you're perceived," he said. "And I can play their game as good as they can."

They walked back through the quadrangle and into the dormitory, where noises could be heard coming from the cafeteria.

A quick look inside at a group of girls hard at work behind the serving line told him they were just getting started on supper preparations.

When he turned to head for the stairs, he noticed the door to the infirmary was open. He thought about taking a look inside, but he hadn't been there long enough to take a chance on being caught snooping around, especially after he had been told there was nothing inside that needed his attention.

He made his way up the stairs, with Sweet on his heels, and into his shared living quarters. The first thing he noticed was his pile of clothes had been replaced by a rather uncomfortable looking fold of cloth. On closer inspection, he found it could pass for a giant potato sack that could no longer serve the purpose for which it was intended. There were too many holes.

"What rack you think they bought this off of?" Doobie said as he stepped out of his jeans. He slipped the sackcloth over his T-shirt and let it fall to just above his knees. Again, he felt like he was being watched. He turned in just enough time to see a shadow pass in the small opening below the door.

"Hope they got their nickel's worth," he told Sweet. Arrianna hurriedly tiptoed down the stairs to her quarters.

She was out of breath when she sat down on the side of her bed, but not from the pace that had brought her there. She lifted the sackcloth and touched the place she wanted Doobie to touch. The place she wanted him to enter. Her breathing became erratic and short and soon her fingers moist. She fell back onto the bed and pulled a pillow to her chest. She held it tight until all she had left was the dream itself.

23

Reid Dalton had stayed at the house just long enough to let Jason retrieve his bike, then followed him safely home before he headed for the police precinct. He wanted to fill Detective Sergeant Montalvo in on Jason's recent discovery. He could have done it by phone, but he wanted to see what the detective had to say about the picture Jason had drawn on the napkin. Maybe another pair of eyes wouldn't see a traffic light in the scratching.

Reid parked on a side street around the corner from the precinct house and stuck the only quarter he had in the meter. It was a slam dunk decision on his part. The MPs, meter patrol, would surely begin their rounds close to home.

Eric Montalvo and Jess Ramsey had stopped in front of the desk sergeant's station on their way out to a late lunch. Ramsey had gotten a call he needed to take and didn't feel energetic enough to negotiate the stairs. The desk sergeant had handed him the courtesy phone and put the caller through. Montalvo saw Reid Dalton as soon as he came through the door. He still had nothing positive to give him, which meant he would have to bullshit his way through a conversation before he could eat.

"Sergeant," Reid said. "I'm glad I caught you."

Montalvo wanted to say, "That makes one of us," but he chose a more tactful approach. "We were just heading out to catch a bite. You want to join us."

"No, thanks. I just ate, which is why I'm here."

Reid Dalton's response made no sense to Montalvo, unless he had Chinese for lunch and his fortune cookie had revealed the

license plate number of a one-eyed car. But that would have been too much to ask. "You lost me there, *amigo*."

"I had lunch with Jason."

"Ah, our little friend."

Neither one noticed Jack Greer, a three-year reporter with the *San Antonio Express-News,* who was sitting on a bench within earshot. Jack Greer had been trying to make a name for himself since he had graduated with a Journalism degree from the University of Texas. He had started out writing obituaries, like most cub reporters, and had worked his way into the city beat. He had spent two years following the mayor around and had jumped at the chance to cover crime in the big city. After a month of fighting to get on the good graces of the detective squad, he had found their inner circle impenetrable. They saw him as nothing more than a snot-nosed kid with a chip on his shoulder, which is basically what he was.

"Before I say anything," Reid Dalton said as he reached into his pocket for the napkin. "Tell me what you think of this." He handed the napkin to Montalvo.

Montalvo looked at the drawing, then turned it sideways and looked at it from a different angle. "You got me. What's it supposed to be?"

"Jason saw something like that on the door of the car."

Montalvo studied the drawing on the napkin some more. "I don't know. What are those things sticking out the side supposed to be?" He turned it again. "Could be a railroad track, maybe. Those things on the side could be cross-ties. What do you make of it?"

"Don't ask me. I thought it looked like a traffic signal," Reid told him.

"Yeah. That, too. Can I keep this? I want to show it around. Who knows? Could mean something. I can stick it in the computer and see what it spits out."

Jack Greer got up from the bench and made like he was reaching for something by the desk sergeant's station. He looked over Montalvo's shoulder as he stretched. He had no idea what he expected to see or even why, but his butt ached from the hard bench. Any movement would be a relief, whether it produced a story or not. He walked a few steps away, took out his notepad and drew a sketch of his own.

"I'd appreciate it," Reid said.

"So, the kid came around again, huh?"

"Yeah, Jason wants to find Bear's killer as much as we do."

Jack Greer wrote two names on his pad. One he vaguely remembered.

"Well, he's the only witness we got."

Jack Greer wrote "witness" beside Jason's name.

When Jess Ramsey hung up the phone, Montalvo introduced him to Reid Dalton and Jack Greer added a third name to his growing list.

"Well, I'll let you guys go eat. Besides, I think my fifteen minutes are about up."

"No problem," Montalvo told him. "I got pull with the MPs."

Reid Dalton was surprised that Montalvo had referred to them as such, not knowing most police slang was the product of squad room in-breeding.

"I'll have to remember that," Reid Dalton said.

* * *

It had taken Doobie every bit of fifteen minutes to decide the sackcloth wasn't going to work. Without the waist of his jeans to stop the movement, his tool belt had the uncontrollable urge to head south. Rather than take a chance on having the jeans disappear like the rest of his gear, he jumped back into them at the first available opportunity. He compromised by cutting a slit down the sides and wearing the sackcloth like a poncho and spent the remainder of the afternoon arranging and then rearranging the tools in the back of the Bronco.

Sweet had spent the afternoon moving from place to place around the silo and scratching at the dirt at the base. Doobie figured he was just digging around, trying to find the coolest spot to bed down.

When the music announced the evening meal, they both took a pass on the groceries. Lunch had been more than enough. Doobie waited for the quadrangle to clear before calling Sweet to the truck. He took a top tray from the toolbox and then removed a row of wrenches that lay on top of an aluminum foil package at the bottom of the box.

"Bet you thought I forgot," he said to the dog when he unwrapped the foil and showed him the supply of dog biscuits. He took out the usual two, as well as the same number of his own brand of home-grown and covered the evidence back up.

"Let's go see what kind of trouble we can get into," he said as he headed toward the front of the church. It had been almost half an hour since Friar Tuck had walked past him on his round. If his calculations were correct, he was somewhere along the back fence. When he got to the front, Doobie opened the box and pressed the button for the gate to roll open. Before it could complete the journey, he pushed the button again and led Sweet through before it closed.

"I got us out," he said as he handed Sweet a biscuit. "You gotta figure out how to get us back in."

Doobie trotted to the nearest hill where mesquite had grown up like a fort among the yaupon. The sackcloth poncho slapped against his legs as he ran. "Ain't exactly home, but it'll do," he said when he sat down on a mesquite trunk growing horizontally to the ground. He took out a filtered joint and lit it. He looked at the lighter where the inscription had been rubbed smooth. It was one of only a few material things he had that meant anything to him and like himself, it too was wearing thin. Doobie leaned against another branch and watched the sun go down behind the compound. Sweet put his head on Doobie's knee and sniffed at the sackcloth. He lifted his head back and sneezed. "Don't worry, boy. They don't come in your size," Doobie told him.

He was about to hand Sweet the other biscuit when Doobie caught movement out of the corner of his eye. He brought the lit joint down below the branch to hide the burning ember. It wasn't yet too dark for him to make out the form of a man as he walked from a thick growth of yaupon in the direction of the highway.

Doobie cupped the cigarette in his hands and took a last deep drag, then stomped the remainder out on the ground. He stood up slowly and peered out through the growth. The man's outfit gave his identity away, but unlike the other two, this monk made no attempt to hide his weapon. He had a rifle slung over one shoulder.

When the man disappeared behind a hill, Doobie handed Sweet the biscuit. "Stay. You understand? Stay here." He patted him on the head and ran crouching around the opposite side.

Doobie fell on all fours when a wide beam of light swept over the hill. He crawled to the top, where he saw a large tractor-trailer rig making a circle in the field just inside the fence. When the gun-toting monk reached the rig, the driver got out like he belonged and lit a cigarette. Doobie watched as the two appeared to carry on a conversation. He was too far away to hear what they were saying and there was nothing between them but open field. He had no alternative but to stay put.

Doobie could tell the trailer was some sort of transport. The kind used for hauling cars across country from the factory to the dealerships, only this one was empty.

The driver moved to the back of the rig and jerked on a handle. Doobie heard the sound of grinding metal as the man pulled out a pair of ramps and let them fall to the ground.

Just then, more lights appeared to Doobie's left. He hugged the ground, thankful for the sackcloth poncho that covered his white T-shirt, and watched two cars drive down the caliche road toward the transport.

It was now too dark to make out who got out of the cars when they stopped single file behind the rig, but Doobie knew they were most likely also wearing outfits similar to the one with the rifle. They shared a few words with the driver, then headed back up the road toward the compound. The driver entered the first car, a small one, and drove it up onto the lower of two rails. He chained it down and pulled the second one up behind it.

Two more sets of lights came around the hill and drove up behind the rig, just as before. This time, the drivers stayed while the cars were loaded and chained.

When the rig driver was done, he lit up another smoke before replacing the ramps with no help from the other three.

"Must be union," Doobie thought.

"Not a bad haul," the rig driver said to Monk James. "I make that a Miata, a Jimmy, an Escort and a Camry."

"All in a day's work," Monk James said as he moved the rig driver away from the other two.

"What'd we say, twenty-four grand?"

"On the nose. Now all you gotta do is move 'em."

"Shit, I had homes for 'em before I left Houston. I just gotta repaint the Jimmy. They want it in red," the rig driver said.

"That shouldn't take long," Monk James said.

"Nab. We'll deliver it day after tomorrow, redder than a pimple on your butt."

"We'll probably have some more this time next week."

"Just keep 'em coming. I got a kid in college and another on the way. If you could lay your hands on a Jag, I can promise you top dollar. I got me a lawyer chomping at the bit for one. Don't even have to be new so long as it's cherry."

"I'll keep my eyes open," Monk James said.

"You do that. Top dollar, you hear?" the rig driver said as he handed him a stack of bills with a rubber band around it. "Don't spend it all in one place."

Monk James had no intention of spending it at all, at least not yet. Four thousand of it would be in his mattress before the evening was done. The rest would go down on the books just like he had told Reverend Daniel it would. Five grand a car, not the six the deal actually called for.

Doobie watched the transport pull away into the darkness and then followed the three forms back up the road until they were only two. Not sure exactly of where the third came to roost, he crawled back down the hill and over to a mesquite line. He followed it on foot until he located Sweet.

"You mind pretty well for a spoiled dog," he said. Doobie yearned for his second smoke, but an open flame would be too easy to spot.

Doobie saw Reverend Daniel waiting just inside the fence. He pressed the button when the two monks arrived and the gate rolled open. "You don't think he'd do that for us, do you?"

When Sweet didn't answer, he followed with, "I didn't think so."

Doobie waited in the original mesquite fort until the reverend and Monk James entered the church building and Friar Tuck began his trek around the perimeter. After half an hour, the coast was clear for them to make their move. They kept the same distance between them and the fence until they rounded the left corner.

Using the garden inside for tall cover, Doobie dug a small trench under the fence. "You need to be doing this since you're so good at it," he told Sweet, just before he forced him through. He followed on his belly, feet first, and brought the loose dirt in behind him.

He waited behind the garden long enough to finish what he had come out for in the first place and buried the filter in the dirt when he was done.

24

The morning papers had built a nest just inside Reid Dalton's front door. Every morning when he was about to leave the house, he would throw the most recent edition inside. Every night when he got home, he would walk by them like they weren't even there. Most of the time, *he* wasn't even there. Physically, yes.

Mentally, no.

The Sunday edition of the *San Antonio Express-News* was like most Sunday editions, over-stuffed and heavy as a brick. While it was true that most injuries occurred at home, what the records didn't show was that so did most hernias, and usually on Sundays.

If lawyers ever got wind of that little-known fact, no newspaper in business would be safe.

When Reid bent down to pick the paper up off the porch, he had every intention of pitching it in with the others, but the paper had other ideas. Or at least Jack Greer had. The reporter's rendition of Jason's drawing stared up at him from the concrete. He grabbed the paper and tore off the plastic wrapper. When it unfolded in his hands, the caption above the drawing jumped out and grabbed him by the throat.

HAVE YOU SEEN THIS PICTURE?

It wasn't an advertisement for a contest. There were no prizes to win if you could identify it. It was the lead into the story about Bear's murder. The story, which began on page one and ended on page twelve of the same section, went on to describe the murder and how the victim's young friend, Jason--no last name as Jack Greer wasn't that good or that thorough yet--had seen it all happen. Reid Dalton's own name had been mentioned and that he and Jason had been working hand in hand with the police in order to solve one of the city's most heinous crimes. The story also included the number of other unsolved murders in San Antonio.

Under other circumstances, he would have considered the story well-written and to the point.

While the story had been about Bear's murder, its intent had been to bring out the fact that too many such cases remained on the books. It had been a direct hit on the San Antonio Police Department and their inability to solve crimes. Jack Greer was getting back at the department for not allowing him in.

Reid read over the story three times, the third time with his hand on the phone. When he was done, he dialed Detective Sergeant Eric Montalvo's number.

Another detective answered. "Detectives. Gamble speaking."

"I need to talk to Sergeant Montalvo." There was no "please" in his request or in the sound of his voice. "He's off today."

"Then let me have his home number."

"I can't do that. It's against policy. I can take a message."

"I'm not leaving a message. I want to talk to him and I want to talk to him *now!*"

"I've already told you he's not in."

"Then find him. You can do that, can't you?"

"I can beep him."

"Then beep him."

"Who's calling?"

"Tell him it's Reid Dalton and I'm at home. He's got the number."

"I'll do it right now." Detective Gamble had read the morning paper.

Reid waited for ten minutes and was about to call again when the phone rang. He grabbed the receiver and jerked it up.

"Where the hell are you?"

"I was in church."

"Have you read the paper?"

"I'm afraid so."

"What the fuck do you think you're doing?"

"I didn't have anything to do with that. It was a little, wise-ass reporter. That's all."

"That's all? What the hell do you mean, that's all? You've just signed Jason's death warrant!"

"You're blowing this thing all out of proportion. I don't think it'll come to that."

"You're damn right it won't! You better have a twenty-four-hour guard at his house."

"That won't be necessary, but we already have a cruiser assigned to go by every hour or so."

"Oh, what, like they're on vacation and need someone to watch the house? That's not good enough, you son of a bitch!" Reid Dalton yelled into the phone. "He trusted me and I trusted you, and you just fucked it up."

"I think you better settle down, Mr. Dalton."

"I think you better go fuck yourself!"

"We're not getting anything accomplished with this. I'm going to hang up now and go back inside. You take a while to cool down. When you think you can discuss this rationally, call me back." Sergeant Montalvo gave him his home number.

"You didn't get anything accomplished before this. I think that reporter was right. You couldn't find your ass if it was parked in front of your face."

"I'm hanging up now," Montalvo said.

"Go ahead. I'm through with you anyway." Reid Dalton slammed the phone down hard enough to crack the receiver.

It was all up to him now. No more cops. They had proved their worth. He never should have trusted them in the first place, and certainly not with Jason's life. Jason had come to him. He had opened up to him and told him his fears. Those fears were now a reality. First and foremost, he had to protect Jason. Nothing else mattered. If protecting Jason led him to Bear's killers, then so much the better. If not, he would just have to deal with it. He could live with that, so long as Jason was safe.

He couldn't live with the fact that he had been responsible for both their deaths.

* * *

When Doobie entered the dormitory, the lingering smell of a supper gone sent a sharp pang of hunger deep into his stomach. While midnight was still a few hours off, a snack was not out of the question. He walked into the dark cafeteria, located the light switch on the wall and headed for the kitchen, where he found three stainless steel doors begging to be opened. Rather than having to choose between the left or the right, he exposed the one in the middle. He stared into the cold cavern until a rather large, sliced ham stared back. He removed it, placed it on the butcher block cutting table in the middle of the room, and then went about locating the proper staff of life to slap the meat between.

Arrianna had just stepped out of the shower and was walking across the hall to her room when the cafeteria lights went on. She wrapped a towel around her and walked down the hall to the door. Across the way, she saw Doobie rummaging through the cupboards. She hurried back to her room, slipped a white cotton camisole over her wet hair and let it fall into place. The bottom stopped its descent about mid-thigh. She pulled the towel up and left the room.

Doobie was walking around the serving line to a nearby table when Arrianna entered, still towel-drying her hair. "I don't believe we've been properly introduced," she said.

Her sudden arrival startled him. The plate in his hand seemed to develop a mind of its own and jumped forward. Doobie reacted fast enough to catch the plate but not the sandwich. It separated in mid-air and landed on the floor in three neat stacks.

"I'm sorry," Arrianna said. "Let me make you another one."

"That's okay," Doobie said nervously as he knelt down and returned the sandwich to the plate. "I should have eaten when I was supposed to."

"I noticed you weren't around," she said as she walked toward him and stopped by the table. She ran the towel over her hair with both hands, intentionally raising the bottom of the camisole.

When Doobie looked up, his eyes caught the dark patch of hair that nestled between her thighs. He gripped the plate tight as he raised himself up and turned clumsily back toward the kitchen.

Arrianna followed with a grin.

He dumped the lost snack into a trash can, took the plate to the sink and rinsed away the evidence. When he turned back around to return the plate to the cabinet, Arrianna was blocking his way. His eyes went directly to her breasts, not that they had been given much choice. The camisole was so light it seemed to snag on the ends of her nipples as they stood there firm and high.

Arrianna knew he was staring, almost trance-like, so she tugged at the bottom of the nightshirt so that the flimsy material stretched tight against the full roundness of her breasts.

Doobie felt an uncontrollable and almost unfamiliar arousal in his jeans as he stood there with the plate in his hands. "Excuse me," he said when his wits returned momentarily.

Arrianna moved ever so slightly to one side and as he passed, she moved back just enough to allow his arm to brush across her breast.

"By the way," she said. "I'm Arrianna, which means you must be Donnie."

Doobie almost corrected her as he set the plate in the open cabinet. Instead, he said, "That's right. And if you'll excuse me, I think I better be getting along upstairs."

"So soon? I was just getting to know you. We can sit and talk a while."

"Yes, ma'am. I mean no, ma'am." Doobie wasn't sure exactly what he meant but he knew he needed to be somewhere other than where he was. Too many doors to too many closets were inching their way open in the dark hallways of his mind. He wasn't ready to see what was behind any of them. He had long since forgotten what he had boxed up and put away.

"I'm not making you nervous, am I?" Arrianna preferred questions she already knew the answer to.

"Yes, ma'am. I really shouldn't be down here."

"It's okay. I do it all the time. They don't care."

"I mean with you," Doobie said. "You're uh..."

"Oh," Arrianna said, turning a counterfeit pose of shyness as she pretended to only now notice the way she was dressed. "I'm sorry. I'm just so used to not having anyone around down here at this time of night. Let me go throw something else on. I won't be a minute."

"No, ma'am. I... I really must be getting along," Doobie stammered.

Arrianna realized she wouldn't be able to hold him in the center of her web much longer, but she wasn't troubled by the thought. He was now caught in the net and the strands were so far-reaching she could drag him back when the time was right.

"Another time then," she said as she walked past him. When she got to the door, she turned. "I'm just across the hall if you ever need anything and I do make a mean sandwich."

"Yes, ma'am," Doobie said. "I'll remember that."

25

Sunday morning had come down hard and late on Carlos Cuevas.

His young head had not yet accepted the fact that beer had become a daily staple. He had rifled the medicine cabinet for aspirin, but had come away empty-handed for his efforts. He had showered in a weak attempt to wash away the misery, but even that had proved to be no match for the pounding in his head and the ringing in his ears. He had dressed hurriedly and left the empty house, before his mother and younger brother returned from church. It was a five-block walk to the nearest store and ten degrees short of the century mark; not unnecessarily hot for a south Texas March.

Carlos was sweating alcohol before he was halfway there.

In front of the store was a newspaper rack and in the rack was the Sunday edition of the *San Antonio Express-News*. When he passed the rack, his knees went limp to the point of buckling. He went with the flow and followed them down far enough to where his bloodshot eyes could focus on the hand-sketched picture above the fold in the paper. He looked from the paper to his arm and back. It wasn't a perfect match, but it was close enough. His headache was all but forgotten. He stood up and dug into his pocket for change. He came out with sixty-three cents, not even halfway there.

He entered the store and went directly to the counter where he laid two ones down in front of him. *"Dar mi feria, por favor?"*

Miguel Para, who owned the store and knew Carlos from the neighborhood, traded the ones for quarters, to which he received a *gracias* in return.

Carlos took the money outside and slipped seven of the eight quarters into the slot. He opened the rack door, looked around, and then took out all the remaining papers, seven to be exact. It was a heavy load, but Carlos was strong and he wasn't going far. He walked around the side of the store and peeled off the front section of each paper and threw the rest in the dumpster. He folded what he had kept under his arm and ran back to his house just as his family was walking in.

"Where have you been, Carlos?" his mother asked. "To the store."

"I wish you had told me. I need some things."

"You weren't here," he said and squeezed his way beside her and through the door.

He went immediately to his room and closed the door behind him. He sat down on the edge of the bed and pulled one of the sections from the fold. He laid the others down beside him. His hands began to quiver, though not from the alcohol, as he began to read. He tore the paper apart, trying to find page twelve where the story continued. Volcanic activity began to stir in the pit of his stomach as he read on. He threw the paper down and ran to the window, where he pushed out the flimsy screen and vomited a yellow mixture of fermented bile on the ground.

He went to his knees with his chin on the windowsill and breathed heavily until the nausea passed. He crawled over to the bed and folded the section he had just read up with the others. He pulled himself up, using the bed as a crutch and left by way of the open window. A trip through the house might have meant another trip to the store and Carlos Cuevas didn't have time, nor did he have the energy left to argue.

Juan Mata was in his backyard, tinkering with an old lawnmower that had outlived its usefulness, when Carlos opened the rickety back gate that led to the alley. It was obvious he wasn't there for a social visit. He looked like death before rigor mortis set in.

"What's up?" Mata asked.

Carlos didn't answer. He shoved the papers in front of him instead, but with the bottom fold out.

"*Que?*'' Mata said when he took the papers.

Carlos grabbed the papers from him and turned them over. "Look." He pointed to the sketch.

"Shit!" Mata said. "Where did that come from?"

"They know about us. Read it."

While Mata read the story, Carlos walked in circles around him. "We've got to do something."

"Wait," he said. "Let me finish."

Carlos continued circling him like a hawk waiting to dive on an unsuspecting rabbit.

"Where did you get this?" Mata asked when he was done reading. "From Para's. I took them all. What are we going to do, Juan?"

"I don't know. I need time to think."

"We don't have time. They're going to find us."

"Just stay cool. The first thing we have to do is take care of the car. Have you called Hector?"

"No, I came here first. You call him. Tell him to get rid of it."

"You can't just get rid of a car. There are easier ways. You go get Eddie and Chuey. I'll handle the rest."

"What are you going to do?"

"You'll see. Just don't go doing something stupid. We'll meet ya'll at the shed," Mata told him.

Carlos Cuevas had already done something stupid. He had taken a life and ruined his own in the process.

* * *

Doobie left Sweet at the silo after breakfast and walked to the Bronco to get his tools. He found the truck sitting at an odd angle, tilted toward the left rear. He shook his head at the flat tire that lay there like a half-eaten donut. He knelt down to inspect the rubber in order to find the culprit and located a nail buried to the head between the worn grooves. He was relieved that it was something he could fix, even though it meant he would have to unload most everything in the back to get to the jack.

While in the process, a cherry red Mustang pulled up alongside him and the monk he had seen from a distance the night before got out. Mo Morley nodded at Doobie. Doobie repaid the greeting in kind.

"Nice car," Doobie said. "Yours?"

"I wish," he answered as he slammed the door. "New arrivals."

"What do you reckon one like that'd set you back?"

"Twenty grand at least."

"Better put it someplace safe then," Doobie said.

"Yeah," Mo answered.

"I was wondering. I picked me up a nail here. You wouldn't happen to have anything inside the garage to make this easier on a fella, would you?"

"Like what?"

"Maybe one of those machines to bust it down?"

"We got one of those hand jobs."

"Mind if I get it?"

"Better let me," Mo said. "I'll help."

"No, I can handle it."

By the size of him, Doobie had no doubt he could but he wasn't about to give up.

"It's my problem. Let me do it."

"You want it or not?"

"Hey, I'm just trying to be neighborly. I know you must have more important things to do," Doobie said.

"You just get the tire off and don't worry about what I got to do," Mo warned.

"Whatever you say."

Mo walked around the building and unlocked a side door. He was back with the heavy tool before Doobie had the flat tire off the ground. "This what you're looking for?" he said as he dropped it beside the Bronco with a loud clank.

"I believe it is," Doobie said. "Much obliged."

"Just set it by the door over there when you're done."

"I can put it back inside if you'd like."

"I wouldn't," Mo said, then walked away.

Doobie worked on the tire for an hour and returned it to the truck as good as new, or at least better than he had found it. He carried the tool to the door and left it there as ordered. Seeing no one around, he tried the handle but found it locked.

On his way to the dormitory to wash his hands, he saw Arrianna usher two young girls in street clothes through the main door.

When he stopped by the silo to scratch Sweet behind the ears' Doobie saw Reverend Daniel and Monk James leave the Austin stone building and walk to the end of the dormitory. He heard a door open, then close just as fast.

"Take off your clothes," Arrianna said to the girls when they entered the shower in front of the one-way mirror.

"Why?" one of them asked.

"It's just a part of what we do here. We have to wash the other world away so you can start fresh," she explained rather methodically. She didn't feel the same excitement that attending this ritual usually brought her. Arrianna's mind was elsewhere.

When the two girls had removed all their clothing, Arrianna stepped back out of the way and gazed into the mirror as the shower began. She watched as the water ran down their bodies like coats of clear paint. She still felt nothing. No arousal. No urge to touch them like before. It was just a shower, nothing more.

And the sooner it was over, the better.

26

Lee and Peggy Watson were not church-goers, but they did follow the scripture that said Sunday was to be a day of rest. Reid Dalton found their copy of the *San Antonio Express-News* on the front porch when he arrived on foot. He picked up the paper and rang the doorbell. Peggy came to the door dressed in a nightshirt and a long cotton robe that she was holding together at breast level. When she opened the door and discovered who it was, she let the robe fall open. Modesty only became her when called for. Reid had seen her in the skimpiest of bikinis at the neighborhood pool. Compared to that, she could have taken the robe off and still been overdressed.

"Oh, hi, Reid. Come on in."

"Thanks," he said and walked in with the paper in hand.

"Are you delivering the paper now?" she said in a weak attempt at humor. She hadn't seen Reid Dalton since the incident and felt somewhat uncomfortable about the fact that she hadn't at least taken something by. Even a small casserole would have made her feel better. Jason had told her that Kathy had stayed in Denton, which meant Reid had been left to fend for himself. Humor was her way of covering for herself.

"I wish that was the only reason."

"I've got some coffee on. Want some?"

"Sure," he said. "Where's Lee?"

"Right here, buddy," Lee Watson said when he entered the living room from the hall.

"There's something here y'all need to see." He motioned with the plastic-covered paper. "Is Jason up?"

"No, he's still asleep," Lee said. "The way things have been, we're grateful for any sack time he can muster."

"I don't doubt it."

"Coffees poured," Peggy said from the kitchen. "You take yours black, right?"

"Yeah, thanks."

"Let's go in the kitchen where we can sit down," Lee told him.

They joined Peggy at the bar that divided the kitchen from the dining room. Reid Dalton took the stool on the end and let the Watsons have the two facing the kitchen. He tore open the wrapper and laid the paper down on the bar, top fold up.

"A reporter has done a piece on Bear," he said.

"Oh, that's nice," Peggy said.

"I don't think so. You better read it first." He slid the paper between them.

Reid Dalton knew when they got to the point where Jason was mentioned by name.

"Oh, my God," Peggy said.

Lee kept reading. He didn't bother asking his wife if she was done when he reached the end of the first page. He quickly flipped through to page twelve and continued reading.

No one touched their coffee.

"This isn't good," Lee said when he came to the end. Peggy took the paper from him and started to catch up.

"My sentiments exactly," Reid told him.

"Damn! Jason's been making good progress and now this."

"I know. I'm sorry."

"You don't have any reason to be sorry. You've been better for him than anything. We're the ones who should be saying we're sorry, with all you've been through."

"I appreciate that, but I can't help feeling I'm to blame."

"Well, you're not, so I don't want to hear any more of it," Lee said.

"What are we going to do?" Peggy asked when she finished with the article.

"You need to get Jason the hell out of here," Reid said. "What about the police? Surely, they'll do something," she said.

"I wouldn't count on it. They haven't done anything yet, and I let them know about it a while ago. They said they would send a squad car by every now and then, but other than that, you're pretty much on your own."

"Typical," Lee said.

"Honey, I think we ought to do like Reid says," Peggy told her husband. "He's on spring break this week anyway." To Reid Dalton she said, "We were going to take him to Fiesta Texas one day and then Sea World."

"That's not going to work," Reid Dalton said. "You'd still be coming back at night."

"Maybe they'll find the car. There can't be too many of them out there with whatever that thing is plastered on the door," Lee said.

"I wouldn't hold my breath," Reid Dalton said.

"He's right, honey. I don't want to take that chance. Not with Jason."

"Well, wherever it is y'all decide to go, don't tell anyone. Not even the cops. You saw what telling them led to. And I don't want to know either."

"You're being a little hard on yourself, buddy," Lee said. "No, just being safe. What I don't know, I can't talk about. If I would have just left Jason alone..."

"Hey, he's in there sound asleep thanks to you."

"And I want to make sure he gets plenty more," Reid said. "By the way, if you leave me a key, I'll put your mail and paper inside. That way, no one'll know you're gone." Reid Dalton had other plans for the house key, but what they didn't know, they couldn't talk about either.

"There's one under a fake rock behind the second bush by the porch," Peggy said. "And I can leave a couple of lights on a timer."

"That'll work."

"I guess now we just have to figure out where to go," Lee said.

"Just call me and let me know when you're about to leave."

"Thanks, buddy," Lee said.

Reid Dalton left his untouched coffee at the bar and got up to leave, then remembered the paper. "Better let me take that with me. I wouldn't want Jason to see it."

Peggy handed it to him and they all walked toward the front door, where Lee opened it.

"Oh, yeah. I need one last favor," Reid said. "When you get to wherever it is you're going, give Jason a hug for me."

The door closed before Reid Dalton could see the tears stream down Peggy Watson's cheeks.

* * *

The rest of the day had passed without event. Doobie noticed that by the middle of the afternoon, the cherry red Mustang had been swallowed up by the garage, leaving not so much as an oil spot as evidence that it had ever been there.

He had been less than enthused when, at the close of supper, Reverend Daniel informed the flock that an impromptu, yet meaningful, sermon would follow in the church building in an hour. Attendance, of course, was mandatory.

"Looks like you're the only one who gets dessert tonight," Doobie said to Sweet when he handed him one of the two biscuits from the toolbox. "Had I known what the reverend had in mind for later, I would've checked myself into sick bay before we ate."

Sweet wolfed down the treat and looked up for the next. "No, you gotta walk that one off before you can have this one." Doobie teased him by popping him on the nose with it and then walked back into the lighted quadrangle.

Arrianna watched from her window across the way as the two walked along the inside perimeter. She knew if they stayed their course, they would pass just outside her room in a matter of minutes. She opened the window so that nothing would be left to his imagination.

Doobie kept Sweet on a straight and narrow path along the side of the garage and then in front of the Austin stone building. The beacon of light that burnished through the open window on the first floor of the dormitory reached out and drew him in like a moth to a flame. Doobie's mouth locked in the open position when he saw Arrianna standing fully nude and brushing her hair into a flowing wave just below her shoulders. When their eyes met, Arrianna made a final brush stroke and then just stood there. It was a contest of who would blink first.

Doobie was frozen somewhere in time. Back before time had lost all meaning. Before someone shut the gate on scenes like this.

For all he knew, it could have been yesterday. The fervor was there but the reason for it had chosen to remain anonymous.

Somewhere deep inside of him, Doobie suddenly felt alive, not just for the sake of living but for the purpose of being.

When Sweet's cold nose touched his hand in search of the biscuit, Doobie blinked. Arrianna knew the moment was over when she saw his eyes fall. While the spell may have been broken, it was nonetheless cast.

<h1 style="text-align:center">27</h1>

Although he didn't yet have a plan, at least not one that would take him more than five minutes into the future, Reid Dalton did have another call to make. He pulled the address book from a kitchen drawer and found Buster Horton's home number. He dialed and got Gay Horton's voice on the third ring.

"Hello?"

"Gay. It's Reid Dalton. Is your ugly husband around?"

"That depends," she said. "Where are you calling from?" Buster obviously brought his work home with him.

"Don't worry. I'm not at work."

"Good. Hold on and I'll get him for you."

Buster had been standing next to his wife when the phone rang.

Reid heard her whisper who it was before he took the phone. "You do understand that Gay will be pissed if she finds out you lied to her."

"And she'd have every right to be, but this isn't one of those times."

"Good. So, what's up?"

"I'm gonna take your advice and take some more time off. I had already scheduled this week to be off anyway. You know, spring break."

"Yeah, I saw it on the board. I didn't think you'd still want to take it, but it's yours," Buster told him. "You heading out somewhere?"

"I thought I might go on out to the hunting lease. You know, spend a couple of days in the trailer. Maybe work on the Bronco some. It doesn't get much use this time of year."

"Good idea. You probably need to take some beer with you, though. I think we pretty much cleaned out the fridge the last time we were there."

"What do you mean, we, Lone Ranger? I seem to recall you being the one who had trouble seeing the cards."

"Maybe that's why I came home broke."

"And drunk."

"A little alcohol never hurt anyone," Buster told him. "I'll remind you that you said that the next time I come to you for authority to settle a DWI liability case."

"I'll take the fifth."

"My point exactly."

"Just go," Buster said. "And if next week isn't enough, take another one. You deserve it."

"Thanks," Reid said. "And tell Gay I was really at the office. She can be pissed at you in my absence."

* * *

Doobie left Sweet by the silo and entered the church building.

The lambs had all flocked in the front pews, leaving plenty of room in the rear for a small army. Not wanting to draw any undue attention, he took a seat with the rest at the end of the last partially occupied row.

Arrianna had been waiting in a study room at the back. When he sat down, she made her move. There was space enough for a small herd between Doobie and the next person but she chose to start a new corral and sat down next to him.

"This seat wasn't taken, was it?" she asked politely.

"No, ma'am," he answered with a surprised quiver in his voice. "Let's make a deal right here and now. I won't call you sir if you stop calling me ma'am. And just in case you've forgotten, my name is Arrianna."

"Fair enough," he said.

"Good," she said and held out her hand. "Let's shake on it."

When Doobie took her hand, he felt a warm smoothness in her touch. It was as if her hand was melting in his. Her fingers were long and nimble. The kind of fingers a pianist dreams of having. When she loosened her grip and took her hand away, he felt robbed.

The congregation grew silent when Reverend Daniel followed Monk James into the room from a side door. He went immediately to the pulpit and James took the chair behind him.

"Let us pray," Reverend Daniel said.

All the heads in the room bowed except one. While Doobie's present role called for him to be someone else, he had no intention of letting it take complete control. The role didn't require him to be a total hypocrite, at least not where some things were concerned.

When the prayer was over, Reverend Daniel jump-started the sermon. "For behold, the Lord will come in fire and His chariots like the whirlwind, to render His anger with fury and His rebuke with flames of fire! So says the book of Isaiah."

"I've seen fire and I've seen rain. So says James Taylor," Doobie said under his breath.

"What?" Arrianna leaned over and whispered.

"Just commenting on his opening," he said. "Don't you just love him? I can see where he could grow on you."

"He did me."

While the reverend continued and Doobie paid little attention, Arrianna thought back to when she had first heard him speak. She hadn't planned on such a meeting, nor had she even heard of him. A disagreement with her father concerning certain sexual advances she had made toward one of his medical partners led to her swift departure from home. She had headed west in her Cougar, driving faster than she could think. With her car somewhere between Pipe Creek and Bandera, and her mind nearing Jupiter, she had failed to heed the speed warning sign and entered a curve forty miles over what the State of Texas recommended as a safe speed to negotiate the road. She had been able to bring the car under control but not before blowing out both front tires when she entered a bar ditch.

It was dark and the road was desolate, neither of which spoke well of Arrianna's predicament. At thirty and looking like a stone fox in a tube top and high-rise hiking shorts, she would have been fair game on the roadway. If she stayed in the car her chances were pretty much the same. It was six of one and half a dozen of the other, with neither holding much promise of a successful, much less safe, outcome.

Arrianna had all but decided to stay in the car, where she could at least hide in the ditch if trouble arose when she heard the music. It sounded like a heavenly choir. The night was still, which made matters worse. The music seemed to be coming from all around her. She checked the road for lights, and finding none, Arrianna scrambled up a small hill on the other side of the ditch. Off in the distance, maybe half a mile away, she saw what looked to be a tent of sorts. She knew it wasn't a circus. The music wasn't right. But she could tell there was a vast number of people attending whatever event was beneath the tent. She also knew there was safety in numbers.

Rather than return to the road, Arrianna jogged the distance up one hill and down another and finally reached the tent out of breath but in better spirits.

Spirits were also what Reverend Daniel was preaching about and to well over two hundred people. She stood by the edge of the tent and listened while she caught her breath. She gasped when a hand touched her on the shoulder.

"Come in. There's a seat over there," Monk James said and pointed to an empty chair two rows up.

"That's okay. I'm fine here."

"You sure? You look a little winded."

"Been jogging."

"This far out at this time of night?"

It wasn't until then that Arrianna noticed what the man was wearing, a brown robe made of a coarse, heavy material much like a potato sack, only larger.

"Actually, I've got car trouble," she admitted. "But I did jog over from there."

"Well, why don't you have a seat and we'll see what we can do to help when the reverend's sermon is over," Monk James said.

"Really?"

"I'm sure we can manage something."

Arrianna thanked him and made her way to the empty chair just as Reverend Daniel made his to the pulpit. When he looked out over the congregation, she was sure his eyes met hers. She was instantly mesmerized. He seemed to be looking directly into her soul for an eternity. To Reverend Daniel, it had been but a brief glance. Eye contact was his forte. He tried to make it with everyone in attendance. They needed to know he was talking directly to them.

Arrianna never took her eyes off him. She sat upright on the edge of the chair so that every time he looked in her direction, he would see her above all the others. She heard very little of the sermon. The words came and went but the eyes came and stayed.

When the revival was over, Monk James asked her if she would consider taking refuge for the night at the Kingdom of Lambs. He promised he would see to it that her car was delivered safely there the following day and if at all possible, repaired and she could be on her way. She accepted graciously.

When she awoke in the reverend's bed the following morning, Arrianna knew she never wanted to return home again.

And the reverend continued. "I will baptize you with the Holy Spirit and with fire. And if your hand causes you to stumble, cut it off; it is better for you to enter life crippled, than having your two hands, to go into hell, into the unquenchable fire."

"He's going a little heavy on the fire, don't you think?" Doobie said.

"It's just his way. You really need to be here during the afternoon scripture readings," she said and laid a hand on Doobie's knee and squeezed.

"I'm afraid I got too much work to manage that," he said when she removed her hand.

"There can't be that much to do around here."

"Nothing serious, except maybe for that old silo out there." Doobie decided it was time to test Arrianna's waters.

"What about the silo?"

"It could use some work, especially down around the bottom. Once those old things start to sink, it's all over."

"Forget it," Arrianna said.

"Why?"

"There's nothing of any value inside. It's just here," she said. "And speaking of which, what brought you here?"

"Peace of mind, I guess," Doobie answered after once again reaching a dead end concerning the silo.

"Good place to find it."

"So, it seems."

"You don't sound all that convinced," Arrianna said. "I haven't been here that long."

"Well, I hope you'll stay around long enough to let me convince you." Arrianna returned her hand to his knee, only this time she left it there.

"But for the cowardly and unbelieving and abominable and murderers and immoral persons and sorcerers and idolaters and all liars, their part will be in the lake that burns with fire and brimstone, which is the second death," spoke the reverend.

"Guilty on all counts," Doobie thought. And like the silo, there was nothing of any value inside him either. He was just here.

28

Chuey Arrendondo was the only other member of the Mayas with wheels; a chopped off, faded purple El Dorado with a white top that was always in need of work. The key was hidden somewhere behind the dash panel. It wasn't lost; he just couldn't get to it without totally removing everything from the windshield back. He had tried to disassemble the dashboard, but Detroit had made it virtually impossible to do without an assortment of expensive tools. He had found it much easier and cheaper to just leave the ignition wires exposed. It also kept him in practice.

Chuey parked the car between two sheds. Compared to the Monte Carlo, his Caddy actually looked like the purple pile of shit Hector called it. Rather than take Hector's ribbing about it, he always parked it outside. He wasn't worried that someone would find the bare ignition wires attractive and make off with it, for two reasons. No one would want it, and they hadn't seen so much as a shadow of another human being since they had started using the old vegetable shed as their meeting place.

The row of dilapidated buildings that stood along three sides of the five-acre yard offered them protection from the surrounding neighborhood. They entered from off Highway 281, just like the produce trucks had done years ago before the company had gone bankrupt. It had been a simple matter of cutting the old lock off and replacing it with their own. From the road, everything looked normal. It was a perfect hideout.

When Chuey Arrendondo, Eddie Bustos and Carlos Cuevas entered the shed, an argument was already in progress. Juan Mata was standing by the Monte Carlo with a sledgehammer in one hand and a belt sander in the other.

"Your choice, Hector. Either remove the war axe or your windshield's history."

"Fuck you, man. You ain't got the balls."

"Juan's right, Hector," Flaco Dominguez told him. "It's gotta go.

"You're just a bunch of pussies. That damn drawing doesn't even look the same. It looks like a fucking traffic light."

"It's close enough," Mata told him.

Chuey walked over and took the sander from Juan. "Fuck him. I'll do it."

"You touch my car and I'll kill you, man."

"Then you better go get some help," Chuey warned him. He switched on the sander that was connected by an extension cord to an outlet below a fuse box on the wall. When the owners had shut down the operation, they had left the power on in order to keep the floodlights going at the four corners of the yard. They had taken the fuses from the boxes, but they had easily been replaced.

Hector Calderon's threat had been empty. He would rather go up against a half dozen *gringos* than tangle with Chuey. He was also outnumbered. "Give me that," he said. "No one touches my ride but me."

"When you get done, there's a rust spot on my car that needs work," Chuey told him.

"Fuck you. The rust is what holds that purple pile of shit together."

Juan Mata set the sledgehammer down when Hector began to work on the door. His threat had not been an empty one, though he knew Hector would back down rather than allow him to damage his car.

He had told Carlos he would handle it and he was a man of his word.

With Hector hard at work, the others gathered around a conveyor belt, far enough away from the sound of the sander in order to hear above the scraping noise.

"That's good for now," Chuey said, "but what about the people who've already seen it?"

"Do you get the paper? Or you, Eddie?"

They both shook their heads, as did Flaco Dominguez, who hadn't been asked.

"Can't afford it, right?" They all nodded.

"No harm. No foul. Very few people around here can afford it either. And thanks to Carlos, the rest won't get a chance. Once it's gone, no one will even remember it was there. And they got no proof if they do. It was all in their imagination, bien?"

"*Si, como no?*" Eddie Bustos said. Plus, it's only been on there, what, three weeks? I don't think we have to worry."

"What about the kid? The one that saw us?" Carlos asked.

"There, we do have to worry," Mata said. "Carlos, you remember where it happened?"

"Not really. Hector was driving. He's the one who wanted to do it up there."

"If he doesn't, I'm sure it'll be in one of the old papers."

"How're we gonna get one of those?" Flaco asked.

"You ever heard of a library, *vato?*"

"Sure, he has," Chuey remarked, "but he ain't never been in one. He's gotta learn how to read first."

"Eat shit," Flaco said.

The shed suddenly became quiet. They looked in Hector Calderon's direction. He had laid the sander down and was running his hand over the bare metal on the door. "Hector. Come here," Mata yelled.

He slapped his hands against his jeans to get the paint dust off as he walked toward them. "Yeah?"

"You remember where you and Carlos went that night?"

"Shit, yeah. Over by Leon Valley, off Bandera."

"Do you know the exact street?"

"Some fucking animal's name is all I know."

"Well, we can always get a map," Mata said.

"Why? What're we gonna do?"

"We got a witness we need to take care of."

"All right!" Hector said. "But I gotta do the other door first and then I gotta paint."

Juan Mata realized he hadn't thought of everything. "That's gonna have to wait. I forgot to get paint. We can get some when we're out later."

"I need some primer and Bondo, too, or it's gonna look like shit," Hector told him. "And you're paying for it all."

"I will. It's probably better that we go in Chuey's car anyway."

"I ain't riding in that purple pile of shit."

"I don't blame you. The trunk's not very comfortable," Chuey warned.

"Up yours, *hoto,*" he said and grabbed his crotch for effect.

"There's no reason for all of us to go," Mata explained. "Eddie, you and Flaco can stay here."

"Do I really need to go?" Carlos asked.

"It was your kill," Mata told him.

* * *

Doobie sat through breakfast for Sweet's benefit only. He had his first cup of coffee while the dog gobbled his way through a plate of sausage. When he was done, Doobie took the plate to the bin and refilled his cup. After trading smiles with Arrianna, he took the coffee and the dog into the quadrangle. Sweet circled the silo, then stopped by the door where he lifted a paw up and scratched on the metal.

"What is it, boy? You smell a rat?" Sweet only whimpered and scratched again.

Doobie looked at the heavy padlocks on the door and shook his head.

"You might as well give up. That thing's locked up tighter than a banker's wallet."

Sweet made two full circles in front of the door, then laid down.

"Just be that way then," he said. "At least I'll know where you are."

Doobie left him there and headed for the Bronco. He lifted the back gate and rummaged through his toolbox until he located a small plastic bag filled with an assortment of rubber and metal washers. He knew his tool belt wasn't necessary for the next job, but he belted it around his waist for show. He grabbed a wrench and dropped it through one of the loops in the leather. He sat on the back bumper and finished his coffee, then walked back through the quadrangle and into the dormitory.

The fourth floor was empty, just like he knew it would be. The girls were required to be up, showered and dressed before breakfast. He found the leaky shower nozzle and unscrewed it with his hand.

Pieces of broken rubber fell out when he removed the head. He was about to open the plastic bag when a voice from behind startled him.

"Oh, I'm sorry," Ashley Jenkins said. "I didn't know you were in here."

"No, no. It's my fault. I figured everyone was at breakfast. Do you need in here? I can leave and come back later," Doobie said, feeling needlessly embarrassed at being caught in the girls' shower.

"No, I've had mine and breakfast too. We just finished, so it's time for chores," she said sweetly.

"Work you hard, do they?"

"Not really, but even if they did, Reverend Daniel says it's good for us to keep busy. Idle hands are the devil's workshop, you know."

"Yes, ma'am. That's why I like to keep busy," Doobie said. "What kind of chores do you do?"

"Oh, mop the floors. Clean the toilets. Stuff like that."

"Nothing to write home about, huh?" Doobie prodded.

"No, but we have other, more important things to write about. Things Reverend Daniel tells us about to help us spread his word."

"I guess I'll learn more about that after I've been here a while."

"Oh, you will. You'll learn all new and wonderful things. I have and I've only been here about a week."

"So, you've written home? I mean, to your boyfriend or whoever?"

"Oh, yes. We all write every night and give the letters to Reverend Daniel to mail for us."

"What do you hear back? I bet he misses you."

"Oh, I don't really have a boyfriend, but I write my mom," Ashley said.

"I bet she writes back just as much," he said.

"Actually, I haven't heard from her, but I expect to any day now. We're pretty close."

Doobie had a fairly good idea why Belinda Jenkins hadn't written. It all had to do with the fact that Ashley's letters had probably been read through thoroughly before being dumped in a trash can along with all the other letters that would never see the inside of an envelope.

"So, you haven't seen your mother in, what did you say, a week?"

"Uh, huh."

"I bet you miss her."

"Sure, I do, but it's nothing compared to what I would miss by not being here."

"Not the least bit homesick?"

"This is my home now. I couldn't think of living anywhere else. It's like nothing I've ever imagined, but everything I've always wanted," she explained.

"That good, huh?"

"Better. Reverend Daniel is the perfect father. He's kind and gentle and teaches us to be just like him. If we could just make everyone understand that. Hopefully, one of these days we will."

"Well, you're still young."

"That's the best part. I've got my whole life ahead of me to be with Reverend Daniel. I want to be a part of him. I want to help him bring his message."

Doobie now knew getting Ashley back home was going to be harder than he had expected, if at all. She certainly wasn't about to leave on her own. "You seem to have it all planned out."

"We all do," she said. "And you will too. You'll see."

"I already do," Doobie told her. "Or at least I thought I did," he reflected to himself.

"Well, I need to get to my chores," Ashley said. "I hope I get to talk with you again."

"I'm sure you'll get another chance," Doobie said as he dug into the bag for a washer. I'm not going anywhere."

29

It had been almost five hours since Lee Watson had called to inform him that they were on their way. Reid Dalton had spent those hours in deep meditation. Not in some transcendental form of yoga trance, but rather the kind he used to practice the afternoon before his high school football games. Back then, he would put an Eagles tape in the deck and lie on the floor with a speaker against each ear, until he had psyched himself into the proper frame of mind to do battle on the gridiron. His taste in music hadn't changed. The only difference now was the Eagles were on CD and he owned an expensive set of stereo headphones.

Reid Dalton had left his house on Polar Bend, dressed in cat burglar black, just after dark and had walked to Jason's house on Buffalo, using the same route Bear had taken. He had given every car that passed the once-over, twice. By the time he reached Jason's, his nerves were shot. Each time a car had passed, he had also expected the worst.

As promised, Peggy Watson had left several lights on a timer inside. She had also left the front porch light burning. Reid ducked in behind the bushes and found the fake rock that held the front door key. He unlocked the door, reached inside and flipped the switch to kill the outside light, just as a police cruiser rounded the corner. He jumped inside and eased the door closed. A few seconds later, a beam of light lit up the living room. It was gone again, just as quick, only to reappear in the hall that led to the bedrooms.

Reid checked his watch and made a note of the time. He wanted to see if "every hour or so" meant the same to him as it did to Detective Sergeant Montalvo. He gave the cruiser a few minutes, in case it had turned around to make a second pass before leaving the vicinity. He went to the window to make sure the neighbors across the street hadn't come out to check out the light display before he ventured back outside.

He bent down between the house and the bushes and replaced the key. From there, he had a perfect view of the street, so he sat down directly behind a bush and waited.

A total of seven cars, none of which paid any mind to the house, passed before the cruiser showed up again. Knowing what to expect, he ducked his head and drew his knees up against his face. He could almost feel the heat of the light as it passed through the bush and into the window above him. He held his breath and waited for it to go dark again. When it did, he relaxed and checked his watch. He had been sitting for an hour and ten minutes, which wasn't bad for an "or so", but not good enough. A lot could happen in an hour or so.

Fifteen minutes later, it did.

Chuey Arrendondo had chauffeured the other three through most all the streets in Leon Valley, at least those on the west side of Bandera Road. The only street named after an animal they had come to was Reindeer, but Hector Calderon had informed them he would have remembered that name. Being unfamiliar with the area, they had no idea that Reindeer continued west into Deer Run. They had only stayed on the street, hoping it would lead them to other animals. Penguin was next but no bells of recognition sounded in Hector's head. They stayed the course but ran out of animals.

"Shit," Hector said. "I know we were here somewhere. Go back to that bird street."

"I'm beginning to think you don't know where you were," Chuey said as he made a U-turn at the next corner.

"Just drive."

They hung a left on Penguin, but again found no animals in the next three blocks.

"Why don't we just go home?" Carlos Cuevas said from the back seat.

"He's right," Juan Mata added. "We can come back tomorrow when it's light."

"Maybe not," Chuey said as he pointed to the next street sign.

Hector stared up at the sign on the corner. "Buffalo! That's it. Buffalo. I told you, man. Turn down that way." He pointed to the left. "Go slow."

Reid Dalton heard the noisy Cadillac before it came into view.

He craned his neck to the right side of the bush. He watched as it inched its way in front of the house, then moved his body to the left as it passed and continued on down the street at the same pace.

Other than having two doors, the car in no way matched Jason's description. This one was two-tone and neither color was black or even dark, and there was nothing on the door. Reid settled back down and decided to give the cruiser one more pass before calling it a night.

"This is it, man. I'm sure of it now," Hector said when they reached the next corner. "I remember that house there. The big one with the fountain in front. I remember we turned here right after Carlos did him. I remember the fountain, man. Turn around and go back. It was about the middle of the block."

Chuey made another intersection U-turn and headed back down the street.

"Go slower," Hector said.

"If I go much slower, it'll die on us," Chuey told him.

"Then put it in neutral and rev the engine a little, stupid."

"Don't call me stupid, you little *pandejo!*" Chuey yelled.

Reid Dalton heard him, but he dared not move. The car was almost at a standstill in front of the house. He could see two people in the car. The one on his side, the passenger, was looking directly at him.

"It had to be here, man," Hector said. "I'm telling you straight. This is where he did him."

"You're sure?" Mata said.

"I'd swear on my mother. This is where he shot the kid."

Reid bit his lip, but he still didn't move. The odds were against him. One wrong move and he was either dead or they would run. He had to wait.

"Then let's go," Mata said. "We got what we came for." When Chuey hit the accelerator, the Caddy leaped forward, coughed once, then died. He tried to start it again as it rolled down the street.

That was all the time Reid Dalton needed. He bolted from the bushes, across the yard and behind a car parked in the street next door. He was close enough to the Caddy to read the plates.

Chuey pumped the accelerator rapidly as he turned the key. "Don't flood it, stupid," Hector screamed.

"I told you not to call me stupid." Chuey swung his right hand around and caught Hector square on the mouth, splitting both his upper and lower lips, just as the car started again.

Reid Dalton watched them drive away. "Your asses are mine now."

* * *

Doobie had spent the rest of the morning, and the noon hour as well, patching the wall in the fourth floor living quarters. Monk James had filled his list of necessities from the garage across the quadrangle. It had taken him two trips, but only because he had refused Doobie's offer to help him with the load.

When it had come time for the scriptures, Doobie had chosen another form of meditation in the way of a power nap on the second floor. The early hour and the one-sided conversation with Ashley had taken its toll. He needed to bring his faculties together, reload and start again. He just wasn't sure where and was even having a battle with why.

Doobie had been dreaming of a shed. It was only too real a dream. Even the gunfire seemed genuine. When the first shot was fired, he woke in a sweat and jumped from the bed. The room spun around him as he tried to gain both his balance and his bearings.

When the next shot reverberated against the far wall, he ran to the window. The workers were huddled together at one end of the field. At the other end, Gonzo Drake held a pistol at point-blank range to the ground where Doobie saw a rattlesnake coiled in the business position. He wanted to yell at him to just leave it be and it would go away on its own, but the third shot ended any hope of that happening.

Doobie shook his head and walked back across the room and looked down. Sweet was still on guard in front of the silo door. Something else about the silo caught his attention. The trunk- like shadow stretched all the way to the church and up the side to the roof. He looked to the left and saw the sun hovering just above the top of the Austin stone building. He realized he had slept the afternoon away. That realization was magnified when the dinner hymn told him it was time to harvest the grain again.

Doobie didn't feel like rejoicing, but he did feel like eating.

The chow line was its usual long self when Doobie entered the cafeteria poncho-less and with Sweet on his heels. He glanced over at the head table but only Arrianna, who was sitting there alone, glanced back. She pointed at him and then to the seat next to her. Doobie countered by pointing to the line and got a quick shake of her head in return.

"Looks like we're moving to the head of the class," he told Sweet.

"Where've you been all day, stranger?" Arrianna asked when he pulled the chair out beside her.

"Earning my keep," he replied. His being there had been based on one lie after another, so he figured that little one wouldn't make much difference. "Where's the boss?"

"You might say he's earning his," she said. "It's revival night."

"You weren't invited?"

"Someone has to stay here and keep an eye on the flock."

"I haven't seen too many wolves lingering about."

"You never know," Arrianna said. "Plus, I have other things to do while he's gone."

A young girl brought two plates of fried chicken, mashed potatoes and green beans to their table. "Could I bother you for some breasts?" Doobie asked her and got a strange look from both women in return. When he followed with, "Boneless, if possible," their looks passed.

"You really love that dog, don't you?" Arrianna said.

"Isn't that what they're for?"

"I guess. I've never owned one."

"You don't own them. They own you."

"I can see that now," Arrianna said when the girl returned with Sweet's supper.

While they ate, Doobie couldn't help but notice the giggling scattered out about the room, even more so when he made eye contact with a particular one. He knew what was going through their young minds and was only too happy to give them something to smile about. He smiled back to add to their fun.

Arrianna smiled also. She was thinking the same thing they were, only she was preparing to make it happen. "Have you called it quits for the day?" she asked when she saw Doobie push his plate away.

While he had mistakenly called it quits about midday, he didn't let on. "I've been known to work after dark on occasion."

"Good. I've got something in my room that needs your attention."

"Nothing major, I hope?"

"Not if you can attend to it right away."

"Well, just give me a few minutes to wash up and get my tools," he said.

"Say, ten minutes?"

"That'll work," Doobie said as he slid his chair back.

"See you then," she said.

When they left the cafeteria, Sweet headed for the front door. "I think we're too late," Doobie told him as darkness met him on the other side of the small window. "Besides, I've got some more work to do."

Sweet scratched hard against the door. "All right. I'll get you one, but that's gonna have to do for now." When he opened the door, Sweet trotted to the silo instead of the Bronco and sniffed at the ground as he circled it. He came to rest in front of the door. "You'll never learn, will you?" he said and walked back inside and up to the second floor.

Doobie went into the bathroom first and washed the chicken grease from his hands and face. He ran his fingers through his long, dark hair as an afterthought and with no ulterior motive. He found his tool belt on the floor by the bed, where he had taken it off pre-nap, and strapped it on.

He met several giggling girls heading up the stairs as he made his way down and when he reached the infirmary door, he knocked lightly.

"It's open," she said from inside.

Doobie pulled the door open and went in, where a long hallway greeted him. Arrianna was standing in a doorway, two doors down. "In here," she said.

Doobie walked business-like down the hall and into her quarters. Just like the rest of the dormitory, it was sparsely furnished, but a bit more comfortable. A couch was against the wall beneath a familiar window, and a throw rug lay out in front of it. On another wall was a well-made, double bed and nightstand. A lone rocker graced the third. "Nice room," he said in polite conversation.

"I like it," she said. "Where's the problem?"

"The couch. I think something's broken." Doobie walked over, pushed against one end and found it steady.

"Where?

"Sit on it. You'll see," she said as she closed and locked the door.

Doobie sat down in the middle, but nothing gave. He looked up as Arrianna began to undress. She slid the sackcloth off very slowly, starting from the bottom and working her way up to reveal her knees first and then her thighs. Doobie sat there like a fly caught in a web of deceit, only worse. This fly had already been stung and was too numb to fight. His brain was locked onto what his eyes were showing him.

As Arrianna rubbed her thighs together with hopeful anticipation of what was to follow, she felt a familiar tingle. She shivered and gasped lightly. She had never before reached a climax without being touched. Never just from the thought. Her inner thighs seemed to crystallize as natural body fluid dripped from her dark brown, pubic hair like melting ice.

By the time she had removed the garment, the nipples on her firm breasts were so erect and sensitive, she wanted to touch them herself. Her body had never felt this hot and her breathing began to increase rapidly. It became heavy, almost to the point of exhaustion. She took Doobie's hands and placed them gently on nipples so hard they yearned for his mouth. She closed her eyes as he fondled them with strong, yet gentle, hands.

Doobie couldn't fight the urge, nor did he want to, but it had been so long since he had been with a woman, his senses could have atrophied. He was unsure of how his own body would react.

His needless concern was answered when he saw the first crystalline trickle flow from her shadowy mound. His erection came sudden and without warning. As he rubbed her firm, yet yielding nipples between his fingers, the skin of his penis stretched until he thought it would tear apart.

Doobie removed his left hand from her breast and ran it down her belly until he felt a satiny wetness between her thighs.

Arrianna spread her legs to allow his fingers to enter. She reached over his shoulders and brought his T-shirt up over his head, even though it meant his hands would have to be momentarily taken from her. She didn't care. She wanted more. She threw the shirt behind her, then placed her hands under his arms and pulled him up. She put her mouth to his and darted her tongue back and forth as she wrestled with the tool belt. Doobie reached down and freed it with a learned hand and let it drop to the floor.

Arrianna unsnapped the button of Doobie's jeans and slipped a hand inside to cover his penis in a protective grip as she brought the zipper down with the other. She moved her hands to his hips and slid the jeans down as far as her arms would allow her to go without having to part their kiss. She lifted a bare foot and sent them to the floor. Doobie toed the heel of each shoe and wriggled himself free, then kicked the jeans to the side, taking the throw rug with them.

They fell to the floor in a passionate embrace with Arrianna on top. She began kissing his neck, then his chest. She ran her tongue over his taut stomach with such vigor that Doobie's heart began to pace like a wild deer running for its life. When she took his penis in her mouth, his hands clenched into fists, not from fear, but from pleasure.

Doobie could feel himself about to explode. He pulled Arrianna up to him and rolled her over. She spread her legs with an anxious anticipation that was short-lived. Doobie entered her immediately. He took her left breast in his mouth and began sucking it tighter with each thrust. Arrianna brought her right hand up and fondled the other. She tilted her head back almost to the point of breaking her neck. It would have been a pain her body would have refused to recognize.

Doobie brought Arrianna to her sexual peak within minutes. Inside her, he could feel the warm explosion of her body. He moved more rapidly until he erupted and felt the sensation, he thought he had lost forever. He brought his arms up and cradled the back of her head and laid his on her shoulder. Their breathing was heavy and erratic as sweat formed a thin blanket between them.

They lay there in silence until the cold floor began to take its toll. Doobie got to his knees, slid his arms under Arrianna and picked her up. He walked over to the bed and laid her down gently, then crawled next to her. It was then she discovered they weren't done. It was going to be even more than she had hoped for. What she had started, he was going to finish but she wanted it to be her way. She eased her way on top of him and, with her right hand, guided him inside her. She rode Doobie slowly and watched the pain disappear from his face. She knew she would be able to do it, she just didn't know that much of her own pain would also be erased at the same time.

When unexpected sleep followed their lovemaking, Arrianna forgot about the "other things" she had told Doobie she needed to do while Reverend Daniel was away.

30

Reid Dalton was at his desk before sunrise. He hit the ON switch and watched as his computer monitor went through its usual hieroglyphic ritual before asking for his password. When it did, he typed in BEAR and gained access to Union Mutual's multi-million dollar system. He could enter a social security number and find out pretty much everything he wanted to know about the owner, short of who he or she had slept with recently. He could, however, find out where they had eaten beforehand. With a driver's license, he could determine if they used alcohol as a form of foreplay.

Reid wasn't interested in the Caddy owner's social life. He just wanted to know where he called home. He entered the license plate and waited. Being that he was one of only a few signed on at that hour, the response time was quick. When the screen gave him what he needed, he hit the PRINT key and swiveled his chair around to face the printer.

"I thought you were taking the week off?" Buster Horton said to his back.

Reid Dalton jumped. "Jesus, Buster, you scared the shit out of me," he said as he whirled back around.

"Then I'd suggest you clean your chair. What are you doing here?"

Reid thought fast. "I forgot about this check I was supposed to issue. I promised the attorney he would have it this week."

"I could have done it for you."

"I know, but I had to come this way on my way out anyway. Besides, I didn't want you to know I'd forgotten. My annual review comes up next month."

"Too bad. Now I don't have to give you that raise," Buster said.

"Oh, well, I'll just have to take you out and get you drunk like I always do."

"Count on it," Buster said. "You get it done?"

"What?"

"The check."

"Oh, yeah. I was just printing the confirmation sheet."

"Then get the hell out of here before you think of something

else you forgot."

"I'm on my way," he said.

When Buster turned and left, Reid went back to the printer and took out the sheet. He read it to make sure no Monday morning glitch had reared its ugly head. He folded the paper up and stuck it in his pocket before he exited the system and shut it down.

"Reid Dalton has left the building," he said to himself on his way out. Little did he know he would never return.

* * *

Arrianna woke euphoric with Doobie's arm around her waist. She rolled over slowly to give him a kiss and saw the clock on the nightstand. Fear enclosed her chest in a grip strong enough to stop her breathing. Her heart pounded in an effort to break free. Reverend Daniel would be back within the hour and no girl was ready. It was too late for the drug to take effect. If she doubled up on the dosage, time would no longer be a factor but the end result would be fatal.

When she pushed herself out of Doobie's arms and rolled off the bed, he woke instantly. "You need to leave," she told him.

"What's the matter? Someone coming?" he asked groggily.

"You might say that," she answered.

Doobie jumped from the bed and found his clothes on the floor.

He dressed quickly and thoroughly, tool belt and all. The added touch would give them an alibi if push came to shove. "Where are they?" he asked when he clamped the belt on.

"Who?"

"You said someone was coming."

"I meant he was on his way. It's nothing for you to worry about. You've got plenty of time. I'm the one in trouble."

"Can I help?"

"No, I'm afraid your tools can't fix this problem," she said. "You gonna be okay?" Doobie asked.

"If not, at least I'll die happy," Arrianna told him and kissed him on the cheek. "Now go."

Doobie presumed he was not to take her comment seriously. When she opened the door, he glanced down the hall just before she gave him a light shove.

Arrianna knew she had no other choice than to confront Reverend Daniel, but certainly not with the truth. She couldn't very well tell him he'd have to postpone his post revival roll in the hay because she had beat him to the loft and pitched a stack of her own. The outcome of such a straightforward approach would produce results she would rather not think about. She'd have to blame it on something or someone.

She lifted the sackcloth over her head and let it fall into place with not nearly as much grace and pleasure as when she had removed it.

She left the dormitory by the side entrance and made her way slowly to the front door of the Austin stone building, thinking as she walked. By the time she had unlocked the door and ascended the stairs to the reverend's quarters, she had developed an acceptable story.

Arrianna was sitting in a padded rocker when Reverend Daniel entered the room. The gleam in his eyes told her the night had been successful. That would be a point in her favor and one he could fall back on when he discovered the party hadn't followed him home.

"What's going on?" he asked when he saw the empty bed.

"First off, it's not her fault. The excitement of being here must have done it to her," Arrianna said as she got up.

"What are you talking about?"

"The girl. She started her period early. She wasn't due for two weeks. That's why I chose her, but when I saw it, I knew you wouldn't approve."

"I thought you knew about those things. What about all your records?"

"She hasn't been here that long. I figured she would adjust after the next one," she explained.

"Well, you figure wrong," he said. He slapped her across the face with the back of his hand with enough force to knock her to the floor. "Why didn't you prepare another one?"

"It was too late," she said as she tasted blood on the inside of her lip.

"Bullshit," he said. He reached down and pulled her up by her hair. "It's never too late."

"I'm sorry. I won't let it happen again," she whimpered. "You're damn right you won't and here's why." He slapped her again with an open palm while holding her steady. He brought his hand back around and gave her the backside.

It was all Arrianna could do to remain conscious. Her feet gave way below her but he didn't allow her to fall. He wasn't done yet.

"You liked it before," he said. "Let's see if you like it now." He gave her a hard shove onto the bed.

The cool sheets felt comforting against her hot and swelling face. She bunched them up in her hands and pressed them against her lip.

Reverend Daniel grabbed the bottom of the sackcloth shift and yanked it up, revealing her bare butt. He dug both hands into the flesh and lifted her into a prone position. He held her there with one hand and with the other lifted his own white robe.

"This should teach you," he said as he entered her mercilessly from the back.

Arrianna bit into the knotted sheet harder with each thrust. The pain was excruciating but she refused to give in to it. Her thoughts turned to Doobie. It was the only thing that would bring her through this.

When Reverend Daniel stopped and withdrew suddenly, Arrianna prayed the worst was over but he was just getting started. He grabbed her by the hair again and brought her face up alongside his. "You want more, don't you?"

"No, please," she mumbled over a split and swollen lip.

He twisted her hair until she was facing him. He grabbed her garment by the neck and ripped it downward. He let go of her hair and with both hands, tore the fabric down the middle.

Arrianna was afraid he was about to hit her again and covered her face with her hands.

"Oh, no. You like to watch. I know you do," he said as he grabbed the top of both her arms and wrenched them free. He pinned her to the mattress and didn't let go. "I've seen you watch from the door more than once. You like how I do it like this." He rammed himself inside her so hard that Arrianna was sure damage had been done, but she was helpless to fight back. His grip was so tight and his thrusts so hard that she fully expected her arms to break at any minute.

When the reverend arched his back in the final plunge, Arrianna promised herself she would never allow him to do that again. Not to her. Not to anyone.

Reid Dalton reached into the glove box for his San Antonio map. The edges were curled and there was a tear in each fold, but he still managed to locate the street he was looking for. He left the lot and headed south. He had to fight the Monday morning traffic, but only until he connected with Highway 281 near downtown. From there, he was going against the flow.

About a half mile south of the 410 loop, he exited and headed east. He had been there before, back when he used to work a territory. Back when he used to ride a car rather than a desk. He stopped and looked at the map again to refresh his memory, then drove on.

He found what he was looking for without having to search the house numbers. He didn't even have to match the plate numbers to the printout. The Caddy was evidence enough and even worse looking in the daylight. He drove nonchalantly by the car and around the block.

It had been a while since he had done any *sub rosa* investigation for the company, but he still remembered a few tricks of the trade. He located a corner store, two blocks from the Caddy. Around the corner from there was a laundromat. Reid parked in front of the laundromat, but before getting out, he mussed up his hair and untucked his shirt. He exited the car and unlocked the trunk, where he kept a light jacket inside for emergency purposes, Texas weather being known for its ability to change without warning. Under that was a dingy towel he had taken to carrying after ruining more than one good shirt changing a flat tire. He took them both out, closed the trunk lid and entered the laundromat.

There were only six washers, one with an OUT OF ORDER sign on the lid, and half as many dryers. The number didn't matter as he was the establishment's only customer. He reached into his pocket for change and came out with three quarters. The washer required only two. He lifted the lid open and dropped the items in the tub and the quarters in the slots. Since there were no witnesses, he didn't bother to add soap. He did notice a dispenser on the wall in case a second washing under more unfavorable conditions became necessary. He also noticed a rectangular spot of a different color paint in the cracked wall next to it, and presumed the change machine had been lifted, either by the owner or an unsatisfied customer.

Reid left the laundromat and walked back up the street to the store. He looked left to make sure the Caddy was still around and then entered. Miguel Para was behind the counter.

"Beer?" Reid Dalton asked.

Miguel Para pointed to the cooler at the back of the store. Reid walked toward it under his watchful eyes. He took out the cheapest brand he could find, returned to the front and laid a five-dollar bill on the counter with the beer.

"Could I get some quarters while you're at it?" Reid asked. "I'm doing some laundry and the change machine seems to be missing."

"You want it all in quarters?"

"Nah. Two bucks should cover it."

"You're not from around here, are you?"

"Nope. Just visiting."

"The Zambranos?"

Something told Reid Dalton to answer in the affirmative, so he did, in a manner of speaking. "How'd you know?"

"Lucky guess," Miguel Para told him. What he didn't tell him was that Santos Zambrano was married to a *gringa,* but if he was visiting them, he should already know that. He handed Reid the change and the beer in a small sack.

"Thanks."

"When you see Santos, tell him not to forget about his overdue bill."

"Oh, how much is it?"

Miguel Para opened an index box by the register and pulled out a card. "Eighteen sixty-four."

Reid Dalton handed him a twenty. "Give him credit for the change."

"*Si, bueno.* I'll do that."

He had no idea who Santos Zambrano was, but he knew how to recruit an ally. If he was lucky, the Zambrano family was not in need of any immediate groceries. Chances are, with an overdue bill hanging over their head, they had taken to shopping elsewhere for the time being.

Reid took a seat on an old church pew just outside the door. The Caddy was still there. He left the beer can closed and only made like he was drinking from it.

After half an hour had come and gone, he got up and walked back to the laundromat. It was still empty, so he left the jacket and towel in the washer. He had already contributed over twenty dollars to the cause and there was no reason to throw good money after bad if the situation didn't warrant it.

When he got back to the store, he saw movement down the street.

A group of people were getting into the Caddy. He didn't have time to count them. He ran back to his car, jumped in and circled the block so that he came up behind them three blocks away. He still had the unopened beer in his hand, so he slid it under the seat. When the Caddy pulled away from the curb, he followed at a safe distance.

The Caddy made two stops and each time another person got in quickly. After the second stop, the Caddy pulled into a driveway and turned around. Reid Dalton turned right at the next corner and drove slowly while watching in his rear-view mirror for the Caddy to pass. When it did, he made another right and kept parallel to the car one block over.

Reid's heart raced as he remembered why he had hated to leave his territory for the desk job. The money and the chance for advancement had won him over, but it hadn't been without a fight.

Ahead of him, he saw the 281 traffic whizzing by. He reached the highway before the Caddy and knew he had either misjudged their speed or they had stopped again. He would soon know if he had been wrong on both counts. They could have turned down another side street.

When the Caddy pulled up to the stop sign one street over, Reid avoided eye contact by looking to the left, as if checking the traffic. By the time he looked back to the right, the Caddy was passing in front of him, heading south. He waited for traffic to clear, then followed. There were two cars between them, but the exhaust trail the Caddy was leaving would have made it easy to follow under any circumstances.

Reid slowed down when he saw the brake lights on the car in front of him, just before the Caddy turned left and stopped at a fenced-in packing shed lot. He drove on by, but adjusted his side mirror in order to keep an eye on them. A highway sign told him the Flores Road exit was a mile away. He doubted they had been paying any attention to him or even noticed him, but he didn't want to take that chance. He needed a little time to pass before he showed up again, so he drove on to Flores Road, where he exited and then doubled back.

When he got to the sheds, the Caddy was gone, but the smoke that still hung in the air behind the locked fence gave their position away.

Reid drove on to the next street and turned off. The shed roofs loomed above the house tops. He continued down the street until they were gone. He took a right and found himself on a dead-end street. He stopped in front of the wooden barricade and got out. He saw evidence that cars had gone around the barricade, so he climbed up for a better look. A rutted path through a field of hay grass lay in front of him. By the width and depth of the ruts, he figured a tractor was the culprit.

He got down and drove around the barricade and followed the path. The ruts were bumpy and caused the beer can to roll out from under the seat. He grabbed the can and threw it into the field for someone's later consumption. The path took him to the back corner of the shed yard before it led off again to the left and further into the field. Another less-driven path had been cut away along the fence line, probably to give the tractor a turnaround alley when it came time to bale the hay. He drove some fifty yards into the alley and checked his rear-view mirror. The land was ridgy enough so that he could barely make out where the alley had started. He turned the engine off and got out.

The chain link fence looked to be in fairly good shape and had been installed blunt end down, in order for the pointed ends to inflict as much injury or damage to someone in the market to five-finger discount a sack of onions or box of tomatoes. Reid kicked at the dirt at the bottom of the fence and found it to his liking. He knelt down and dug in the soft dirt until he had enough room to slide under.

Once inside, he stayed to the rear of the sheds. He peered around the corner of each building in search of the Caddy and spotted it on his fourth attempt. It was parked between two sheds, but on the opposite side of the yard. Rather than chance being seen, he stayed behind the buildings as he made his way around to the other side.

Reid stood braced against the side of the shed to his left and moved his head just enough to allow him to see into a dirty window. The shed was dark. He suddenly heard voices, but not from inside. He hit the ground in front of the Caddy and crawled under.

"Brilliant. Just fucking brilliant," he thought. "All they have to do now is back up and you're dead meat." It was too late for him to move. All he could do was lie there and listen. He could still hear the voices but when he got up the nerve to open his eyes, he saw no feet. He listened harder and discovered they weren't close enough to inflict pain. He crawled backward and then over to the opposite shed.

The voices were clearer. He looked up and saw that one of the panes in the window was loose and had slid down from the frame. He got to his feet against the shed and reached for the bottom of the glass.

The frame was rotten and the glass came out with no resistance.

The odor of paint reached him through the new opening. He leaned over and carefully looked inside, but a stack of pallets hampered his view. He moved his head up and down and caught different parts of the people through the pallet openings. With his eyes at the bottom of the window ledge, Reid Dalton saw the car.

When he made out the figure of one of them working on the

door, he understood why he smelled paint. The figure was running a spray gun back and forth along the car door. He wondered if he would ever know what the emblem Jason had drawn was supposed to be. It was obvious they knew and had recognized it in the paper.

"Good job, Jason," he whispered.

"Hey, mother fucker. At least when I killed mine, I didn't leave no witness behind," Flaco Dominguez yelled at Juan Mata, who was taking up for their newest member's blunder.

"It wasn't his fault. You could just as well blame Hector. He was driving."

Hector Calderon was too busy making sure his job was done right to hear their conversation.

"Yeah, Flaco. Leave him alone. You were just lucky. Anyone could have seen you cut that kid's throat."

"Oh, big man. You ain't nothing but a faggot killer. I bet you did let him suck your dick before you killed him. You probably had to pay Eddie not to rat on you."

"No, man. It happened the way Chuey said it did," Eddie interjected.

"Shit. What do you know? You can't even kill a nigger right. You gotta do it twice to make it count."

"Hector was driving too fast," Eddie told him.

"Yeah, blame it on Hector. Anybody who would shoot a girl in the back and then fuck her dead pussy deserves it."

"That's enough," Mata said. "We have to stick together in this, or we're all dead. It's called accessory."

"Fuck you, man. I know that," Flaco said. "I watch TV."

Reid Dalton had heard enough. In fact, he had heard too much.

In his attempt to locate his son's killer and bring him to justice, he had stumbled into a pack of animals. Animals of the worst kind. The kind that don't feel, don't think, only act. The kind that lashes out at anything that moves, rabid.

These animals that Reid knew of, only one may deal with a rabid animal. He had seen how the Animal Control officer had done it when he was a boy. His father had explained to him how it was the humane way, but he hadn't bought it then and he wasn't going to buy it now. It hadn't been humane, but it *had* solved the problem.

Reid Dalton had to solve the problem. While watching and listening, he estimated he had five problems to solve, but not now. Like the Humane Officer, he needed help. He couldn't just walk in and throw a rope around them and expect them to come peacefully, nor could he throw a net over them and drag them to an awaiting caged truck. He had to have the right tool.

Juan saw Hector stand up on the other side of the car and yelled at him in an attempt to move them on to the matter of what had to be done. "Hey, Hector. When you gonna be finished?"

"Right now, but it needs a day to dry correctly. Otherwise, it's gonna run and look like shit."

"Then we go tomorrow," Mata told the others.

Reid Dalton knew he would be back. He made his way along the fence to where he had dug the hole and crawled back out. He wanted to see if the mowed alley led to where he thought it did, so he put the car in drive and negotiated the bumpy ground until he reached the highway. If he could exit, he could enter.

He turned right onto Highway 281 and headed north. When he passed the street he had taken that morning, he suddenly remembered his laundry. He turned at the next corner and drove through the *colonia* until he came to the store. He turned left and parked in front. He left the door open and the motor running. He didn't plan on being there long.

He was, once again, the establishment's only customer. He lifted the lid to the washer but only the towel was there, and still just as dingy.

* * *

Monk James counted the stacks of money three times to make sure he was right. The crowd just outside Kerrville had filled the tent to capacity and spilled out for almost a half-acre around it. It had been made up of mostly older people, retirees who spend the season in travel trailers and motor homes. The kind who leaves lavish houses and large bank accounts behind in order to see what they had missed while they had built up their nest eggs. They also left behind their church communities, but never their will to congregate ever so often for a habitual religious fix. The closer their second foot got to the grave, the more money they were willing to part with in an effort to buy eternal peace.

"Damn," Monk James said as the third count ended with the same figure. He slipped five grand under his gun belt and left a little over forty grand on the table. Absent was the usual haul of jewelry. Money was just money to the previous night's crowd. Jewelry, on the other hand, was a status symbol to be flashed around. Most of them would even take those possessions to the grave or at least until the mourners were all gone and they were left with no one to protect them from the temptation of others not so fortunate.

"I do hope I'm not to take that as a remark of discouragement," Reverend Daniel said as he closed the door behind him.

His sudden entry startled Monk James. "I wish you'd learn to knock."

"It *is* my house."

"Yeah, but I'm the one carrying a gun and accidents do happen."

"The Lord would never let that happen," the reverend told him. "He watches over me."

"I thought that only pertained to drunks and fools," Monk James said.

"Quite the contrary, I assure you. Maybe I should have you attend our afternoon scripture readings since you are so inclined to quoting from the text," he warned.

"Thanks, but I'm content just counting your money."

"You mean the Lord's money?"

"You think the Lord will be happy with forty, though?"

"Are you serious?"

"Well, you saw all them old geezers out there. What'd you think they were putting in the plates, their dentures?"

"I never expected that much," Reverend Daniel said. "And to think they want to hear more tonight. Praise the Lord."

Those who had been unable to get inside the tent to actually see Reverend Daniel's sermon had crowded around him when it was over and actually begged for an encore. Most, it seems, had been Southern Baptists and to them a revival meant at least a week of fire and brimstone. The reverend had agreed to only a second night, claiming he had other flocks to attend to elsewhere after that. As it was, he only had one sermon set to memory. With a little movement of passages and different hymns to start the program, he figured he could get away with the same material. Now that he knew the take, he would throw in a few extra verses of scripture for good measure.

"They were a little light on the jewelry, though," Monk James informed him.

"How light?"

"Would you believe nothing?"

Doobie figured he had nothing to lose by just waltzing into the Austin stone building unannounced. He didn't plan on being around there long enough to wait for an engraved invitation. He needed to find something he could use against the reverend to get Ashley's train of thought back on the right track. Something to derail the train before it picked up speed on the downhill run and took her away forever.

When Doobie opened the front door, a buzzer sounded in the office. Monk James paid it little attention. Reverend James paid it more. "Go see who that is," he told him.

"It's probably just Arrianna."

"I don't think so."

"Sure, it is," Monk James said. "She always comes over about this time."

"Not today, she won't. Now do as I told you," he ordered.

Monk James was taken aback by the reverend's statement and even more so by the tone of his voice. "You're the boss."

"And you remember that, unless you want to go back to handling prisoners every day."

Monk James figured his job hadn't changed that much. He was still handling prisoners, only they didn't know it. But he wasn't about to argue with the unreported pay increase. He left the office and walked down the hall, where he expected to find Arrianna going over her daily routine of scheduling who would be assigned to what duty the following day. She liked to work a day in advance, but not more than that. Too many things could happen to a girl over a twenty-four-hour period and usually involved a period.

Monk James found Doobie just inside the front door instead. "What are you doing in here?"

"You said I could have a look-see when the time came," Doobie told him. "I'm done with everything else, so I might as well get started on the reverend's balcony."

"You couldn't be finished with everything I showed you."

"All but the mirror and the table. I'll need to find a glass shop for the mirror and you might as well junk the table. It'd be cheaper to just replace it. Now, I could always build you another one but then it wouldn't match the others. It'd be a lot sturdier and last you a lot longer, but then you'd just want me to do the rest the same way and you'd have all them other tables you'd have to find a place for and..."

"Okay. Okay. I get the picture."

"I figured you would, money being what it is and all," Doobie said, laying it on thick. "Besides, I know how anxious the reverend is about getting that there balcony built so he can get started on his meditation. That'll put him a little closer to the Lord, if you get my meaning."

"What will put me closer to the Lord?" Reverend Daniel asked from the end of the hall.

"Your balcony," Doobie said. "I'm ready to get started on it."

"It seems Brother Donnie here is better with his hands than we expected," Monk James said.

"I told you I loved doing things with my hands and it's so peaceful around here a man could get lost in his work. Food's not bad either, I might add."

"I'm glad to see you've settled in so quickly. We try to be accommodating," the reverend said, then he noticed Doobie's attire.

"You seem to have done a little accommodating yourself."

"What? Oh, this. I'm sorry but I couldn't work dressed that other way. Every time I tried to bend down to grab something, it would pull on my shoulders and over I'd go. I got more freedom this way, but I couldn't very well be walking around out there with all them young girls open like this and no pants on. That just wouldn't be the Christian thing to do," Doobie explained, then added. "Plus, I don't really have the legs for it. This way, I can still wear what you want me to, only different. But if you want me to, I'll pay to have this one fixed back the way it was, only it'll slow me down some."

"It'll be fine the way it is," the reverend said. "And I admire your ingenuity."

"So, can I get a look upstairs now?"

Reverend Daniel knew what would be taking place in his quarters later and wasn't about to give him free access. "Maybe tomorrow. I have other things to do at the moment."

"It won't take me long. I just need to look around and take some measurements. You don't even have to be there. I know you're busy."

"It can wait," the reverend said.

"Okay, if that's how you feel. I can always get started on that old silo out there."

"I beg your pardon?"

"The silo. Didn't he talk to you about that?" Doobie said. Reverend Daniel looked at Monk James, who never had any intention of bringing up the subject of the silo.

"He says it's falling over," Monk James said.

"Oh?"

"No, I believe I said it needed some work. You said the reverend here didn't care if it fell on some of the girls or not."

"James?"

"Now wait a minute. You're twisting things around a little," Monk James said.

"Nevertheless, it wouldn't hurt none for me to get in there and shore it up. I could have it good as new in no time and then wouldn't none of us have to lose any sleep over it. Ya'll wouldn't have to worry about the girls and I wouldn't have to worry about that dog of mine. He seems to have taken a liking to it. Lays there in the shade all day long. If that thing fell over on him, I'd never be able to forgive myself for letting it happen."

"I'm sure no one is in any danger," the reverend said. "Let's just leave it the way it is. I'm sure your dog can find another shady place to lay."

"I don't know. He used to follow me around everywhere. Now all he wants to do is sniff around that old thing and dig him a place to light," Doobie said.

"The silo stays the way it is," Reverend Daniel warned him. "If you can't find him another place, then I would suggest you think about getting rid of him."

Doobie knew he had hit a nerve as the reverend's true colors began to show. He also knew he might have just stepped over a line he didn't want to cross. A line with Sweet's name etched into it. He back-peddled across. "I'll have a talk with him. Like you say, there's plenty of other places he could spend his time just as comfortably." Then he edged back closer. "And a lot safer."

32

Reid Dalton was up before the sun. He laid the semi-loaded Weatherby Mark V Magnum rifle, he had spent most of the previous evening cleaning, in the trunk with the safety engaged and no shell in the chamber.

With very little traffic on the road, he turned off the highway at the entrance to the mowed alley just as the sky to the east began to brighten. He drove a car length past, put the gear in reverse and backed into the alley until he reached the hole.

The rifle went through first and Reid followed. He stopped long enough to look across the yard to make sure he was the first to arrive. The Caddy was nowhere in sight. The direct approach would have been quicker but not necessarily safer, so he took the route along the fence line until he came to the shed with the missing pane. He went to the window and looked inside. Only darkness looked back.

The large bay doors were separated just enough to allow him entry without having to make a sound. The paint smell hung in the stale air like a bad reminder. Shards of light began to break through the higher windows as Reid walked around the car that fit Jason's description perfectly.

Reid froze in his steps when he heard a sound behind him. He knew full well the rifle wasn't ready to do business. He hadn't expected a confrontation this quick. He whipped around, hoping the sight of the rifle would be ominous enough, and caught the tail end of a large rat as it scurried into a nearby trash pile.

"Settle down," Reid told himself.

As the inside of the shed grew lighter, he walked it over from all directions. He was careful not to move anything, not even the smallest empty beer can. Everything had to be just as they had left it, whether they would notice or not.

After an hour's worth of examination had passed, Reid decided to set up camp behind a fortress of pallets in the back, where he could stand or sit without being noticed. The location also gave him a panoramic view from wall to wall.

After another uneventful hour, Reid wished he had taken the time to eat or at least grab a coffee on the way over. Five minutes in a drive-through wouldn't have made that big a difference, especially when he knew the others wouldn't be making their trip in broad daylight. If nothing else, his hunger would keep him alert, but coffee would have kept him awake.

* * *

Reverend Daniel left the Austin stone building and entered the dormitory by the door that led to the infirmary. Arrianna had been conspicuously absent at breakfast and he wanted to make sure she understood that what happened last night was never to happen again. Tonight especially. He was glad to see that none of the beds were taken, which meant his workforce was at full capacity. He walked through the spotless examining room and ran his hand across the paper-covered table. He had never paid much attention to what Arrianna did. He had left it all up to her and very seldom visited her sanctuary outside of his clandestine visits to the mirrored shower room. He could easily see that she kept a clean house.

Reverend Daniel found the door to Arrianna's room closed. A quarter-turn of the knob also found it locked, which was against the rules. He owned the buildings and the tenants as well. To refuse him entry was considered a sin and not to be dealt with lightly. "Open the door, Arrianna," he said without knocking.

"Go away," she said from the bed.

"If you don't let me in, you'll force me to request the assistance of Mo and Gonzo and I'll see to it they're rewarded for their efforts," he warned.

Arrianna wanted no part of the reverend, but she wanted no part of those two even more. She slid off the bed and unlocked the door. He could do the rest himself. She turned away when he entered.

"The girls missed you at breakfast."

"It's better for you they did," she said. "Why would that be?"

When she turned, he saw why. Arrianna's lower lip was cracked and swollen to three times its size. Both cheeks were a reddish purple with marks outlining where his fingers had made violent contact. She had no intention of leaving her room, at least not for his benefit, and had yet to apply the proper amount of makeup necessary to hide what he had done to her. No amount of makeup could hide the shame she felt.

"I didn't realize I had hit you that hard."

"And you didn't mean to rape me either, I suppose?"

"It isn't rape when it's between two consenting adults," he informed her.

"Consenting?"

"You were there waiting. What would you call it?"

"You almost beat me to death. What was I supposed to do?"

"Your job."

"I explained to you what happened."

"And that was my way of explaining what you could expect if it happens again. I believe I got my point across, wouldn't you say?"

"All you had to do was tell me," she said.

"Which brings me to why I'm here. The outpouring was so generously overwhelming, we're having another revival tonight."

"Tonight? That's too soon."

"On the contrary. It comes at just the right time for you to prove yourself worthy and I'll expect only the best."

Arrianna thought quickly. "She has the same problem as last night, or do I need to go into more detail about her situation?"

"It isn't her I'm speaking of," he said. "I've chosen one this time. There was a redhead who came in last week, I believe. She should do nicely."

"What if she's the same way?"

"Then you better find out now so you can make suitable arrangements; otherwise, I may not be so understanding," he warned. "I'm sure the monks would like nothing better than a little quality time with their favorite nurse."

"You wouldn't."

"Not if given a choice but offhand I'd say the choice is yours."

"What's happened to you?"

"Nothing that you can't cure and that is what you're here for."

"And that's all I mean to you?" Arrianna asked.

"We all have our crosses to bear. Yours is to make sure mine will continue," Reverend Daniel said. "And now that we understand each other, I look forward to returning tonight."

33

The scraping sound of the bay doors opening woke Reid Dalton from an uneasy sleep. He grabbed at the pallet he had been leaning against to keep from falling. It too made a scraping sound as it slid toward him. He bent down and peered through the slats as the group entered. His watch told him it was after five. His knees told him he should have fallen asleep sitting. He made a quick but accurate count of the arrivals. All five were present and accounted for. One was rubbing his hand across the door of the car.

"She's done," Hector said.

"Good," Mata told him. "Let's get ready," he told the others.

Reid was ready. He had been ready for hours. He hadn't seen any weapons when they walked in and hadn't found any in his earlier search, but he knew they had to be around somewhere. His guess was the trunk of the Monte Carlo, where they needed to stay. He slid the rifle from under the pallet and walked out of the shadows.

"What the fuck?" Mata said.

"I've been called worse," Reid said as he brought the rifle to his shoulder and aimed at the middle of the group.

"Who the hell are you?" Mata continued.

"I'd say your worst nightmare, except for what I've heard, I doubt you have any."

"Cop, right?" Mata again.

"You should be so lucky. Now why don't y'all just back over there against the wall and we'll talk about what's gonna happen next."

"He's gonna kill us," Carlos screamed.

"Not if you don't give me any shit," Reid said. He motioned Hector away from the car with the barrel of the rifle.

"You can't get all of us," Mata told him.

"You're right. The way I got it figured, I can probably only shoot three of you. In here, that is. The other two, well, let's just say unless you can put three hundred yards between us by the time I walk out the door, you're gonna see Jesus; and I don't think He's gonna be in any mood to listen to what you have to say." Reid didn't feel it necessary to explain that he would also have to reload. No one was that fast.

"You're bluffing," Mata said.

Reid half-circled the group and had his back to the bay doors. "You must be the leader."

"What if I am? What's it to you?"

"Just looking for a little help," Reid said. "I'd kinda like to know who I should take out first."

"Too late," Mata said.

Reid only felt the blow for a split second before everything went black. Chuey Arrendondo had spent the afternoon slamming down one beer after another to get his courage up. He had stayed outside the shed just long enough to empty his bladder, then a little longer to locate the pipe he had introduced to the back of Reid Dalton's head.

"Way to go, Chuey," Mata said.

"Who is he?" Chuey asked, with the pipe still clutched in his hand.

"He never got around to saying," Mata told him as he bent down and took the rifle. "Check his pockets."

Chuey threw the pipe aside and began to dig into Reid's jeans.

"Nothing here."

"Is he still alive?" Mata asked. Chuey felt at his neck. "Yeah."

"Then kill him and get it over with," Hector said.

"Not before we find out who he is and what he's doing here."

"What difference does it make?"

"We may need him later."

"For what?"

"In case someone knew he was coming." Mata lied. He had something more deadly in mind.

* * *

Doobie waited until the noon meal was over before tackling the table in the cafeteria. He knew it was a lost cause, but this way he could at least look busy. He had inspected every inch of the compound he was allowed access to and found nothing else in need of repair. When he turned the table on its side, the jagged edge of the broken metal brace tore a chunk of flesh from the palm of his left hand. He jerked back and bit his lip to keep from saying something the two girls on dish-washing duty might take offense to. He knew it wouldn't be something they hadn't heard before, just not lately.

Blood dripped from his hand and onto the floor. "I knew this was a bad idea," he mumbled as he gripped the edge of the poncho in his hand to stop the bleeding. Doobie knew Arrianna would be in the

326

church up to her elbows in scripture reading, but his hand needed attention. He left the cafeteria and walked across the hall to the infirmary, where he figured to find a sufficient amount of peroxide and gauze to doctor the wound himself. When he passed Arrianna's door, he was sure he heard the sound of something hard hit the floor inside. He gave the door a solid rap.

"Who is it?" Arrianna snapped. "It's me. Doobie."

"Go away. I'm busy."

It wasn't the answer he expected, but he dealt with it in his own way. "Fine, but can you tell me where I might find some bandages?"

"Why?"

"I'm wrapping a mummy." Even with the door between them, he still heard her laugh.

"Just a minute," she said.

"I don't got a minute. I'm bleeding to death out here."

Arrianna opened the door just wide enough to look through without showing her entire face. "Let me see."

Doobie let go of the poncho and showed her his palm. "Table bit me."

"Better let me tend to it," she said and opened the door.

Arrianna had managed to cover the facial bruises with an extra layer of makeup, but no amount of base coat could hide the fat lip.

"What the hell happened to you?"

"I walked into a door," she said, knowing he wouldn't believe her.

"I don't think so," Doobie said when he caught sight of the bruise on her upper right arm. "Not unless you wrestled with it first."

"Don't worry about it. It's not your problem."

Doobie looked over her shoulder and saw what it was that had made the noise. A suitcase lay on the floor by the bed. "Going somewhere?"

"I thought I might."

"Does the way you look have anything to do with it?"

"I told you it's not your problem. Now, do you want me to take care of your hand or not?"

"Not until you tell me what's going on," Doobie said.

"Fine. I'm leaving. Okay?"

"For good?"

"For good and for real," she said. "I'm tired of this shit."

"And what shit is that?"

"Just shit. And you'd be wise to do the same."

Doobie reached back and closed the door behind him. Something told him he would be there a while and not for the reason he had intended. He had already forgotten about his hand. "I think it's time for show and tell," he told her.

"I think we've already played that game, twice as I recall."

"That was for different stakes. Now, why don't you tell me what really happened?" Doobie said. "The rules say I can't leave until you do."

"And if I don't agree to those rules?"

"Then you won't leave either."

Arrianna was in no position to argue. She wanted out and there was only one exit. She turned and walked over to the couch and sat down.

"How much do you know about this place?"

"Only what I've seen the last few days." Doobie chose to play his cards close to his chest.

"Then you better sit down and rest, cause when I'm through, you're gonna need all the energy you've got just to high tail it out of here."

"It's your move," Doobie said as he took a seat on the end of the couch.

"When I came here, I did so with the intention of doing something good, just like you, but I got caught up in all of it. First, it was the reverend. I think I actually fell in love with him or maybe it was just his ideas. I wasn't any different than any of the other girls he's managed to manipulate into coming with his smooth talk and good looks. Then there was the money. You wouldn't believe how much he rakes in," she explained.

Doobie had a pretty good idea. He had a fish hook in over two grand himself.

"He gets thousands every time he holds one of his revival meetings, plus whatever people bring with them when they come here. They turn everything over to him, but then you probably know that. I'm sure he wouldn't have just let you walk in on a promise."

"I did my share," Doobie said.

"You're just lucky you didn't drive up in a Cadillac, cause it wouldn't be here now. As far as he is concerned, what's his is his and what's yours is his. He hauls the cars out of here as fast as they come in. I don't know what he gets for them or where they go, I just know they don't stay around long."

"You sure?" Doobie had already been witness to such an event, but he had become a master at playing dumb here of late.

"Sure, as I know my Cougar is gone." She nodded her head back toward the window.

"They pulled it into that garage over there and I haven't seen it since. And I've been in there."

"How?"

"That's the bad part. Once he found out my father had been a doctor, he figured I knew enough about medicine and stuff to put me in charge in here. After that, I was sort of part of the inner circle. I could pretty much do as I pleased and I'm sorry to say I enjoyed it. Now it's too late. I'm up to my ears in what's going on."

"At least you could help. I mean, they do need someone to look after all the girls," Doobie said.

Arrianna bowed her head and took a deep breath. She brought her head back up and looked Doobie square in the eyes. Nothing she had told him yet was going to hurt as much as what he was about to hear.

"Yeah, that's what I did all right. I took care of the girls. I made sure they kept themselves clean, just the way he likes them. It wasn't enough for him to take everything they owned. He had to take them too."

"What're you saying?"

"He's had sex with almost all of them. Some of their own free will." She paused. "Like me. The others, well, let's just say there's more in that medicine cabinet out there than over-the-counter drugs. They never knew what hit 'em. Still don't for that matter."

Doobie was glad he was sitting down. Had he been standing, he would have surely injured his other hand, hitting the closest thing to him.

Arrianna continued. "Every night after one of his revivals, I get one of the girls ready for him. I'm close enough to them to know who should go next. When the only ones left are those who wouldn't want to go, I give them what they need. That's why I look this way. When I was with you last night, I let myself go and forgot about the girl. By then, it was too late for the drug to work, so he took it out on me."

"He did that to you?"

"And then he raped me. I was his girl last night. And now I'm glad I was. At least he didn't get to do it to another one of them. But after what we had, he had to do this to me." Arrianna could hold back no longer. Tears began to stream down her cheeks. When she wiped at them, her makeup smeared, and the bruises began to show through. Doobie wanted to hold her but he had heard too much.

"He's got another revival tonight. He's never had one two nights in a row before. He told me he wants the newest redhead, but I can't do it anymore. I just can't. That's why I have to leave. Maybe with me gone and no one to get them ready, he'll leave them alone."

Doobie had only one redhead on his mind. "Ashley?"

"Yeah. How did you know?"

Doobie knew he had the hand won, so he laid his cards on the table.

"She's why I'm here."

"What do you mean?"

"I'm here to get her out."

"Are you her father? No, you couldn't be. She would have said something."

"No relation. Her father doesn't even know I'm here."

"I don't understand," Arrianna said.

"You're not supposed to," Doobie told her. "Well, why haven't you done something?"

"I had to see for myself what was going on. Once I did, I found out she wouldn't go, at least not without a fight. Even if I did get her out, she would just be on the next bus back. I have to do something to change her mind," Doobie explained.

"If I were you, I'd just call the cops. They'd put an end to all this."

"Right. Who here would testify against the reverend? Even if some of them had a change of heart, their parents wouldn't want the embarrassment of it all. I know Ashley's wouldn't. Besides, with all the money he probably has stashed away somewhere, he could hire any number of shysters capable of getting him off."

"There's still one more thing," Arrianna said. "The silo. They'll never let you inside."

"Why?"

"There's a girl buried in there. A suicide."

"Shit!" Doobie said. "That's why Sweet's been hanging around there."

"Would that be enough to hang him?"

"I don't want to take that chance. I've gotta do something and not just to get Ashley out. This maniac's got to be stopped."

"You want some help?"

"I thought you were leaving?" Doobie said.

"The game's not over yet," she informed him. "I don't leave until you do."

"How dangerous is that stuff you give the girls?"

"Not dangerous at all, with the right dosage. It just puts them in la-la land. But double it up and they might never come back. That's the only thing that bothers me about leaving. He could give them too much," she explained.

"Then you're gonna have to hang around for one more dose."

"You're not serious?"

As much as Doobie hated to admit it, it was the only way he could think of on such short notice. Ashley was next in line. She had to be the bait. Sure, Arrianna could always give her something to make her sick and put someone else in there instead, but who was he to decide? Another girl was just as important. Just as innocent as she was. And this way, he could be sure she would leave without a fight.

"Don't worry. He won't hurt her. He won't even get a chance to touch her. If he does, there won't be anything left of him to identify," Doobie said.

"What are we gonna do?"

"That depends on you. Where do they keep the money?"

"There's a floor safe in the office. It'll have whatever they took in last night. The rest he's got in several banks," she informed him.

"That'll do. What about guns? I know the monks carry them."

"They're in a closet there too, but it's got a big lock on it and only James has a key."

"Lock's no problem," Doobie said.

"You still haven't told me what we're gonna do," Arrianna told him.

"We're gonna see how he likes the taste of his own medicine."

34

Reid Dalton woke to pain and total darkness, with no idea where he was or how he got there. The last thing he remembered was calling Buster to tell him he would be taking the week off. When he tried to lift his head, all he got for his effort was more pain. A numb right shoulder told him he was lying on his side somewhere. When he lifted his left hand up to feel the back of his head, it hit metal.

"Hey, Mata. I think he's awake." Hector hadn't liked the fact that the trunk of the Monte Carlo was being used to hold their prisoner. A sharp kick could damage the quarter panel and mean more painting. He had chosen to stand guard for that reason.

"Open it up," Mata ordered.

Hector slipped the key in and popped open the trunk. The light hurt Reid's eyes. He blinked back the glare, still lost in the fog of forgotten memory. He felt a pair of hands on his shirt as Chuey pulled him from the car.

"Hey, don't scratch the paint, stupid!" Hector said.

Chuey stopped in mid-lift. Reid's head jerked and sent a hot poker pain to the back of his eyes.

"I didn't mean it," Hector said and ran his tongue between his split lips. "Just be careful... please?"

Chuey dragged Reid the rest of the way out and held him up by his shirt. Things began to come back to him in bits and pieces, like a half-finished jigsaw puzzle. His legs were asleep from being crammed into the trunk for so long. They tingled, almost tickled, as the feeling returned, but Reid was in no mood to laugh.

"Who the fuck are you, *gringo?*" Mata asked. "And don't give me no more of your nightmare shit."

"Nobody," Reid mumbled.

Mata hit him in the ribs with the barrel of his own rifle. "Wrong answer."

When Reid looked down at the familiar Weatherby, the rest of the pieces fell into place.

"Eat shit," he said.

"You're gonna have to do better than that," Mata said and poked him again.

"You're supposed to shoot that thing or am I too old a target?"

"Ah, so you know. Good. That'll make it more interesting."

Reid noticed the tattoo on his arm. "You work for the street department, asshole?"

A blank look came over Mata's face. "That thing on your arm."

Mata looked at the tattoo, then stuck his shoulder **in** front of Reid's face.

"It's a war axe, *boboso*."

"Looks like a traffic light to me." Reid hadn't bothered examining the tattoo. His eyes had been focused on the rifle, more specifically, just above the bolt action on the right side. The safety was still on.

Mata brought the butt of the rifle around and buried it in Reid's stomach. Chuey's strong grip kept him from doubling over, but it didn't stop the pain.

"We're the Mayas. It's our sign," Mata said proudly. Reid was too busy gasping for air to comment.

"And you, my friend, are our next sacrifice."

"What's the matter? Run out of children to kill?"

"Shoot him, Juan," Hector shouted.

"He's not going to shoot. Your fearless leader ain't got the balls."

Reid knew at that range, he would take both Chuey and the Monte Carlo with him.

"No, we're going to do like we planned. What do you know about the Mayas, *gringo?*"

"I know enough." All Reid could remember was what he had studied in History class in junior high or maybe high school. And that could have been the Incas or even the Aztecs. He had only remembered long enough to take the test.

"Then you know about the ritual of human sacrifice."

"Murder is still murder, no matter how you practice it."

Mata pointed at a waist-high stack of pallets that hadn't been there before.

"We've built you an altar."

"Oh? You making me a god now?"

"No, we're gonna make you dead, *hombre.* And it's gonna hurt you like shit."

"It's not supposed to," Reid told him when the sight of a case of beer on the floor brought back a long-forgotten History lesson.

"*Que?*"

"I thought you knew something about the people you claim to be," Reid said. "I was obviously mistaken. You don't seem to know shit."

"Then why don't you tell me?" Mata said.

"They always drugged their victims first," Reid explained.

"Too bad. We don't got no drugs."

"You got beer." Reid nodded toward the floor.

"Why would we waste it on you?"

"I just figured you'd want to play by the rules."

"He's right, Juan," Chuey said from behind Reid, his hands still clenched tightly on his shirt. "What would it hurt? It would be like his last meal."

"Then he can have one of yours," Mata told him. He handed the Weatherby to Carlos and broke open the case. "Bring him over here by the altar."

Chuey let go of Reid's shirt and shoved him forward. Mata walked over and handed Reid a can of beer with one hand. He pulled a knife from his belt with the other and showed it to him. "For later," he said.

Reid opened the can and took a slow drink while scoping out the others. One held a nickel-plated pistol and another a rifle that looked to be a 30-30. The other two, one standing within arm's length and the one he had come to know as Chuey, had come to the dance alone.

The beer tasted good. Warm, but still good. He felt the liquid fall all the way to the empty pit of his stomach. He squeezed the can as he drank. When he switched hands, he crimped the aluminum flat along one side. When he finished, he asked for another.

Mata looked discouraged, but took another from the box anyway.

He brought it to Reid and held it out. "Drink fast. It's your last."

"I don't think so." Reid twisted the empty can and tore it in half. In one swift move, he grabbed Mata by the hair and ran the sharp aluminum edge across the right side of his neck. Mata's hands emptied and grabbed at his throat, where blood was pumping with each dying heartbeat. "I told you would be first." He shoved a foot in Mata's chest and sent him reeling across the room.

Eddie Bustos' first mistake was watching too long. It was also his last. Reid Dalton grabbed for him just as Hector brought the 30-30 up. By the time he fired, Reid had a shield. The bullet entered Eddie's chest, shattering his breastbone and exited out his left shoulder with pieces of his heart muscle along for the ride.

"You stupid, fuck! You killed Eddie," Chuey yelled and tried to grab the rifle from him.

Carlos Cuevas looked on in horror as Reid ran for the front of the Monte Carlo. Flaco Dominguez fired a round from the pistol that bounced off the concrete floor. Reid dived around the far side of the car and scrambled toward the trunk on all fours.

Flaco followed the same route, but was too late. Reid had already gotten what he hoped he would find. Flaco had both hands on the pistol and was about to take aim when he died. Reid had aimed for the pistol with the tire iron in hopes of knocking it from Flaco's hands. The pointed tool had missed its mark, but had found a more favorable one in the process. Flaco stood with his mouth open. His eyes were crossed as they stared blindly at the metal object protruding from his forehead. He was dead before he hit the ground.

Reid was about to go for the pistol when a deafening sound filled the shed. He looked around the left side of the trunk where Hector and Chuey had been fighting for control of the 30-30. The top of Chuey's head was gone. Hector watched as his body slid down the side of the Monte Carlo. "Get away from my car, stupid!" he yelled.

Reid remembered the pistol at the same time Hector remembered him. He fired wildly in Reid's direction. The bullet entered the side and ruptured the gas tank. The force of an explosion sent Reid back against the bay doors.

"No!" Hector screamed. He threw the rifle down and ran to the rear of the car. He tried to fight the flames with his bare hands, but the flames fought back. Reid watched as they licked out and touched Hector's shirt. Hector whirled around and began slapping at the flames that now engulfed him. He bounced off a stack of pallets and fell into a pile of burlap bags. The flames soon became a bonfire as Hector's thrashing around did nothing but kindle the blaze.

"Welcome to hell," Reid Dalton said when all movement from Hector's charred body stopped. He looked over to where the last one stood with the Weatherby clutched in his hands.

Carlos Cuevas' feet felt as heavy as lead. His hands ached from gripping the rifle. He had wanted to be a Maya and now he was one. The last one. He also wanted to live and only one thing stood in his way. He still didn't know who this man was. The others had died not knowing.

Reid got to his feet and staggered across the floor. He knew it was over. It was time to take the last one in. He stopped not five feet in front of the boy. "So, shoot."

Carlos pursed his lips and squeezed the trigger, but the trigger refused to budge. He squeezed again. Nothing.

Reid saw the boy's muscles clench each time he tried to fire. "The safety's still on, son."

Carlos turned the rifle over in his hands. "It's right there on the side," Reid told him.

Carlos found the button, pushed it and squeezed the trigger again. When he felt it give, he jumped, expecting a recoil, but all he got was silence.

"Not a hunter, are you?" Reid said. "Just a killer." He stepped forward and jerked the rifle from his hands. He lifted the bolt and slid it back.

Carlos saw the shell enter the chamber. He wasn't ready to die, but death was ready for him. It had been from the night he had signed the pact.

"Why?" Reid asked.

"I'm a Maya," he answered with a scared sound in his voice. "So were they and look what it got them." When Reid turned his head in the direction of the destruction, he saw that the fire had spread to half the shed. "You want to die in here?"

"No."

"I didn't think so. Let's go."

"Wait," Carlos said. "Who are you?"

Reid had already reached where the 30-30 lay on the floor. He bent down and picked it up. He knew who it had been used on. He could feel it in the wood. "Y'all killed my son."

"Which one?"

"Does it matter?" he asked with his back to the boy.

"Yes," Carlos answered, though he already knew.

"His name was Bear. Bear Dalton. He was only twelve."

Just then, Carlos saw the knife Mata had dropped. It was his last chance. He bent down and scooped it up.

Reid heard the sound of metal against the concrete floor and turned.

"You don't want to do that, boy."

"It was me," Carlos said. "I killed him."

At that moment and holding the gun that had killed his son, something good in Reid Dalton died. He knew the knife was no match for either rifle he was holding, but when Carlos lunged at him, he lifted the 30-30 up and sent a bullet through his brain. The impact jerked Carlos' feet out from under him and what was left of the

346

back of his head made a splattering thud when he hit the floor.

Reid Dalton turned and walked slowly toward the bay doors. On the way, he dropped the 30-30 into the burning trunk of the Monte Carlo. He followed the fence line back to the hole, pushed the rifle through first, then followed. He kicked the loose dirt back in, as best as he could in the dark, and laid the Weatherby gently in the trunk.

He drove down the mowed alley with his lights off and stopped just short of where the field ended. Cars had already stopped along the roadside to gawk at the fire. Reid turned the motor off and got out to join the throng. It would make leaving easier when the time came. He would just be another astonished face in the crowd. No one would pay any attention when he left with the rest.

* * *

Arrianna had no choice but to show herself at the evening meal. To those who asked about her lip, she told them she had taken a fall and hit her face on the side of a cabinet. One had been Ashley Jenkins. In return, she told her she looked a little pale herself and told her to report to the infirmary after she ate. When she was sure

347

everyone was present and accounted for, Arrianna left the cafeteria. She met Doobie at the front door of the Austin stone building and let him in. He followed her down the hall to the office, where she punched in the correct sequence of numbers in the panel by the door to gain entry.

Arrianna stepped in first and turned on the lights. "The closet's over there," she told him and pointed to a door by what looked to be some sort of radio equipment.

Doobie hadn't seen an antenna on the grounds, so he asked, "What's that, some sort of ham radio?"

"No, that's where the music comes from. You just stick the tape in and switch it on."

"You mean the dinner bell?" Doobie said.

"Yeah, or if you just wanted to make an announcement, like in the cafeteria, you'd just flip on this switch."

Doobie knelt down and saw that all the switches were marked. "That easy, huh?"

"Yep. There's even an intercom right there above it. He can talk to the monks' quarters or even his own, for that matter."

"This is going to be even better than I thought," Doobie said. "When you're upstairs with Ashley, turn it on."

"What're you thinking?" Arrianna asked.

"I won't know for sure until it plays out," Doobie said as he lifted the poncho up and took out the bolt cutters. He made quick work of the padlock on the door and found an arsenal of weapons inside. "Shit," he said when he laid the bolt cutters on the desk.

"What's wrong?"

"I don't know what he carries."

"Who?"

"James."

Arrianna thought for a few seconds. "It's a three-fifty something, I believe."

"Three fifty-seven?"

"Yeah, that's it."

Doobie located a box of shells and emptied them on the floor. "I need to get back over there. I told Ashley to meet me in the infirmary when she was done eating," Arrianna told him.

"Okay. Make sure the door is locked when you leave."

"You gonna be all right in here? It'll be a couple of hours before they're back."

"I'll need every bit of it. You just make sure Ashley's taken care of."

"Oh, yeah, I'm almost forgot. Here's your dinner." She pitched Doobie several packages of condiments.

"You got yours?"

"In my underwear."

Doobie just shook his head and when the door closed between them, he went to work turning a jury of deadly hawks into doves.

Arrianna was in the infirmary when Ashley walked in. "I don't feel bad," she said.

"There's a bug going around," Arrianna informed her. "I've already given these out to some of the others. I'd rather get the jump on it than have all of you bedridden at the same time. We're not equipped to handle an epidemic, which means some of you would have to go to the hospital in town."

"Oh, in that case, I'll take them. I don't like hospitals," Ashley said.

"Good girl," Arrianna said as she handed her the pills. "Get a glass of water to wash them down with, then lie down over there."

"I have to lie down, too? Why can't I just go upstairs?"

"These are pretty strong. They'll make you dizzy at first. When that passes, you can go on up. It won't be long."

Ashley took a plastic cup from a dispenser by the sink and filled it halfway-up. She threw the pills into her mouth, took a sip from the cup and tilted her head back to swallow.

"Take another drink to make sure they went down," Arrianna said.

Ashley did as she was told, and in a few minutes, she was out of it. The plastic cup fell from her limp hand onto the floor.

"You'll be the last one," Arrianna said. "I promise."

When Doobie finished with the shells, he cleaned the floor with the bottom of the poncho, then played with the switches on the speaker panel to make sure he knew which ones to throw. The digital clock below the switches told him it was after ten.

Arrianna should have had Ashley upstairs by now. He reached up and turned the knob. "Beam me up, Scotty," he said into the speaker. A few long seconds later, he received a reply.

"Cool it, Doobie. They just drove up."

Doobie turned the knob back off and took his place in the closet with the door slightly ajar. He suddenly remembered the lights were still on. He ran to the door and flipped the switch. Without windows, the room was pitch black. He ran his hand along the desk and reached out for the corner of the door just as the buzzer sounded. "Now, what the hell did I do?" he thought. His mind raced. He reached over to the far wall and padded it until he found the knob and turned it on.

"Arrianna. I set a buzzer off. What the hell do I do now?"

He could hear the sound of movement on the floor above him just before she answered. "It's just the front door. That means someone's come in. Get hid. Now!"

Doobie reversed the knob and jumped into the closet just as the office door swung open. He flinched when the lights came back on. Through the crack, he could see Monk James was alone and carrying a large bag. He set the bag on the table across from the desk. Doobie noticed a strange look come over his face and when he stepped toward the desk, he knew why.

Monk James picked up the bolt cutters with both hands and studied them. His eyes went instinctively to the closet door where the lock should have been. He laid the tool back down and started to reach under his robe. His hand became tangled in the fold.

Doobie saw his chance and sprang from the closet with another .357 in his hand and hit him square on the jaw. Monk James grunted and fell to the floor in a large brown heap. Doobie turned him over, lifted the sackcloth and, with work-gloved hands, took the gun from his holster. He made quick work of exchanging the shells and holstered the gun again. He gave him a nudge as he replaced the robe to make sure he was out enough to leave. When he got no response, he moved over to the speaker panel and switched on just the right ones. Before he left, he turned the intercom on high. He could hear faint voices coming from Reverend Daniel's room.

"Show time," he said to himself when he grabbed the bag of money from the table. He closed the door to the office and headed north.

"Maybe I'll forgive you now," Reverend Daniel said to Arrianna as he viewed the nubile body of Ashley Jenkins on his bed.

"Everyone should be allowed one mistake," Arrianna told him as she walked near the intercom, realizing what it was Doobie wanted played out.

"Just see that it doesn't happen again," he warned.

"I won't. I promise it'll never happen again. I've learned my lesson. When you want to fuck one of the girls, I'll have them ready."

"What's with the language? Have you forgotten where you are?" he asked sternly.

"I know I'm in your quarters. I'm sorry."

"Not as sorry as you're gonna be though," Doobie said when he entered with a sack of money in one hand and a pistol in the other. He grabbed Arrianna around the neck with the gun hand and pulled her to him.

"What's going on here?" Reverend Daniel yelled.

"I'm taking what doesn't belong to you," he said and lifted the sack. "Look familiar?"

Reverend Daniel stared at the sack. "Where's James?"

"Taking a nap. He's had a rough day."

"I see. You know, I wondered about you. Who are you really?"

"Nobody important. I figured you were running a scam out here. I just didn't know how far it went."

"Far enough. Why don't you dump that sack out and see for yourself?"

"This is peanuts. You're gonna take me downstairs and empty out the safe for the rest."

"Not on your life."

"I'll kill her if you don't," Doobie twisted his hand so that the gun was pointing at the side of Arrianna's head.

"Go ahead. She means nothing to me. Who do you think gave her that busted lip?"

Doobie wasn't worried about the reverend's attitude. He had expected it. "Then I'll shoot the girl."

"By all means. She's so doped up she won't even know she's dead. Plus, I've got plenty more where she came from. Kill them all if you want to. It isn't going to get you what you want. I can have a new batch in here by next week. That is, if I don't decide to burn it all down around them."

Doobie figured he had given the reverend just about enough rope to hang himself. He imagined all the ears in the dormitory were no doubt tuned to the speakers he had switched on in the office before he left. It was time to move on. "Now," he whispered in Arrianna's ear.

On cue, she jerked at his arm and Doobie let the gun fly in the reverend's direction. Arrianna jumped out of the way just before he grabbed the gun and fired. Doobie dropped the bag and slapped his hand against his chest. When he removed his hand, he looked down to see the results and then fell forward onto the floor.

"Stupid son of a bitch thought he could get away with something like that," Reverend Daniel said. He picked up the bag and headed out of the room.

Arrianna went to the doorway and stood for a good minute. "He's gone," she said.

Doobie turned his hand and let the partially opened packets of catsup fall out. "They'll never look the same on a hot dog again," he said. "Your turn."

"You're a tough act to follow," she said as she reached under the sackcloth and removed her own packets of fake blood.

"Damn it, James. Get your fat ass up," Reverend Daniel said as he kicked at his side.

"What? Shit, what hit me?" he asked groggily. "Your carpenter friend tried to rob us."

"Where is he?"

"On his way to hell. I shot the bastard. Now get up. We got a mess to clean up here."

"What are you gonna do with him?" Arrianna asked when she appeared just outside the room.

"We'll bury him in the silo like we did the girl. His damn dog, too, since he wants to get in there so bad."

"You don't have enough time for that, asshole. I just called the cops. I figure you got about five minutes before they get here and nail you to the wall for all you've done. I hope you fry." Arrianna began to squeeze the catsup packages in her hand.

"You bitch," Reverend Daniel said. "I should have killed you last night when I had the chance."

"But you didn't. You were too busy trying to get it up."

Reverend Daniel did what she was waiting for. He raised the gun and fired. Arrianna played her part to the hilt and soiled the sackcloth valley between her breasts with catsup as she fell backward.

"Why'd you do that?" Monk James shouted.

"She deserved it," the reverend replied.

"Well, what the fuck are we gonna do now? You heard her. The police are on their way."

"We'll tell them she was in on it with him. They got no witnesses. The girl upstairs sure won't be able to say anything."

"Damn," Monk James said. "I didn't sign on for nothing like this."

"Shut up and help me get this money into the safe. We can..."

"What?"

"Who did this?" Reverend Daniel asked and pointed to the speaker system. "Someone's turned the speakers on in the dorm."

"That ain't all," Monk James said. "Look." He pointed to the intercom knob.

Reverend Daniel ran out of the office and down the hall.

Arrianna cringed as he jumped over her supposedly lifeless body. Through the front window, he could see a quadrangle full of lambs.

"The moneys in the safe," Monk James told him from the hall. "Get it back out. We gotta get the hell outta here."

Monk James leaned into the room and saw why.

"Shit. We're screwed."

"Not yet, we're not," he said as he barreled his way around him.

Arrianna held her breath as the two stepped over her a second time. She wanted so badly to open her eyes and see the expression on their faces, but was too afraid. If they knew she was faking, the next time would be for real.

"How're we gonna get out?" Monk James asked nervously. "The cops'll be here any minute."

"Just fill the bags and let me worry about that," Reverend Daniel ordered.

Monk James crammed the contents of the safe, two nights' worth of giving and an assortment of leftover jewelry from previous revivals, into a pair of canvas sacks. He guessed the haul would be in the neighborhood of a hundred thousand dollars. The figure rang a bell in his head and he remembered his mattress. He had at least that much stuffed inside but it was too late to do anything about that now. He was going to have to leave with nothing to show for his efforts.

When the bags were full, Reverend Daniel grabbed them both up. "Out the back," he said.

"And do what, dig a hole and bury ourselves?"

"We're going over the fence. They won't be able to find us in the hills."

"We can't get over that fence. That's why we put it up," Monk James reminded him.

"You got a better idea?"

"No, but..."

"I'm not wasting any more time," Reverend Daniel said. "You can stay or go. It doesn't matter to me." He took the money and ran from the room. Monk James had no choice but to follow the money.

They ran the fifty yards to the back fence. It was dark and the ten feet of chain link, topped by three strands of barbed wire that lay outward, looked menacing when they arrived. "There ain't no way," Monk James told him.

"There's always a way," the reverend said as he jumped onto the fence with a bag of money in each hand. His sandals slipped as he tried to get a hold. "Push me up," he yelled.

"Who's gonna help me?"

"I will when I get on top. Just do it."

Monk James got up under him and with a foot on each shoulder the reverend steadied himself and pitched the bags onto the barbed wire for protection. "You got me?" he said.

"Yeah. Hurry up." Monk James grunted under the weight. Reverend Daniel bent at the knees and jumped onto the bags, landing on his stomach. Monk James looked up at him and placed a foot against the fence. "Give me your hand."

"I don't think so, James. You'd never make it."

"You son of a bitch. You help me up or I'll kill you."

"Too late for idle threats," he said.

Monk James lifted his robe and came out with his gun. "You call this idle?"

"You wouldn't shoot me. You aren't smart enough to explain your way out of it when they find me."

"Not hardly. I'm just a guard, remember? Me, Gonzo and Mo. We just worked for you. We didn't have no idea what you were up to."

"No one's gonna believe that," he said as he slid his way to the top.

"Another inch and you're dead."

When one of the bags slipped under the weight, Monk James took it for an escape attempt and fired. Only sound emanated from the gun, but that was enough. The reverend lost what balance he had and fell onto the barbed wire. His long white robe became entangled as the barbs bit into his skin. The more he tried to free himself, the worse it got. "Help me, you fool."

"Not on your life."

"The money. You can have the money. All of it," he begged. "Throw it down," Monk James said.

"I can't," he said as he tried to lift his arms. The jerking movement made his body slide forward. The barbs cut deeper lines into the skin of his back.

"What do I do?"

"Cut the wire. Do something."

Monk James remembered the bolt cutters. "Hold on," he said as he turned and began running back to the Austin stone building.

Doobie and Arrianna had been watching from the second-floor window. "Oh, shit," Arrianna said. "I should be down there."

"Too late," Doobie said as Monk James hit the back steps. Monk James had only one thing on his mind and it wasn't Arrianna. He didn't even notice she was gone. He grabbed the bolt cutters and ran back down the hall. He stopped at Arrianna's desk and picked up her small clerical chair. He wouldn't have to depend on the reverend to help him through this time.

By the time he reached the fence, the reverend's white robe was no longer pure. Splotches of red covered it like a bad case of measles. He set the chair below the money bags that covered the bottom two strands of wire and climbed onto it. The rollers dug into the dirt under his weight. He punched at the bags with the tool but they wouldn't budge. He wanted his payment up front.

"Cut the damn wire, you idiot," the reverend ordered.

Monk James saw that if he cut the bottom two strands first, the money would more than likely fall on the other side of the fence. With only one strand left, the reverend had a better than even chance of falling free himself on that same side. He wasn't going to let that happen. The money was rightfully his. He reached high, connected the business end of the cutters onto the top strand and squeezed the handles together. The line snapped with ease and made a whipping sound just before it circled the reverend's neck. The once taut wire caught him off balance and jerked him backward. Flesh and fabric ripped as he fell within inches of the ground and hung there choking while the barbs bit into his jugular. He clawed at the wire but to no avail.

Monk James looked on in horror. He tried to reach through the square holes in the chain link but his hands were too big. In less than a minute, the reverend's body went limp. It wasn't the outcome Doobie had expected, much less intended. It was, however, final. Whether it was fitting or not wasn't up to him to judge and he didn't plan on being around when the jury came in.

"Time to go," Doobie told Arrianna when he saw Gonzo running down the back fence line. He walked over to the bed and scooped Ashley up in his arms. She felt like dead weight but he knew better. He followed Arrianna down the stairs and waited while she picked up the phone from her desk and dialed the police.

"Wait a minute," she said after she cradled the phone. She turned and opened a file drawer behind the desk. She rifled through the folders, stopping twice and then a third time to pull something from their ranks.

"What's that?" Doobie asked.

"Us," she said.

The crowd in the quadrangle met them as they exited the front. "Ya'll get back in the dorm," Arrianna yelled. "Reverend Daniel's gone crazy. The police are on their way. You'll be safe there until they get here."

When the crowd ran one way, they ran the other. "Come on, Sweet," Doobie said as he passed the silo. "Time to go for a ride."

Sweet understood "ride." He bolted from his position by the silo door and ran for the Bronco.

Arrianna opened the passenger door, tilted the seat forward and climbed in the back. Doobie eased Ashley through the opening and onto the seat with her head in Arrianna's lap.

"In, boy," he said to the dog when he tilted the seat back up. Sweet didn't have to be told twice. He bounded into the seat and laid a paw on the dash.

When Doobie walked around the rear of the truck, he saw the last obstacle coming down the road in a slow trot. "Trouble," he told Arrianna when he reached the door.

"Let me handle it," she said.

Doobie opened the door and helped her out. "Be careful. I think *his* gun is loaded."

"You just stay here till I get back." She ran around the side of the building and reached the front gate at the same time as Mo Morley reached the other side, out of breath. She opened the box and punched the button. "You gotta hurry," she said to him as the gate began to roll open. "Someone's trying to kill Reverend Daniel."

"Where?" he said between gasping breaths. "Where are they?"

"Behind his house. Go around the dorm. James is over there."

"Thanks," he said and loped toward the left side of the church.

Arrianna waited until he had rounded the corner of the dormitory before she returned to the truck.

"How'd it go?" Doobie asked as he helped her into the back seat.

"Piece of cake," she answered. "Now get us outta here."

Doobie jumped in behind the wheel. The Bronco hadn't been started since the day he arrived but he wasn't worried; still, he held his breath as he turned the key. The engine answered with a resounding and familiar hum.

"You ready to go home, dog?"

When Sweet removed his paw from the dash and settled back into the seat, Doobie knew the answer was yes.

35

Reid Dalton was sitting in the green, metal lawn chair on the back patio when Detective Sergeant Eric Montalvo rang the doorbell just before noon. He heard the chime through the open patio door. He left his empty coffee cup by the chair and walked inside.

"Mister Dalton," Montalvo said when the door opened. "Hello, Sergeant," he said with very little feeling in his voice.

"Mind if I come in?"

"Sure," he said. He stepped aside and allowed him to enter. "I'd offer you some coffee, but I seem to be out. I guess I need to think about getting around to shopping one of these days."

"That's okay. I've had my quota."

"Listen, Sergeant. About the other day."

"That's history," Montalvo said. "You were only speaking your mind."

"Still, I..."

"Forget it. I didn't come here for an apology. I think I may have some good news or at least news."

"You find something?"

"We found a lot of something," Montalvo said. "You work for an insurance company, am I right?"

"Yeah."

"You wouldn't happen to insure that big packing shed out on South 281, would you?"

"I doubt it. We're not really into that sort of thing, why?"

"The whole place burned to the ground last night. I mean every damn building and even some of the fields next to it. It's a wonder some of the houses on the other side didn't go up with it," Montalvo explained.

"I don't understand."

"I'm sorry. I was rambling. It looks like it was started by some sort of gang war, near as we can figure it. They found six bodies in the rubble of one of the sheds. Ugly mess. The coroners only had a chance to examine one of the remains, but it appears it wasn't the fire that did them in."

"What're you telling me?"

"Well, we matched the serial numbers from two cars we also found out there to what's probably gonna turn out to be two of the bodies. Course we're gonna have to rely solely on dental records to be able to do that, but neither one has been seen since yesterday, so my guess is it's them. Anyway, one of the neighbors said one of the cars, a black Monte Carlo, had some sort of painting on the doors. We also found what was left of a paint sprayer in the shed where we found the car. Looks like your little buddy may have been right and they were trying to cover up the evidence."

"Did you ever find out what it was?"

"The picture? Yeah, it was supposed to be some sort of Aztec, no Mayan, weapon or something like that."

"Huh. Could've fooled me."

"You and me both, but I guess you had to be there."

"I guess," Reid said.

"I think we've found what we were looking for, though. It's just a shame someone beat us to them."

"Yes, it is. I'd still like to know why?"

"Well, the thing is, it's over," Montalvo told him. "I know it won't bring your son back but at least it'll make him rest easier."

"Thanks," Reid said. "I'll remember that."

"You, uh, you wanta tell the kid yourself?"

"Jason? Yeah, if you don't mind. He's away on spring break but I'll tell him as soon as he gets home."

"I guess that's about it then," Montalvo said. "I wanted to tell you in person."

"I appreciate it, Sergeant."

"By the way, how's your wife doing?"

"Day by day."

"I understand," Montalvo said. "Give her my best, okay?"

"I'll do that."

* * *

When Doobie pulled into the bus depot in Boerne a half hour later, Arrianna had a bad feeling about it. She knew why but she had to hear it from him.

"You gonna be okay?" Doobie asked when he turned in his seat. "If I said no, would you let me go with you?"

"Can't do that. I've got nothing to offer you."

"I don't want much."

"Maybe not now, but you deserve better."

"Not after what I've done."

Doobie had been dealing with his own demons long enough to understand.

"You're gonna have to live with that."

"What if I can't?" Arrianna said.

"You will. You were gonna leave anyway. I just came along for the ride."

"And now the ride's over."

"For me it is," Doobie said. "It's up to you to decide where you'll go from here. I'd recommend home, wherever that is."

"You don't mind if I change in here, do you?"

"I'd recommend it. You're likely to shake up a few people if you walked in like that."

Arrianna slid over and laid Ashley's head gently in the seat.

She reached into the back for the small suitcase Doobie had managed to sneak from her quarters.

"You got money?"

"I've got enough to manage," she told him as she slipped the sackcloth over her head. "He always made sure there was enough on hand for me to keep the medicine cabinet full."

After a few minutes, Doobie heard the suitcase snap shut. He got out and tilted his seat forward. "I don't guess I could talk you out of this?" she said when she stepped out.

"It'd never work," Doobie said.

"Well, here then," she said and handed him the folders.

Doobie saw she had given him all three. "Don't you want yours?"

"No, you keep it," she said. "That way, you'll know where home is if you ever change your mind. I'm guessing it wouldn't do me any good to keep yours?"

"Nope."

"I didn't think so. You just don't look like a Donnie." Doobie smiled. "I'm glad you waited until now to bring that up."

Arrianna reached up and kissed him lightly on the lips. Any more than that would have been too much for her to handle.

Doobie watched her walk away, knowing it was the right thing to do. At least for now.

36

When Montalvo had mentioned Kathy, Reid remembered he had another matter to deal with. He went to the desk in Bear's old room and opened his briefcase. The divorce papers were right where he had left them. He took them out and read over them slowly. It was the usual legal mumbo-jumbo. Twenty-five-cent words dictated at two hundred dollars an hour. He switched on the computer and electronically dictated a letter of his own. He wanted very little to close their marriage and had no intention of paying a second attorney to try and convince him otherwise.

In his letter, which he directed to Kathy's attorney and a copy to her at her parents' house, he asked for five of the six things he required: his personal clothes, the green metal lawn chair which he had brought into the marriage, Bear's bed, the soccer picture and his retirement from Union Mutual. He had made the decision not to return.

The sixth item would not be spelled out. He would take possession of that on his own.

He ended the letter that would eventually end their marriage and sent it to the printer.

* * *

Cliffdweller Drive was dark and deserted when Doobie brought the Bronco to a stop just down the street from Ashley Jenkins' house. She moaned groggily when he eased her from the seat and into his arms. Sweet jumped from the Bronco and led the way down familiar territory. When they got to the porch, he realized she had nothing on under the flimsy negligee Arrianna had dressed her in. He laid her down gently, then removed his catsup-stained poncho and wrapped it around her. He stood there a minute and watched her sleep, then reached down and brushed away the auburn hair that covered her eyes.

The sound of the doorbell woke Belinda Jenkins from a worrisome sleep. Her husband continued his rhythmic snoring next to her. This late at night, she should have feared the worst, but she didn't. Instead, a feeling of relief followed her as she hurried through the house to the door.

She didn't need to hear the sound of the Bronco's motor as it made its way up the hill to tell her who had brought her daughter back to her. She knew the day Doobie left he wouldn't be returning alone.

37

Reid Dalton sat in the green metal chair at the edge of the cliff and gazed out over the valley before him. He watched the shallow creek below as it meandered slowly around the nearest bend. It was early afternoon and the sun was blazing hot. The drive from Denton had been a trying one, but he and Bear eventually made it to the fifteen acres of hilltop land he had purchased with most of his retirement check.

When he had packed his belongings two days before, a folded, plastic bag had fallen out from between some lesser-worn shirts. He had totally forgotten hiding it there after Bear was born, and had to laugh when he saw the six small rolls of paper.

There on the cliff, with the hardest part still ahead, Reid pulled the bag from his pocket along with the Zippo lighter Bear had given him. He opened the bag for the first time in over twelve years, took out one of the thin sticks of paper and fired up a doobie.

After the second one had come and gone, Reid felt relaxed enough to finish the journey that required a quick trip into Boerne. The granite-hard, hill country stone had proven too much for his shovel to handle. He left the chair, returned to the rented car and headed the few miles into town.

He drove through a residential section and stopped at the first store he came to. It wasn't much to speak of but the name, Bradley's Grocery and Bait Shop, meant the owner probably carried an unusual assortment of items not normally found in the run-of-the-mill convenience store. He parked in front and went inside.

"Afternoon," the man behind the counter said.

"Appears so," Reid said politely. "You wouldn't happen to carry a pick, would you?"

"Garden variety or are you lookin' to bust up some rock?"

"I need the biggest you got."

"Right over there next to the shovels," the man said and nodded toward an aisle where Reid saw a small grove of wooden handles sprouting up above the shelves.

Reid made his way to the display and took a large pick ax from the rack.

"You new around here?" the man asked when Reid laid the tool on the counter.

"Starting today," Reid said.

"Thought so. I know most of my regulars," the man said as he rang up the price. "Ah, that'll be twelve forty-four."

Reid pulled out his wallet and handed him a twenty. "Wait. I think I might have the forty-four cents." He was about to reach into his jeans pocket when the man offered a form of introduction.

"My name's Jake Bradley. What do your people call you?"

Reid felt the plastic bag as he was digging around for the change and smiled. "Doobie," he said while he counted out the change.

When he got back to his fifteen acres, Reid drove the rented car around to the cliff-side of a grove of pine trees. He got out and leaned the pick ax against a lone sycamore on the outer edge. He took a deep breath before he opened the trunk and took out the heavy, canvas tarpaulin he had folded around his son's body when he reclaimed it from the grave.

As a young boy himself, he had once carved his own initials in a sycamore tree, not much different than the one he would soon carve Bear's into.

THE END